EVERLASTIN' LOVE . . .

brings to true life the f[illegible]gth of love from its bittersweet beginn[illegible]

Jaz had everything . . . A scholarship to Berkeley, a magical marriage to her handsome high school sweetheart and a future full of kept promises, until the Vietnam War shattered her idyllic life. The dramatic conclusion will shock you!

The following Titles in the INDIGO SERIES are available through Genesis Press:

Entwined Destinies by Rosalind Welles
Everlastin' Love by Gay G. Gunn
Dark Storm Rising by Chinelu Moore
Shades of Desire by Monica White
Reckless Surrender by Susan James
Careless Whispers by Rochelle Ayers
Breeze by Robin Lynette Hampton
Whispers in the Sand by LaFlorya Gauthier
Love Unveiled by Gloria Greene

This book would not have been possible without my
Trinity: Patrice "the Connection" Gaines, Denise
"You'll fix it" Stinson, and Charlotte Sheedy.
Thank you all for your continued belief and support.
Much gratitude to the wind beneath my
wings Marvin, Tre' and Marc Gunn.

To Iva, Dottie, Leslie and Derek Ross, and Dan and
Linda Hartley thanks for the West Coast Wanderings!

To My Inner Circle... Evelyn, Ulonda, Tira, Cheryl, Connie,
Joyce and Mike. . . . And my "daughters," Jennifer,
Stephanie, Debi, Melanie and Lauren.

Indigo Love Stories

are published by

Genesis Press, Inc.
315 Third Avenue North
Columbus, MS 39701

Everlastin' Love

ISBN: 1-885478-02-X

Manufactured in the United States of America

First Edition
Second Printing

Everlastin' Love

Gay G. Gunn

The Genesis Press, Inc.
406A Third Avenue North
Columbus, MS 39703-0101

Characters

Jaz	*Jasmine Bianca Culhane*
Qwayz	*Quinton Regis Chandler IV*
Akira	*Qwayz's Irish Setter; a gift from Jaz*
TC	*Tavio Culhane; Jaz's older brother and Qwayz's best friend*
AJ	*Aubrey, Jr.; Qwayz's second cousin who prefers being referred to as his nephew; son of Melie and Big Aubrey*
Gladys Ann	*Jaz's best girlhood friend*
Mel	*Jaz's older sister*
Hud, Jr.	*Mel's son*
Selena C. Fluellen	*Jaz's paternal aunt*
Zack Fluellen	*Selena's husband*
Denny	*Denise Chandler Hodges; Qwayz's older sister*
Yudi	*Denny's first husband*
Ma Vy	*Vilna; Qwayz's mother*
Hanie	*Qwayz's and Denny's baby sister*
Hep Culhane	*Jaz's father*
Lorette J. Culhane	*Jaz's mother*
Scoey	*Ellis Carlton Scofield; TC's and Qwayz's friend*
Tracy	*Jaz's old friend; Scoey's wife*
Amber	*Oldest daughter of Scoey and Tracy*
CC	*Chiam Cooper; Jaz's friend at Berkeley*
Sloane Yeager	*Jaz's friend at Berkeley*
Addie	*Jaz's secretary*
Zeke	*Executive elevator operator*
Nick Santucci	*Award-winning novelist*
Lloyd	*Denny's second husband*
Avia Checole'	*Hep's assisstant at the Italian Embassy and later at Culhane Enterprises (CE)*
Kyle Jagger	*Hep's right hand man at CE*
Dory	*Landscape architect at CE*
Marc	*Architect at CE*
Derek	*Architect at CE*
Tre'	*Finance consultant at CE*
Cass	*Kyle's cousin and best friend*

Chapter One

1968

Music. There was none where it had always been. Singing into the mike at Champion Studio. Singing to each other as they strolled the beach stealing kisses and hidden touches, harmonizing as they furnished their apartment from Antique Row, before and after they made love. Music, as much a part of them as breathing, was yanked from their lives, and the silence screamed between them.

It was a familiar sight. A red Karman Ghia speeding up coastal highway from Watts to San Francisco. A guy, a girl and a dog. The guy and girl had been inseparable since high school, since she was sixteen; now he was graduating from Stanford, law school bound, and she was finishing up her junior year at Berkeley. You seldom saw one without the other, him in red baseball cap with a white S covering curly brunette hair, and a brown leather bomber jacket clinging to the torso of one of the west coast's most sought after athletic bodies. She, wearing her father's 1940 fudge fedora, her mane of copper hair matched the billowing of the fringe flying from her buckskin jacket.

Until now, the sojourns to Watts had been pleasure trips, to see family and old friends, to participate in the Annual Watts Boys Club

Christmas Show, to attend the New Year's party at Club Oasis, to record at Champion. But now there was loud quiet. To turn on the radio was to risk reminders of happier times when his Raw Cilk songs rivaled Motown's best. When Raw Cilk's "Everlastin' Love" and Percy Sledge's "When A Man Loves A Woman" were hailed as *the* love ballads of 1966. When the stars were in their heavens and all was right with the world. What a difference a year makes.

Now his hypnotic hazel eyes set in deep bronze skin were fastened to the nothingness of the road. The car seemed guided by the stars as the moon shimmered silver on the ocean and played hide and seek with the terrain. She touched his hand, sadness flickering in her honey-colored eyes. He managed a glance and quick smile before returning his gaze to the highway. The silence was deafening and all that could be heard was the whiz of rubber on asphalt.

He parked his car beside her 1957 pink T-Bird, a sweet sixteen gift from her parents. They climbed the front steps of the Victorian house on Alta Vista, and she stopped to get the mail as he opened the vestibule door. After tackling the three flights in silence, he unlocked their apartment door and hung her hat and jacket on the halltree, while she went over to the wall of windows. The San Francisco skyline twinkled before her, calming her much like the ocean always did. As he went to get the dog's leash, she folded her arms and gazed at the city's lights dancing below.

"You want some light?" Qwayz asked when he returned to the room.

"No thanks," Jaz answered.

"I'm gonna take Akira for a walk." He kissed her cheek and opened the door for the beautiful Irish Setter named for its master's old karate teacher.

Her brother's handsome image superimposed itself on the San Francisco vista and Jaz washed the windows with her cascading tears. What had TC, this young music mogul, this black genius, been doing in Vietnam, and why did he have to die? Whether killed at Khe Sanh or in TET Offensive, it was January 1968, and her big brother, Tavio Culhane, was dead. Until Qwayz's brother-in-law, Yudi Hodges, went over, Vietnam was known only as the thief who stole young black men from urban ghettos to fight the yellow men in a distant land for the white man. The lure was steady money and benefits. The catch was few made it back and those who did, like Yudi, where in no condition to enjoy it. When TC went, it put Vietnam right smack dab in the middle of the Culhane/Chandler world.

Now, just back from TC's funeral, Jaz, in her mind's eye, replayed the day her idyllic life shattered. She and Qwayz had just driven back from a ski trip in Tahoe, their Christmas gift to AJ, whom they'd put on a plane back to L.A. and called his parents with the flight info. She and Qwayz called dibs on a hot shower as they raced up the steps to the vestibule, grabbing the mail before jockeying up the first flight of steps. Jaz tripped Qwayz and laughingly climbed over him until they reached the second floor. They tipped past two apartments, before they bolted up the final flight to their love nest in the sky. When Qwayz unlocked the door they both tried entering at the same time before Qwayz's long legs took four giant steps to the bedroom door.

"Foul, foul!" Jaz protested. "Your legs are longer than mine."

"But yours are prettier." He gleaned as Jaz sidled up to him, gyrating her body into his. When Jake, Jaz's nickname for Qwayz's manhood, responded, she bypassed him and ran for the bathroom.

"Foul, foul!"

"You use your advantages and I use mine!" She closed the bathroom door.

"How 'bout we share?" he said through the door.

"No way, I've had enough of you guys and the cold. I'm never going skiing again."

"You didn't go this time," he joned. "I'm going to the store to get Akira dog food, anything else?"

"What I want from you you can't buy in a store, babes. Hurry back!"

When Qwayz returned he snatched up the ringing phone and set the groceries on the counter.

"Hey, Mr. C." He eyed the bedroom. No sight of Jaz meant she was still in the tub.

"Well, I'm clean, prunie and hot." She stood in the doorway wrapped in her fluffy robe, her wet hair hidden beneath a thirsty towel. "How about some loud lovemaking on the magic carpet of our big, brass bed." Qwayz didn't respond as he finished putting things away. He's tired, she thought. "You take a shower while I rustle us up something delicious to eat." Her husband was transfixed by something out the kitchen's stained-glass window. "What is it?" Jaz looked out and saw nothing but a strangeness in her husband's eyes.

"Qwayz, what's the matter?"

"Your dad called..." His mouth was open but nothing came out. Jaz thought her father had blown her anniversary gift, but the painting was to be shipped directly to the landlady. "Jaz..." Qwayz gripped her shoulders for support and it scared her.

"What?" She implored, his face looked as if it were going to explode under the pressure. "Qwayz what?" She almost screamed as her heart pounded, her breath shortened, and a queasiness churned in her stomach. *And she knew.* There was only one thing her father could say that would hit Qwayz like this. "What Qwayz?"

"It's TC..."

She began to cry uncontrollably matching the silent tears streaming down his face. "No... no, no, no." She wailed like a wounded animal. Forehead to forehead, nose to nose, honey on hazel, tears to tears. They collapsed, huddled and locked in each other's arms. Akira circled them before resting by Qwayz's side.

"It was instant, painless—" he began as Jaz jerked at the idea of death being painless. "He received a Bronze Star for Valor. After most of his company was killed, he lay in ambush until the VC came around and took out four before they...got him." The last word mixed with a new wave of tears, and they cried together until all moisture drained from their bodies.

It had been a horrible few weeks that followed, and now with her brother buried in the Culhane family cemetery in Colt, Texas, Jaz just wanted her life with Qwayz back to normal. She just wanted him to finish up his pre-law studies and her premed. She just wanted her Qwayz back. The fun-loving, optimistic, crazy Qwayz. The guy whose handsome face would split into a wide smile, whose laughter would fill his eyes and then the room. Her Qwayz. Girls wanted Quinton Regis Chandler IV and guys wanted to *be* him. His gait as easy as the licks he'd put on Amber, his dad's old guitar. She wanted popcorn and old movies from their brass bed on Saturday nights, bubble baths in their claw-foot tub illuminated by a thousand candles perched on its ledge. Chilled apple cider and satin sheets. She wanted to make love again any time, anywhere. Didn't matter how much lovin' they enjoyed through the week, Saturday night was always a marathon and twice on Wednesdays, their hump day, when afternoon delight between classes was capped with an after dinner flesh-fest. She wanted lazy rides north to Napa or south to Carmel, where love pulled them off the road demanding release. She wanted strolls along the beach, special celebrations at Giuseppe's, cuddling by their fireplace munching pecan bark from Ghiradelli Square, and purchases from Fisherman's Wharf to be cooked and devoured in the privacy of their own home. She wanted her perfect life back when it was all sunshine, laughter, music and love.

And Qwayz's lovin' was ... supernatural. He knew the how, where and what of pleasuring her. He was talented, adventurous and insatiable, crediting his West Indian heritage for his "gift." After all this time, being with him was still magical. Making love in their big brass bed was like climbing onto a magic carpet, Qwayz her passport to ecstasy. Soaring high above the earth, they flew among the stars, tumbled through heaven and somersaulted into paradise as Qwayz brought her to an indescribable, unendurable pleasure. He was her FLO– First, Last and Only love. It had taken him a full year and a half to consummate their relationship because he wanted it to be special for her. "You're only going to have one first time Jas-of-mine. It's gonna be magical like we are. No backseat, sand dunes or green grass motels for us." Jaz's best friend, Gladys Ann, had told her that Qwayz could pull it off since he'd "had enough poontang to last him till he's thirty!" Jaz and Qwayz had discovered inventive ways to relieve sexual tension while maintaining her virginity. Finally, during her graduation trip to visit her aunt and uncle in Paris, France, Jaz was deflowered in a French hayloft deep in the Champagne region. The second and third time was during the Fourth of

July celebration at Chateau Jazz; once in the Fluellen limo while TC's "Night Moves" tape played, and the other in their chateau's gatehouse. They had intended to make love all across Italy too, but the Watts riots had called them home.

Jaz blew her nose and walked into their bedroom and ran her fingers across the "friggin' heirloom" as TC had called their gleaming brass bed with its ornate, curved headboard and footboard. It had been the first bed she and Qwayz had ever made love in. Over the last few weeks they had existed in an isolated togetherness, still sleeping intertwined as usual, but brought together by comfort not desire, and Jaz missed his touch, spontaneity and craziness. She missed coming home to a passel of balloons after a tough exam or a candlelit dinner set for two with a centerpiece of pink roses. Or a cord of wood obstructing the doorway and lining the walls because he thought two cords would keep "his Lady" really warm in the winters. Or coming home and finding him stretched across the hearth wearing nothing but a smile, strumming Amber. He'd put the guitar beside the driftwood from Paradise Rock, open his arms and say, "Show me you know me, girlie." And she would.

Yeah, she wanted her Qwayz back so they could "not mourn" like TC said. TC was the big brother Jaz had followed everywhere for years. Before he went to Vietnam, TC was her only blood relative here on the west coast, but TC and Qwayz had been womb-close since they were 10 and 8. Despite a two year difference in age, Qwayz was TC's equal athletically and musically. They were closer than most brothers, and once Qwayz revealed his newfound feelings for Jaz, they both often reminded her that they shared a relationship "over and beyond" her, which she had to recognize and respect.

With her parents in Italy, where her father was Ambassador, her sister Mel in New York, and her jazz diva aunt Selena and her husband the legendary saxophonist Zack Fluellen back in Paris, Qwayz was all she had in this world. He had always been there for her and promised that he always would, and she never had reason to doubt him. He needed time to grieve TC's loss and to heal.

"I'm back," Qwayz said, as he hung his red cap and jacket on the halltree and headed for the bathroom. Jaz only wished it was so as

Akira stretched out in her usual posture. "Ready for bed?" Qwayz climbed in and opened the covers for her.

Jaz crawled into him and he enveloped her body with his. They lay there in the darkness, the reflection of San Francisco bouncing back at them from the dresser mirror. A distant fog horn bellowed as she paced her breathing with his. They both feigned sleep, begged for it to come and go, come and go, signifying the passage of time when all would be right with their world again.

Jaz pulled into a space and noticed Qwayz's car. It was their first anniversary, and she had stored their wedding portrait in the never used bedroom closet. It had been such a weird few weeks, with both of them preoccupied with TC's death, while trying to catch up on their studies. As Qwayz kissed her goodbye early this morning, had he wished her Happy Anniversary or Happy Valentine's Day or Good Luck on her Biochem exam? Jaz hoped today was the day they would find their way back to each other.

Opening the door and announcing her arrival, she stopped, then convulsed with laughter. In her grandmother's rocker, a few steps from the door, sat a gigantic teddy bear holding a red and purple balloon bouquet in one paw, and a dozen pink roses in the other.

"I couldn't find gardenias to save my life," Qwayz said, leaning against the bedroom doorjamb.

"You're a trip." She fell into Qwayz's waiting arms. "I love you."

"Me too. Happy Valentine's Day, Jas-of-mine."

"That sounds so good." Jaz let her head crane against his neck soaking up his Jade East scent.

"And this feels good too but we've got reservations at Giuseppe's at six."

"Oh, boo coo de bucks."

"Nothing's too good for my lady." He flashed his familiar smile, even toothed over a sensuous bottom lip.

They dined royally at their favorite neighborhood bistro where Mama Aruzzo always hired a roving violinist and gave each woman a rose for Valentine's Day. When Qwayz told her it was their anniversary, she announced it to the entire room and gave the couple a bottle of champagne.

They staggered lazily up the hill to their apartment. Inside, they patted Teddy on the head, and rounded the fireplace to the bedroom where Qwayz had more champagne on ice ...water.

"No more champagne," Jaz protested weakly, "or I'll get a headache, and I don't want a headache tonight." She began peeling off her clothes as Qwayz threw the champagne out of sight. "Oh, I look a mess." Jaz stood in front of a free-standing, antique Cheval mirror absently moving a big red bow from her field of vision. "I always loved that mirror." She flopped on the bed.

"Happy first anniversary." Qwayz stroked her bare, brown thigh.

"Ah!" Jaz said, jumping up as she realized the antique mirror she'd admired for so long was hers. "You devil!" She fingered the beveled glass as Qwayz saddled up behind her, his image captured behind hers.

"It's hard to shop for the girl who has everything." He brushed his lips across her cheek and kissed her.

"As long as I have you, I do have everything." She squeezed her hands over his.

"Well, I'm gonna give you something memorable every anniversary."

"That reminds me." She wrestled herself loose of his grasp, rolled the television out of the way.

"Hey, watch it." He ran to help. "What's in there?"

"Put it over here. Prop it on the bed. Now, you unveil it."

"Oh, sweat!" He was speechless.

"Oh, Qwayz, it's beautiful. We're beautiful." They both stared at their wedding day image captured in oil, their eyes shinning brightly. Jaz remembered his proposing during one of their study play-breaks ....

"Valentine's Day has always been super special for us and I think we oughta do something extraordinary to commemorate it," he said, his sensuous bottom lip tucked under even white teeth, devilishness dancing in his eyes. Jaz, who lay straddled on top of him, murmured.

"Yeah? What?"

"Marry me." He rode her to the other side of the couch, her questioning eyes never leaving his. "Why not? I love you, you love me, I can't see any part of my future without you in it. Somewhere on this planet I want it written that you and I cared enough about each other to make it legal. I've thought about it alot since your father discovered our living situation, and it's what I want. You and me for eternity, Jaz. I want you to be my wife." He kissed her.

"Qwayz, you're a trip. In a time when folks are running from marriage and commitment—"

"I've never gone along with the okey-doke, Jas-of-mine. Isn't that why you're so crazy 'bout me?"

"You're pregnant!" Jaz teased. "In love and trouble, tsk, tsk."

"I'd be in trouble if you said no, Jaz. That'll mean I was wrong about us all along. Am I?"

"No, Qwayz. I'd be honored to be your wife for the rest of my life." Qwayz then sprang the ecru Victorian tea dress with the leg-o-mutton sleeves that Jaz had loved in Memories Boutique. "How can I refuse?" She smiled through tears of happiness.

Qwayz was willing but Jaz nixed the idea of inviting her parents, knowing her father would be vehemently opposed to his daughter marrying so young. So they swore their friends to secrecy, and the Chandler wedding party took off for Tahoe one weekend. TC orchestrated the ceremony with Nat King Cole's "Too Young" as their wedding march. TC hosted the wedding dinner before dangling the bridal suite keys in front of the newlyweds. Qwayz carried his bride away from their friends and into the suite, where the first thing they noticed after he staggered and dumped her on the bed was the beamed ceiling –a reminder of the first time they made love in that French barn. They'd convulsed with laughter and fell to sleep in their wedding clothes, she in that gorgeous lace dress with the gardenia wreath on her head, and he in his tux ....

And now their wedding day images stared back at them. Two blissfully happy newlyweds with a glimpse of the gardenia bouquet. The artist had captured Qwayz's full lips, the little indentation between his top lip and his narrow nose, his high cheekbones, hazel eyes, skin tone and curly hair.

"I didn't expect this masterpiece." Jaz moved closer to inspect their larger-than-life selves. "You are one fine brother!"

"It's perfect of you." Qwayz was mesmerized by his wife's intelligent, honey eyes, hooded by dense, long eyelashes, and topped by her thick, naturally arched eyebrows. Her curly mane which fell below her shoulders was crowned by the halo of gardenias. "Unreal. Who did this? Michelangelo?"

"Close, Luchesi Tretoni. He did the painting of us as children that hangs in Dad's office. It's as awful as this is magnificent."

"He captured us, Jaz ...the love, the hope, the promise. This is a for-sure bonafide heirloom. You hadn't seen it before?"

"No." Jaz slid her arms around Qwayz's waist. "I wanted us to see it together—for the first time on our first anniversary."

"Our kids are gonna laugh," he chuckled. "What is it about you, me and Italy? We're gonna get there one of these days."

"Our second honeymoon. I'll get pregnant there." They laughed into each other's arms.

"Oh Jaz, thank you. I needed this ... to remind me of how sweet our life together is."

They made slow deliberate love, with not an inkling of urgency from the weeks of deprivation, but long, languorous, sinewy love.

"Welcome back," she said as they lay spent and satisfied.

"It's good to be home." Qwayz kissed her as he interlocked his legs with hers. "If I'd played my cards right we'd be making love at Paradise Rock for our first anni–"

"Everything I want, I have, whenever you hold me tight," Jaz said.

"We are magic, Jaz, and we'll last until the end of time." They giggled and kissed. He thought of the place they'd found after one of their trips to Carmel, where they had regularly stopped to make love until somebody built a house on it."But it was perfect, Jaz – that secluded granite peninsula jutting out over the Pacific. The sound of the ocean pounding five hundred feet below."

"We have a lifetime to discover another special place. Maybe even the Myrtle Beach your dad was so crazy about."

"Yeah, but he hadn't seen Paradise Rock. If I'm ever missing, that's where I'll be. Our one bedroom hideaway from little Q-5 and Amber and Shane."

"Oh, Negro, please. We'll name our daughter after your dad's guitar, but I'm not naming our second son after a movie."

"Shane Chandler? Sounds ... athletic."

"Sounds dufuss."

"As cool as we are, we'd never have dufuss kids." He stretched out his long, brown legs and Jake protruded. "I'm kinda cool, how 'bout warming me up?" Qwayz said, and Jaz climbed on top of him, covering his body with hers. She raised above him and held onto the brass headboard, with San Francisco's diamond sky approving beyond. She let her engorged breasts fill Qwayz's passion-soaked eyes. "Have mercy, girlie," he managed before treating each of her chocolate drops to the rough-smooth texture of his tongue.

"I love you Jas-of-mine, don't ever forget that."

"Don't ever stop. Promise?"

"Promise."

Chapter Two

The NCAA basketball final drew a SRO crowd to the immense stadium and Jaz pried Denise Chandler Hodges, Denny, away from the house to see the last game of her brother's college career. As they settled into their seats, Jaz recalled, sadly, that last year TC had been there, and Yudi, Denny's husband, was expected home from Nam. This year TC was gone, and Yudi had disappeared somewhere in America, a broken shadow.

Qwayz's second cousin, AJ, who preferred being called his "nephew," sat with Jaz and Denny. Qwayz's mother and sister, Ma Vy and Hanie, and AJ's parents, Melie and big Aubrey, sat in front of them. Qwayz's boys from Champion Record Studios, the neighborhood, and Roosevelt High kept up noise and spirit to the far left. The excitement was high. All those who had scored the coveted tickets revelled in their good fortune and felt privileged to witness the final game of 'Magic' Chandler's college career.

The TV commentators relayed second-handed plays to all unable to beg, borrow or steal a ticket and bantered on about how 'Magic' Chandler's leaving would hurt the team. How before him, Stanford hadn't played in the NCAA since '42, but Magic had brought them there twice. How he epitomizes 'grace under pressure,' even with 7 foot Alcindor on his back, "Magic just adjusts and scores." Now he was giving up the game to go to law school.

Even though Stanford lost to UCLA, Qwayz was high scorer with 38 points, 12 short of his personal goal to tie with Wilt Chamberlain's 1962 record. As the two teams shook hands Stanford ran off while UCLA remained on the floor.

It began on the far right, a hum like a swarm of unearthed bee's and became rhythmic and distinct. "Qway-z! Qway-z! Qway-z!" Like a Zulu chant, it spread through the crowd, until everyone in the bleachers stood chanting his name. "Qway-z! Qway-z!" Folks had stopped in their tracks, in the aisles, at the entrances, and on the floor the UCLA team joined in to give a great one his due. "Qway-z! Qway-z!"

The crowd wasn't going anywhere until it got another glimpse of #24, the best college player of the century. Qwayz appeared and the crowd thundered with applause, cheering and whistling. He raised both hands over his head like a prizefighter who'd just been declared champ; his clenched fists alternating with waves. When the crowd refused to cease, he threw kisses to his mother and his wife, bowed graciously from the waist to his adoring fans and jogged off. Tears of pride, joy and pain graced Jaz's cheeks as her husband bid farewell to a segment of his life he'd lived and breathed ever since she'd known him. He'd surely miss it and basketball would miss him ... and TC had missed it all.

Even though UCLA won the NCAA championship that year, and Alcindor was named Player of the Year, it was the picture of Qwayz "Kissing Basketball Goodbye," that made the cover of Sports Illustrated.

"I think we oughta move?" Qwayz had said casually as they prepared fondue for guests one night.

"Where did that come from?" Jaz swirled the melted cheese as Qwayz arranged seafood around the vegetables.

"After graduation." She eyed him curiously as he continued. "It'll be better for you once I start law school. I don't wanna worry about you coming and going from campus to here."

"I do it now."

"Yeah, but I'm here now. I thought we'd moved to Berkeley. A nice apartment with a balcony for Akira, maybe a fireplace in the bedroom." He yo-yoed his eyebrows but Jaz wasn't amused. "I'll get it." He answered the door for their dinner guests.

Jaz loved this apartment, their first home with its handpicked heirloom furniture, beamed ceilings and fireplace. She assumed they'd stay here until they bought a house. She wasn't sure what to make of this move idea, but maybe he would read her reaction and drop it. Things were much better between them since their anniversary celebration, but he still kept more to himself than usual. She thought that after the basketball season and his last game, he'd be more the old Qwayz, but he remained slightly preoccupied. For all she knew, she could be to. They were still adjusting to the lack of TC in their lives. Things would happen and after sharing it with one another their natural reaction was to "call TC." Maybe this apartment reminded Qwayz of TC, maybe San Francisco did. Maybe it was Qwayz's attempt to move on.

If Qwayz brought it up again, she wouldn't balk. He'd always been there for her. He was there when her parents threatened to move her to Connecticut so the family would be closer to her dad in Washington. When her aunt and uncle came from Paris to take care of her, he'd called her every night at 11 through her senior year and came down from Palo Alto whenever he didn't have a game. He was there at her prom and graduation, taking her pictures, and beside her every step of the way as she discovered Paris. He was there when she had her first brush with prejudice in her Phi Sci class. It was Qwayz who comforted and told her "Jasmine Bianca Culhane had the GPA, SAT scores and the right to be in any class on Berkeley's campus ...and the only relationship you have to worry 'bout is between you and the teacher. Period." He'd held her and said, "Some of us are born to ride against the wind– I guess we're just a pair of the lucky equestrians." He was there for her when TC died. He'll be there with her forever. It was her turn to be there for him. She loved this apartment but she loved Qwayz much more.

Qwayz's graduation was full of pomp and circumstance. His mother and his sister Hanie stayed in her parent's suite at The Fairmont, Melie and Aubrey in a room at The Mark Hopkins, and AJ on Jaz and Qwayz's sofa. Jaz's father, Hep, hosted a reception for his "son" in The Riverton Room where members of the old L.A. crew came up and mingled with the academicians, former teammates and college friends.

Jaz still had a few more weeks of school, so Qwayz took it upon himself to apartment hunt. He often waited for her at school after an unsuccessful day of inspecting possibilities. She didn't know which was worse, his apartment hunting or his going off to L.A., which he'd done twice without her. They never did anything apart except during basketball season and that was over.

"I found the perfect place!" He told her one day, beaming with excitement, and took her by.

"It's new!" was her first objection to the apartment.

"It's a year old and really close to campus."

When the door swung open, she hated it instantly. Straight ahead was the balcony. To the left was a closet door, the next opening was the exposed kitchen with the countertop, just like her childhood home on Alvaro Street. To the right was a closet door, then another door to the bedroom. The living room was the space in front of the balcony and the dining room was the space in front of the kitchen counter. It was small with no character and thin, white walls. "It has a dishwasher, disposal and a washer and dryer," he pointed out. "The bedroom has a fireplace."

Jaz took the two giant steps from the front door into the decent sized room with a long window on one wall, and the two closets and bathroom doors on the other. "Where are we going to put all our furniture?"

"Well, the bed on this wall opposite the fireplace and the armoire and wardrobe ... over here. We'll work with it Jaz."

She stepped back into the living room, shaking her head at the thought of all their gorgeous pieces being crammed into this tiny apartment.

"Over here we can get that new dining room suite you wanted–

the all glass one on the brass pedestal and the matching chairs."

"Where do we put our parlor set?"

"On the balcony."

"The balcony?!" Jaz smelled a rat. Was Qwayz so anxious for this move that he was bribing her with the "too expensive" glass and brass dinette set. If she could only determine why he wanted to move so badly, then she could counter it, ease his worries, and they could stay on Alta Vista. But this was as animated as he'd been since graduation. His sister Denny had said that the death of TC probably conjured up some long buried feelings from their Dad's death. Stir in his giving up basketball and ending his musical collaboration, graduating and beginning law school, it all must weigh heavily on his mind. As his wife, Jaz would have to adjust and make the transition more palatable for them both.

"Is this the best you've seen?"

"Trust me." His hazel eyes locked with her honey. Jaz swore she saw him flinch.

What they didn't cram into the new apartment, they put in storage. The bedroom accommodated all their furniture including the lingerie armoire and the Cheval mirror, but the living room had to forfeit some furniture. Still, once they hung their wedding portrait over the couch, it seemed like home.

"I could stare at it for hours," Qwayz mused, sitting on the coffee table facing the painting.

"Why do that when you got the real thing?" She kissed him on the nose pivoting into the kitchen to unpack condiments. "Think Scoey and Tracy will be as happy as us?" She spoke of their best friends who were about to marry. Scoey had unselfishly shared his friendship with TC to include Qwayz. From their days at The Watts Boys Club right on up through Raw Cilk, to Scoey's receiving a football scholarship to USC and beyond.

"No one could be as happy as us. I gotta go down to L.A. to make the last plans for Scoey's bachelor party."

"Can't you do that by phone?" Jaz noting the frequency of his trips to L.A., including one last week.

"I've got final fittings for the tux and a bunch of us are helping

Scoey move into his new place. 'Sides you'll be busy. You are taking that special program at the hospital? That's quite an honor to be recommended as an incoming senior."

"That's only because I'm so brilliant and talented," Jaz teased, returning to sit next to him on the coffee table. "I thought I'd pass it up and we'd spend the summer together–Carmel, Napa, Tahoe–"

"The program is only six weeks. Think how far ahead of everyone you'll be with this project. A shoe-in for med school."

"I just thought it was important for us to spend some serious time together." It bothered Jaz she couldn't read his expression.

The wedding was gorgeous. Tracy was radiant in the most exquisite gown and train ever to grace St. Theresa's. Jaz as matron of honor, a maid of honor, six bridesmaids and a flower girl were all decked out in a symphony of muted pink and green. Scoey, his best man, Qwayz, and the other groomsmen were handsome in their black tuxedos.

Jaz took the bouquet from her old friend, Tracy Renee Summerville, the petite, pretty girl with the graham cracker complexion framed by black hair, whom she'd met in dance class before Mrs. Terrell put Jaz and Gladys Ann out. A parochial school girl, Tracy had refused to attend an all-girl high school, and had ended up at Roosevelt with the notorious pair. Right then, she'd set her designs on the older, star football player, Ellis Carlton Scofield, and slow walked him until she got him. "Shoulda given that girl more credit," Gladys Ann once said of the quiet, naive Tracy.

From the packed church, guests followed the limos to the reception where the champagne flowed from fountains like water, and the food as plentiful as the cache of gifts, which required their own room.

"Did I tell you I've just bought and revived a pepper farm with a pimento plant?" Hep asked Qwayz. Next to his children there was nothing Hep Culhane enjoyed discussing more than his investments, and Qwayz was the only interested family member. "My foreign holdings now include the cocoa plantation in South America, tin in Sumatra, bauxite in the Caribbean and in Sri Lanka–" Hep chatted on as Qwayz drank in the pink champagne along with the image of his wife posing with the bride. Don't-give-a-damn-gorgeous, and phatness personified had been used to describe her physical beauty—the copper skin, the voluminous, nutmeg hair shot with blond from the California sun. The Cherokee rise in her profile was also responsible for her pronounced cheekbones which plunged into hollows and were rescued by full, bow lips that rendered her mouth in a perpetual pout. Jaz had always been mature-looking, even at ten, when, tired of the constant comments and comparisons, she had plopped her father's too big fedora on her head in an effort to hide her looks, but instead drew more attention. Jaz took no responsibility and therefore no credit for her looks, and had no time for folks who responded to her based solely on her appearance. Jaz hated the comparisons others made between her and TC to Mel. At seven, to the delight of Hep and the chagrin of Lorette, Jaz punched out many an older classmate for calling her big sister, Mel, "bug-eyed," "gorilla nose," or "adopted." But Miss Thang found her beauty niche when she went off to Juilliard. In the gene-pool roulette black families inherit, Mel would never have mountains of long hair like her sister, or her height, or "apple-jelly eyes" as AJ called them, but Mel learned to play up her features. Those "bug eyes" rimmed with professional makeup became her trademark, she grew to her nose and adorned it with an 18 carat gold ring, and the hair her mother had croquignoled every Saturday now formed a short, airy natural halo around her mocha skin. The Culhane sisters favored but the most beautiful one was his wife, Qwayz thought.

"Young man, you haven't heard a word I've said," Hep chastised Qwayz who was smiling at his wife. "But I approve of my competition. You love her very much."

"More than life itself."

"I hope you don't have to prove that one day."

"I hope I prove it everyday, Mr. C."

"What are you two jawjacking about?" Jaz insinuated herself between her favorite men.

"We're buying a house in San Fran, Punkin'. Three bedrooms on Knob Hill. The head of Culhane Enterprises needs a house in the city," Hep informed his daughter.

"Are you keeping the Connecticut-house museum?"

"No, my New York business will be moving to the coast, too."

"What about that poor old fossil you brought out of retirement to run it for you while you were in Italy–Kyle? Was that his name?" Jaz watched her father's eyebrows knit together in a question, then relax with recognition.

"Tipton Kylerton has been a trusted friend and associate–"

"Can he still walk, Dad?"

"So like the young to have no mercy for the old."

The photographer called for the best man, and Qwayz left to pose for pictures with Scoey. Jaz couldn't help but remember that it used to be three extraordinary black men: TC, Scoey and Qwayz, the trio.

And then there were two, Jaz thought.

"Glad this circus is over," Qwayz said, as the bride and groom got into the limo, to catch a plane bound for two weeks in Hawaii.

"You'll do the same for our daughters," said Jaz.

"No question, and they'll be as beautiful as their mama."

"This is just what the doctor ordered." Jaz slid her arms around her husband, thinking of the changes and horrors of 1968, beginning with the death of her brother in January.

In March, Howard University crowned a homecoming queen with a natural, like the one Mel had been wearing since her days at Juilliard. In the My Lai massacre the U.S. had slaughtered a whole village of unarmed South Vietnamese, and fifteen days later LBJ announced he would not seek reelection. Four days later, on April 4th, Dr. Martin Luther King Jr. was shot on the balcony of the Lorraine Motel in Memphis and died an hour later. Two days later, 17 year old Black Panther Bobby Hutton was shot and killed by police in West Oakland. On May 13th, delegates from the United States and North Vietnam held their first formal peace meeting in Paris. Then Robert Kennedy was assassinated. One step forward then two steps back.

But personally, all was not lost. Mel had the lead and hit song – with a nightly standing ovation – in the Broadway hit, *Hair*. Qwayz had graduated with honors from Stanford, and Mr. and Mrs. Ellis Carlton Scofield, Scoey and Tracy, had entered the ranks of the blissfully married.

"Well, after six long months this year is finally looking up," Jaz said, to which her husband made no comment.

The alarm blasted Jaz awake and she opened her eyes. Ugh! this hateful apartment, she thought. She missed the wall of windows at the headboard, and making love with their silhouettes' reflecting in the bureau's mirror, and the starry San Francisco skyline as their backdrop. She missed the wide open spaces. Here poor Akira had a balcony but she had to sleep on the threshold between the bedroom and the living room. It was awful, but Qwayz made it bearable. The move was good for him, he seemed to be coming around.

Jaz stood on the balcony watching him wash their cars down below. Akira sprinted back and forth in the park across the small one-way drive. Jaz watched Qwayz's biceps ripple as he applied pressure to her car's roof. The way the sun caught and ricocheted off his brunette curls.

"Hey foxy mama," Qwayz greeted, swinging his arm up over the car roof in pure adoration of his wife's beauty. She wore her sleep-T shirt with scanty panties underneath, her hair still tousled from last night's lovin'. "Have mercy! Girlie you do look fine in peach."

"Everything you buy me is peach." She teased by rocking her legs and body suggestively.

"You wear it well next to that deep brown skin."

"Thanks for the wake up alarm." She leaned over, taunting him.

"Your interview is at three."

"I don't need three hours to get ready. What else did you have in mind?" She licked her lips.

"I'll be up in a few." He winked, as Mr. Sanchez, the super, greeted them both. An embarrassed Jaz quickly disappeared.

Showered, dressed in jeans and a sweatshirt, Jaz answered the ringing phone, and talked to Denny as she seeded a cantaloupe.

"I report directly to the chief psychiatrist," Denny said. "I've only got my thesis to complete. Gotta keep busy." The name of Yudi hung, unspoken, between them. "As for you, I hear it's quite a coup to even be approached for Dr. Brock Williams' summer research program."

"True, but I was hoping Qwayz and I could spend the summer together, maybe even Myrtle Beach."

"Where is that baby brother of mine anyway?"

"He should be hanging his cap and jacket on the old halltree any minute now. How does he seem to you?"

"How do you mean?" Denny hedged and Jaz heard it.

"He moved us over here for one–at least he stopped his solo trips to L.A., which means the other woman lost to the wife."

"Nothing like that."

"You know somethin' I don't and should?"

"No, he's been taking care of things ...with the recording rights for TC's–"

"Denny what's going on?"

"Hey, girlie." Qwayz and Akira came through the door, hanging his cap and jacket on the brass knobs.

"Saved by the bell," Jaz said to Denny, "Catch you later."

"Who was?"

"Denny."

"So how's she doin'?" He asked evenly as Jaz surmised that blood was thicker than semen.

"OK, but I still can't get her here to visit. So, we gonna get AJ before or after his summer in camp? He's a teenager, how long do they think this camp crap will last?"

"His parents don't think. That's why he has us ...at least–" he stopped. "I thought we'd spend some time together, just the two of us."

"I like the sound of that." Jaz slid her arms around his neck as he sat on the coffee table facing their portrait. "I'll make you blaff tonight. I'll pick up the ingredients on the way home from the interview." She kissed the side of his salty cheek.

"I better go shower."

"Good idea." Jaz released him. "Qwayz," she called after him. "You don't have anything to tell me?" Her honey eyes fixed upon his hazel; the longer the gaze the more worried Jaz became.

"Well," Qwayz could hear his sister's voice prompting him, *You better tell Jaz.* "It can wait."

"Why don't you tell me now." She walked slowly to him without blinking once. She was getting bad vibes and he looked uncomfortable. Quinton Regis Chandler the 4th never looked uncomfortable.

"OK." He relented, motioning for her to take a seat on the couch. He sat facing his wife and their oil images upon the wall.

This was going to be far worse than Jaz had thought. Qwayz was deathly ill and dying or impotent–nope. The area of lovemaking remained supernatural. If anything their problems began once their feet hit the floor. Were they broke? Impossible. He wasn't going to law school? That was his choice and not as grave a situation as he was making her feel.

"Qwayz, you're scaring me."

"How do I begin," he said, as he played with her folded hands.

"At the beginning."

"I've spoke it in my mind a thousand times."

"No more dress rehearsals, this is it, spit it out."

"Better or worse," he chuckled, twirling her circle of diamonds wedding band. "I've already lost two people I cared about most in this world. Don't be number three." He looked at her.

"I'm not going anywhere, Qwayz."

"It has to do with TC's death. I've remained more tied to it because I've handled most of his affairs. He was a complicated and talented man." He sensed Jaz's disguised impatience. "I know you've noticed my preoccupation at times and that's partially the reason for it–that I couldn't put it to rest as quickly as you thought I should have."

"So what you have to tell me is about TC?"

"Yes and no. I mean, I couldn't believe that he had so much to give here in the States, but he wanted to give in Vietnam where his country needed him."

Jaz didn't hide her confusion. His eloquence had served him well as a songwriter and would do so as a lawyer, but right now it was driving her up the wall.

"I've felt the need to do more." He raked his hands through his curls, rose and strutted across the room, looking out the balcony window down at their cars parked predictably side by side. "Before TC went over, we knew about Vietnam from Yudi going over, and the guys we knew who came back and didn't. We saw it on television, able to turn it off if we wanted. We see the demonstrators, pass right by them with their handouts and protest songs. What it mean to us? The future doctor and lawyer? But TC's death brought the war right into our house, sat it down and said, what are you gonna do about it? And I gotta do something, Jaz." He looked back at her from the sliding glass door. "I just haven't felt comfortable with this whole thing—that TC died fighting to protect our freedom over there, while we enjoyed it free of charge here. I just had to do something."

"I think that's admirable." Jaz joined him at the door, stroking his arm and taking his hand. "Everyone has their own way of contributing to the same cause–different roads to the same end. We're all fighting for freedom. Your role in life isn't in Vietnam it's here, fighting in the courtrooms for justice. It's to protect Ma Vy, me and our children."

"But how do I look our children in the eye when they ask about Uncle TC and ask what I did?" He broke from her grip and paced across the room to the other side and back again. "How did you get out alive daddy?"

For the first time in their relationship Jaz felt as if she and Qwayz were seriously out of sync—a bizarre twilight zone of lapsed communication. Something that seemed so important and all-consuming to him, didn't mean diddley to her.

"Qwayz, it'll be alright. We're talking years from now, the war will be long over. There are peace talks in Paris now, LBJ isn't running again, we'll elect a president who'll stop the war–"

"I need to do something NOW. Something definite, concrete, something I can feel good about as a man, so I can contribute and move on with my life." He led her to their original seat with him on the coffee table and her on the couch. "I feel confident about my decision. It's your reaction to it that has me worried."

"What? You volunteered to work with vets?"

"I want you to look at the long term benefit of this for me as a man, a husband, a father. It's important to me, and I really have no choice.

It's something I have to do if I am to look at myself in the mirror with any pride for the rest of my life. It'll throw our plans off for about a year, no more than two tops, but we'll be healthier as a couple–a family because of it." So he'll work a year or so before going to law school, Jaz thought, could be worse. "I've joined the Air Force." Hazel eyes unflinchingly pierced honey brown ones.

"What?" Jaz managed without blinking, her face frozen, and Qwayz repeated his statement with such calm relief it was frightening. Qwayz seemed almost boyish after the release of the news, and Jaz felt ancient.

He continued eloquently as if presenting a case before the Supreme Court. Jaz felt as if she were trapped in a nightmare which grew more macabre as she caught snatches of his soliloquy like "As an officer ... equivalent to law clerking ... trying cases of military indiscretions ... court martials ... a special task force ... Saigon is a fortress ...well-protected ...

"What did you say?" Her horror found voice. Qwayz had mistaken her quietness for reluctant acceptance. She slid her hands from his as if his were contaminated with acid. "You're crazy." She rose from the sofa pacing the room's perimeter like a caged feline.

"I've made up my mind, Jaz."

"You're certifiable." Her heart pounded and her head split wide open. "Didn't you see TC? His body riddled with bullets, the jungle funk that filled that room. Did you hear the sobbing? The words? Did you see the pain? And you're signing up for more of the same?"

"Jaz, I told you this place is a secure–"

"That's what Yudi told Denny about GRU, all he'd be doing is what he did at the funeral home, and she hasn't seen him since he got back! No one gets back alive from Vietnam, haven't you learned anything from the neighborhood? Zombies come back. The minds are gone, the body parts missing, and flesh that survives is hooked on morphine and heroin. If you wanna kill yourself just get a gun and blow your brains out. Save us the prolonged agony and trouble." Tears streamed down her face and she yanked a napkin from the holder.

"Jaz, I can't imagine living without you. You are my world, but something heinous has crawled into it and I have to deal with it the best way I can ... or it will destroy us both."

"Save it, Qwayz." She resumed pacing. "You're going off to avenge my brother's death. It would be funny if it weren't so sad. This isn't back in the day when some rival cross-town team sold wolf tickets to the Dragons so y'all gonna go over there and whip ass for the big payback!"

"I'm doing this for both of us, Jaz–" Qwayz stood.

"Don't hand me that shit! And please spare me the Gary Cooper 'a man's gotta do what a man's gotta do' bullshit. Well, I gotta another quote for you Qwayz." Her face was inches from his. "I think it's from Dr. Zhivago–'Only an unhappy man volunteers to go to war!' If life is so bad for you here with me, you don't have to go to Vietnam to get away. No! I release you." She began throwing things into an overnight case, and Qwayz followed her without realizing what she was doing. "You selfish bastard!"

"I could say the same about you."

"You're doing this because it's right for YOU. To hell with everybody else! They don't count, they don't get a vote. Jaz is strong. Jaz is resilient, she'll bounce back. Jaz heats up and cools down. She'll adjust, she'll get over it. Hell, I'll be back home by that time. Well, little Jaz isn't going along with the same-o, same-o shit this time." She yanked her shoulder bag, fedora and jacket off the halltree. "Let Qwayz go off to war so he can feel better about himself. To hell with me, Ma Vy, AJ ... those you leave behind."

"Jaz, where are you going?"

"Like you even care." She shifted her shoulder bag. "Tell me shall I bury you next to TC so I can visit both graves at once? That'll be real considerate of you."

"Jaz, I'm comin' back."

"Yeah? Think so? In what condition?" she challenged and when he started to speak again she yelled, "Stop it! Just stop it OK? You are leaving me for no good reason but to chase some macho male bond shit thing you had with my brother. Well, I can't compete with my dead brother's memory. I have sense enough to know that."

"Jaz let me go with you–"

"I have to learn to live without you ... might as well start now." She dodged his attempt to hold her. "You still don't get it," she said with precise clarity. "I don't want to be around anyone who cares so little about me and my feelings ... as a wife, a person, a human being."

"I'll make it all up to you."

"That is so typically male of you." She stopped at the door. "You have demonstrated to me just how much you care for me–the living." She opened the door. "It's too late. You can never make this up to me. Never in a million years." She slammed the door shut. Qwayz watched her sling her things into her car and drive off without a backward glance.

Jaz tore around the streets of San Francisco before she ended up at Ghiradelli Square for a chocolate fix. Absently munching on pecan bark, she strolled too close to Antique Row where she and Qwayz had spent most of their Saturdays, so she hopped into her car. What the hell am I doing? She gassed up and headed down the coast turning off the radio which played too much Raw Cilk. She needed to talk, but Tracy was still on her honeymoon, and she wouldn't understand anyway, not like Denny, whom Jaz resisted seeing. She longed to talk to her oldest best friend, Gladys Ann, but she was in Washington at Howard U. They'd joke about the "stiff dick club"–the way guys stick together no matter what.

Unconsciously, she drove to Gary's Seaside Restaurant in Carmel, where she cried in her soup, played with her lobster, passed on dessert, and was propositioned by the waiter as she left. She strolled Carmel's quiet streets before ending up on Ruidoso Road. She pulled carefully off the main highway, taking the treacherous turn with aplomb, cruising to a stop about one visible mile from Paradise Rock and the house that occupied it now. The couple who lived there came out and peered in the direction of her '57 T-bird perched on the look-out before they climbed into their car and pulled off.

Jaz gazed out at the ocean cast silver, not knowing how long she'd been there. The sun had set long ago, and the moonrays skated on its dark glass. What is it they say about full moons and crazy people, she thought as she drifted off to sleep. Awaked by the chill in the air, she got out to retrieve the quilt from her trunk and thought she saw an outline of a car further down road, but decided it was a rock formation. She locked her doors and let the ocean's roar soothe her back to sleep.

"Dag," she said aloud, unfolding herself. She rubbed her neck, vowing no more nights spent in the car. Maybe she'd head south; stop in the coastal sights she'd always whizzed by in the last few years. The couple hadn't come back last night, and the tap on the car window startled her.

"What do you want?" She asked rolling the window down only a crack.

"I want you to come home," Qwayz said simply. "So we can talk this thing out."

"As I see it, the time for talk is over. You're going. Goodbye." Jaz started up her car and drove off, a cloud of dust swirled around him.

He wouldn't follow her, to what point? When he called to postpone her interview, he found that Jaz had already canceled. He just had to wait for her to come around, to see his side of it. He hoped it would happen before he left for Saigon.

"Hi" Jaz said simply as the door whined open, and Denny smiled.

"I've been expecting you."

"I took the scenic route, Big Sur, San Simeon. You ever been to Hearst Castle?"

"Nothing on the Culhane Estate in Connecticut," Denny said, with a chuckle.

"I've always liked this house." Jaz looked around the cozy decor as Denny poured soda over ice.

"It's been four days. Folks arc kinda worried."

"You mean, Qwayz."

"And your father. Qwayz thought you'd caught a plane to Italy."

"Left my passport at the apartment. Besides, Pops was the first one to leave me. Then TC, now Qwayz. Seems I can't hold on to a man."

"Yeah, I know the feeling."

"I'm sorry, maybe I shouldn't of come."

"Nonsense. I want you here. Who else would understand better than me?"

"Is this Denny the friend, the sister-in-law or the psychologist?"

"A little of all, but more of the first."

For a couple of days, the two women just lounged around, goofed off and went to the movies; "Barefoot In The Park" and "The Graduate," enjoying each other's company and steering clear of the old gang who'd ask after Qwayz. Jaz called her father and convinced him not to leave the Embassy in Italy. Denny convinced Qwayz of the same.

"I don't know when I lost control of my life," Jaz said quietly. "When it all shattered into a million pieces." She grabbed a throw pillow, cradled it into her hands as Denny sat across from her. "The very foundation of our marriage, the love, the honesty, the trust was all a sham–violated and replaced with deceit and manipulation. That whole Berkeley move was part of it. He knew back then, but didn't tell me. I was happier on Alta Vista. You know, I shoulda laughed in his face that cold winter night on Papa Colt's porch when he told me he loved me. Thrown this gold star in his face." She fingered the necklace he'd given her. "I woulda been spared all this. I wonder where I'd be now? TC used to say, 'Same thing makes you laugh, can make you cry.'"

"I think you've had many an enviable time or two as I recall."

"Yeah, we did have a charmed life–a crystal stair," she borrowed from Langston Hughes.

Denny left Jaz remembering the good times, while she fixed them a snack. She saw a faint sad smile on Jaz's lips when she returned.

"During his weeks of soul searching Qwayz turned to me, his sister," Denny explained. "With TC gone, I guess I was second pick. He wasn't moving past the death of his best friend, his brother. He didn't say it, but I knew he felt six years old and powerless again. And there's nothing worse for a man to feel. So without judging or offering guidance, I listened to him try to make sense of it, sort it out and then self-prescribe his course of action." Denny stopped staring out the window. "It was hard to hear. As his sister, I can't endorse it, but as an objective psychologist, I understand that it is important for him to do something, and this is what he's elected to do. What he needs now from us is the unconditional love and support that our grandmothers gave our grandfathers. The way our mothers did our fathers. I guess that's why we're here now because of forgiveness and compromise." Denny looked at her friend who didn't respond as she twirled the glass of soda on the coaster. "It's easy to love somebody when everything is smooth and cool runnin'. The test of real love is when you can hold on through the rough times. Better or worse ... until death do us part." Denny looked at the door. "It's hard to sustain love with no contact, but I still love Yudi. I always will, couldn't stop if I wanted. If he were just to walk through–" Denny's voice broke.

"How do you get pass the hurt and anger?" Jaz asked.

"Maybe you don't. Maybe you just put it on hold until later the way a parent does who's crazy with worry when their teenager has broken curfew. You imagine all sorts of grisly things but then you see them ... that they're alright–you're instantly relieved and mad at the same time. Maybe you can put this aside until Qwayz comes home safe and sound, then give him hell for the rest of your lives," Denny chuckled. Never have two people been so much alike as her brother and his wife, she thought. "Worse scenario," Denny continued, "He leaves with you all like this. Him guilty, you mad ... and he doesn't come back at all." Bingo, Denny thought as Jaz jerked her head towards her. "Then all the guilt and anger will be yours alone, my friend." She touched her sister-in-laws shoulder. "The nicest thing you all did for TC was to put aside personal feelings and give him a good send off, with great memories ... a reason to come back."

"Lotta good it did," Jaz mumbled.

"You'll never know. I just hate to think of you and Qwayz wasting this time apart when you two should be building memories, not tearing them down. Don't regret forever not spending these last few weeks–"

"Few weeks?"

"You didn't know? He's leaving on the third of July."

"July!? But I thought ... August ... like TC. Oh shit!" She scrambled for her things. "He'll miss his birthday."

As Jaz tore up the highway the anger melted, evaporating with her need to see Qwayz, be with him. "Oh please be there," she prayed when she stopped for gas and called home, but there was no answer. "I'm coming home Qwayz just as fast as I can." The faster she sped, the slower it seemed as if the car were on a treadmill going nowhere.

Chapter Three

"Qwayz! Qwayz!" Jaz slammed open the front door, jarring Akira to her feet. "Where is he?"

"Right behind you." He let the towel fall around his neck and over his bare chest.

"Oh, Qwayz!" Jaz flew into his arms. "I'm so sorry I acted that way. I was so mad and scared–"

"Jaz, Jaz." He rocked her in his embrace, as happy for her safe return as for her changed state of mind. "I was scared too, not about going, but that I'd lost you in the process of finding my answer to this crazy mess. I never meant to hurt you or make you feel—"

"I know, I know." They stood wrapped in each other's arms, joy filling their hearts, and the week-long separation creeping into their groins.

They began kissing, while Qwayz removed Jaz's shoulder bag, then her outer jacket. As they dropped to the floor, the knowledgeable Akira took her seat next to the balcony window. Undressing each other, they remained connected by tongue and tongue, tongue and neck, tongue and nipple, until he lifted her in his arms and carried her the few steps to the couch. While they made love, bathed in the moonlight, crowned by the wedding portrait over their heads, Akira yawned at the familiar scene.

Luxuriating in each other's embrace, they sat on the floor with the couch as their back rest.

"What will I do without you?" Jaz asked nuzzling his chest.

"I'll be back before you can figure it out." He brushed his lips across her forehead.

"I'll never understand Qwayz, but I don't have too. Just come back so we can get on with our lives."

"I will Jaz. We've got degrees to get, children to have and a lot more memories to make."

"Promise?" Jaz implored with her honey eyes.

"Promise. Never broken one yet have I?"

"No! And now's not the time to start."

"No argument here."

Satisfied, secure, warm and protected, Jaz fell asleep with the familiar rhythm of Qwayz's heartbeat as her usual lullaby.

There was nothing between them now, only the cloud of Vietnam hung over their heads as they crammed a year of life into two weeks. They went up to Napa, over to Tahoe, down to Carmel and passed Paradise Rock. They ate out most nights, sometimes capping the evening with a movie. Paul Newman's "Cool Hand Luke" for her, and Sidney's "In The Heat of The Night" for him. It was Sidney again in "To Sir With Love," that stirred Jaz to tears as Lulu sang about someone taking you "from crayons to perfume." That's what Qwayz did for her, helped her grow up and allowed her to be.

Sometimes they stayed home partying on their own, playing old records and dancing all the moves of their youth until the wee hours. Mostly they went to bed early and slept late, until the time drew nearer and nearer.

"We'll go down to L.A. tomorrow." Qwayz adjusted the covers over Jaz's bare behind.

"No, you go. I think you should go say goodbye to your mom and sisters alone. I've had my private moments with you and so should they."

Reluctantly Qwayz went alone to L.A., spent a couple of days before returning to Jaz. He had nixed a farewell party proposing a big all-out welcome home bash.

"With a devil's food cake with white icing, balloons, flowers, champagne, and tickets to Myrtle Beach."

"You got it. What did AJ say?"

"He wanted to know who was going to take care of Aunt Jaz and Akira? Not necessarily in that order," he chuckled.

* * *

Jaz clung to him at the Alameda Air Force Base, the airplane engines threatening their last moments.

"This is so weird. Send me your hair." She felt the sides that would soon be shaved.

"What about the rest of me?"

"It's not too late to go AWOL."

"You decide where you wanna go for our R&R–Tokyo or Hawaii?"

"Hawaii, no question. I want that place Elvis had in 'Blue Hawaii', with the single cottages so we can make lots of noise."

"Have mercy, girlie." When the commanding officer gave him a final stare, he kissed her.

"Stay safe." Jaz held his hand, then his fingers until the very last touch possible.

"I will. I got promises to keep." He walked backwards, hazel eyes on honey, a sensuous bottom lip tucked under even white teeth. Up the steps and at the opening, he threw a kiss and yelled something Jaz couldn't make out but guessed. The more tears she wiped away the more came, and it blurred her vision as the watery image of the plane shivered down the runway.

"And babies to make." She held her stomach hoping that she was pregnant. It would make it all so much more bearable.

Like a seasoned opera goer, she came in and took a seat in the middle on the aisle, knowing that to be her best vantage point–not in the first few rows of the immense auditorium where the eager to impress sat. Two weeks late, due to some family crisis, Doctor Williams awaited the arrival of Jasmine Chandler, partly because of her academic reputation and partly because she was black, the only one in this class of sixteen.

She sat poised with glasses perched upon her nose and a tell-me-all-you know attitude. She took few notes, her intelligent eyes absorbing the words before he spoke them, and she jotted down a word here and there. When something was complicated, she'd lean a little forward, asking pointed and focused questions, sitting back only after she had a complete understanding. She acted visibly impatient when another student masqueraded inquiry as an opportunity to show off his knowledge, as if she resented his wasting her time. The doctor would lose her to daydreams out the window when he repeated something a pupil should have already known. It was always hard to draw her back in after one of her interludes.

In the lab, the white coat accented her copper skin, and Dr. Williams stared at the long braid that divided her back as she worked tirelessly with accuracy and precision, staying as long as it took to render textbook results. She needed little assistance, and under her own volition, she had made up the two weeks of lab work she had missed.

Jasmine Chandler was unlike the other black students he'd taught in this advance placement course; the too few, too hard women, and the men who felt the brother-man should cut them some slack. The rigors of this program, first to be invited, then to excel, took its toll on minorities and they became obsessed with achievement; an admirable quality in the classroom, when balanced with some normalcy. Miss Chandler didn't seem obsessed, but quietly enthusiastic and supremely confident without arrogance. It was a delight to have her in his class with her quick grasp of new material, her dedication and commitment to problem-solving. Dr. Williams was smitten with Jasmine Chandler, and no one would believe it was only her mind that excited him.

Jaz breathed easier after Qwayz's first letter. From a local florist, he'd sent her flowers on his birthday, pink roses and a card in his handwriting saying, Happy Birthday to me! I love you! She'd hoped to surprise him for his birthday with an announcement of her own, but it had been only stress and nerves that delayed her period, not a little Chandler.

Jaz talked to him twice by phone, and was cautiously reassured by claims that his assignment was far less dangerous than combat. He was in "the American Embassy in Saigon for chrissakes!" He talked, laughed, told weak jokes and made kissing sounds goodbye. He was safe and challenged by the work, maybe he would be all right. Jaz just wanted him to make it past November, TC survived only four months over there. If Qwayz made it past that she promised herself to relax about it.

"Excellent as usual Miss Chandler." Dr. Williams corrected her lab work as she was leaving one evening. She always wore the same jewelry; the gold star around her neck, gold non-pierced earrings, and her watch and gold bracelet of interlocking hearts shared her left wrist. But he never seemed to notice the thick, initialed gold cigar band ring mounted on a circle of diamonds.

"Mrs. Chandler," Jaz corrected for the umpteenth time.

"Are you considering research as a career?"

"No. Pediatrics or OB-GYN."

"Good choices, wide open field for a woman. I hope your husband doesn't mind your long hours here at the lab."

"No. He's in Vietnam. Goodnight, Dr. Williams."

Dr. Williams sat stunned and puzzled by her information. He wondered how a young, beautiful, brilliant girl ended up with a husband in Vietnam. Had he misjudged her? Was she so academic that she'd fallen for the rap and game of a street dude? Maybe he was in ROTC and was over there as an officer. It did not correlate.

When the summer was over, and Dr. Williams' recommendations on candidates were made, he offered Jaz a work study in his lab. But she declined. "I've enjoyed your mind, Mrs. Chandler. I hope you'll return to the program next summer."

"I'd like to get into the surgical program, but thanks for everything, Dr. Williams. I've enjoyed your class." She extended her hand and they shook. Dr. Williams watched her saunter down the hall. "Have a nice life Jasmine."

* * *

Summer was over and Jaz's senior year began along with CC's and Sloane's. The three had been friends since they were freshman. CC, Chiam Cooper, was the rambunctious product of an East Indian mother and a black, military father who had retired after a stint at the Presidio. Being the fourth daughter born next to the coveted first son, CC had learned early to work her personality, and the art of making and forgetting friends fast. She was a study in soot-black from her waist-length wiry hair to her lips; the only white was around her ebony eyes and when she flashed a smile. The depth of her skin color seemed to exempt her freedom from it. CC dated any boy she took a fancy to, black or white. It was a bone of contention for Jaz, but no biggie for CC. "Keep dating gray boys and no decent black man will have you," Jaz had seethed.

"Honey, there are forty-nine other states and several continents where I can be a born-again virgin. I am not pressed," CC had replied.

CC was the first truly free spirit Jaz had ever encountered and she did so with awe and envy. The pretty 'high yella' Sloane Yeager with the sandy-colored hair, was from Atlanta where her father had unsuccessfully run for mayor in 1967 and was regrouping for a win in 1969. Sloane and her brother at Morehouse would be the third generation of Yeager college graduates. Sloane was a dedicated officer of The Black Student Caucus, and had recruited her two reluctant friends. During Qwayz's road-games the two girls would visit Jaz on Alta Vista. They'd eat junk food, talk about folks, do hair and nails and party which often started with forty-fives and CC asking Jaz to sing something like "Tell Mama" or "Bye Bye Baby." On Sunday, CC would leave to attend church with her family, and jet back to be with her friends until Jaz put them out.

"Y'all got to go, my man is coming home," Jaz would say, changing the sheets from blue percale to pink satin.

"I guess we've served our purpose," CC teased, as Jaz opened the apartment door while singing "Dr. Feelgood" to them, much to CC's delight.

But now Alta Vista was gone, Qwayz was gone, and Jaz purposely took an overload of courses to keep her mind occupied. She sprinkled her premed studies with architectural courses, and was pleased when her model of South Hall won a first place ribbon. It had been heralded as one of the most exquisite replica's of a building from any student, architectural major or not.

At home she received phone calls from Denny, Tracy, and AJ, who would call to ask a homework question in Biology and then talk on as if he were just around the corner. Her father would call to discuss process and progress on the Culhane building and his Frisco house. He'd already planned to be in San Francisco, and host their traditional Christmas/New Year's Eve parties from their new house. Mel was coming and Jaz agreed to as well, since she "had nothing else to do."

Jaz didn't betray Mel's confidence, but she knew her sister had finally left Hud, the actor who'd lured her from Juilliard to audition for a Broadway play. Her three octaves outshone him, and despite their having a son, nothing could stop Mel's meteoric rise or Hud's despair. So Mel was moving into a three story brownstone in the Village with Hud, Jr.

CC and Sloane remained Jaz's closest friends, but sometimes all human contact was too much to bear, whether by phone, at home or on campus. None of them was the right human being.

"Mrs. Chandler, please." Jaz halted at the super's insistence. "There is something for you in your apartment. From the florist. I let them in, I hope you don't mind."

"Anytime, thank you." Jaz ran up the steps, knowing exactly who sent her flowers on this Monday, the fourth of November.

"Hi Akira," she spoke, and then stopped in her tracks to admire the two dozen pink roses arranged in a vase poised on the coffee table under their wedding portrait. Jaz cried as she reached for the card which unfolded into a letter of familiar handwriting.

"The jinx is off. We broke the curse! I'm still here, though you are there, but I couldn't love you anymore. I miss you goo-gobs. Much love always, your husband Qwayz. P.S. tape to follow."

"He's a fool," Jaz said to Akira. "A crazy wonderful fool." She sniffed the roses, imagining what it took for him to arrange all this with the florist before he left. "I wonder how many more surprises Marchetti Florist has for us?"

The tape full of news and sentiment arrived two days later. Slowly, she was beginning to believe in his safety as well. He sounded like he was just visiting Ma Vy or away at law school. "The work was meticulous, tedious but invigorating," his voice revealed. "There were horrors and atrocities but I'm not given those cases. I'm on the Tan Sun Hut basketball team and we're crushing all opposition. I help the guys write letters home to their girls. I write and record songs for them using the base piano, a far cry from the studio equipment. I know you don't understand," he continued, "but I feel I am making a contribution here. I'm not fighting, not in the bush or running up against Charlie, but I am giving something, Jaz, and that makes me feel good. Once off the U.S. compound you don't know who to trust. Kinda like being in Watts ain't it?" he chuckled. "Make no mistake, I'd rather be with you, but just think I'm four months closer to being with you forever. I love you so much. I wish I could show you." At the sound of the kiss, she wiped her tears. She propped Teddy Bear by the headboard and wrapped herself around Qwayz's pillow, pretending she heard his heartbeat as she fell to sleep.

Jaz and Akira drove to Carmel for Thanksgiving, missing the holiday invites from Mel, her Dad, CC and even AJ who had invited her on his usual ski trip. On the way back she stopped by Ruidoso Canyon Drive, taking the murderous curve with ease and parking on the same look-out where she had blasted Qwayz for his betrayal. Jaz got out and let Akira relieve herself on a nearby rock. She wished there was some way to access the beach below, but that's what they'd liked about the property, the natural prohibitive boundaries. The owner's car wasn't in front of the house on Paradise Rock, a lifeless aura hung in the air. Jaz summoned Akira to the car, and drove slowly up the private driveway to the house perched on the tongue of granite. As Jaz passed the front entrance she noticed the setting sun shinning straight through. White folks never use drapes, she thought. No cars in or out of the garage and when Jaz peered inside the house looked uninhabited.

"I'll have Daddy check this out," she said to Akira, as she returned to the car and started the motor. "Wouldn't that be fine? What a surprise if I could get Paradise Rock for us. He'd come home and I'd surprise him with this new address. He'd love it!"

Greetings, presents and salutations from her parents, Selena and Zack from Paris, Mel and her son, and AJ, celebrated Jaz's twenty-first birthday. Qwayz sent her the most exquisite authentic peach kimono that shimmered into a pale lavender, with intricately embroidered birds and flowers and a note. "You're legal now, girlie. I have something for you to wear under this during our second Hawaiian honeymoon. Love you beyond all words, Your husband Qwayz. XXOO." Red and purple balloons came from Marchetti's. Her girlfriends threw her a surprise birthday party at the Black Student Caucus, complete with devil's food white icing cake and chocolate ice cream.

As Jaz devoted her time to finals, her parents made the final arrangements to occupy their San Francisco house and return from Italy for their two-week Christmas vacation. Fifty year old Joe Virgil Tennyson, the valued Culhane butler from Connecticut, consented to move to San Francisco with his wife Mildred as the maid. The seasoned Tennysons comprised the Culhanes sole staff for the house's day-to-day operation. Additional staff was hired on an as-needed basis for special occasions.

Jaz managed to stay clear of the house until Mel, and her son, Hud Jr., arrived. Jaz entered the small semi-circular driveway in front of a substantial, old, elegant brick house with gracious draperied windows and a small flagstone stoop. Upon entering, a stone wall, with indirect lighting highlighting its granite texture, showcased the poinsettias in its flower box. To the left was an immense living room with livable furniture, and a beautiful split rock fireplace wall as its focal point. A series of sliding glass doors led out onto a long narrow side yard, well secured by the eight foot brick wall that surrounded the entire property. Across the room opposite the fireplace was the door to Hep's office.

To the right of the entrance, black and white tile was the base for a two-story foyer. A curved staircase cradled a mammoth Christmas tree. Through the archway, she saw an ample, elegant dining room with sliding glass doors that revealed a flagstone patio and a small manicured yard beyond. The kitchen reminded Jaz of a ship's galley until the neat built-ins gave way to an immense but quaint breakfast room of sturdy white wrought iron and glass tables.

Jaz climbed the stairs using the rope on the non-bannister side of the staircase, noting the master bedroom, to the left, two good sized bedrooms with baths, and the back stairs down to the kitchen and up to the Tennysons.

"Merry Christmas, baby. So what you think?" Mel hugged her sister hello.

"They done good." Jaz eyed her father as he beamed. "Where's my nephew?" Jaz started to the bed.

"Don't wake him!" Mel and Hep yelled in unison.

The party was going full swing, the sound of the band wafted up to where Jaz and Hud played peek-a-boo for the zillionth time. The pair had used the back stairs to raid the goodies and steal back upstairs unnoticed. Jaz liked Millie Tennyson; salty hard and tough on the outside, but a soft touch for babies, dogs and sensible folk.

"Jaz, won't you come downstairs?" Lorette said. "You didn't used to be so antisocial."

"I don't know or care about those folks down there." Sloane had gone home for the holidays. CC was to come and spend the night, but had fallen victim to the same malady that cut AJ's annual Christmas ski trip to Sun Valley short–the Hong Kong flu.

"As a doctor, you're gonna have to work on your bedside manner." Lorette smoothed her hands over her dress, pirouetting at her reflection in the mirror without looking at her daughter.

"I don't think any of your friends will be having babies when I'm a doctor," Jaz said. She'd tried to be nice to her but she was starting that tap dance on her last nerve.

"You can bring Hud down," Lorette said as she left.

"C'mon sis, it's not right for me to be partying while you babysit," Mel came in and lifted Hud.

"Lorette send you up here?" Jaz asked as Mel wiped her son's mouth with a wet washcloth. "I've been damn tolerant, staying here when I have a perfectly good apartment of my own."

"Akira loves the yard."

"I've endured the Christmas carols, the celebrating 'all together as a family,' the whole bit. Well I'm twenty-one and it's a new year in about an hour. So tell yo' mama to back off!"

"Look, I accept this thing you and mama have. You don't see me tryin' to change not nare thing. Now, when are you coming to New York to see me and your nephew's new house? You have your own room this time."

"Jaz!" her father boomed over the crowd, the phone in one hand, summoning her down to him.

"Hello?" Jaz couldn't hear, so Hep pushed her into the powder room and closed the door. "Hello?"

"Hi yourself. Happy New Year, girlie."

"Qwayz?!" Her voice lifted and tears fell.

"Jas-of-mine, you partyin' while I'm here all alone on the telephone?"

"You're crazy."

" 'Bout you ...yeah. How you doin'?"

"I'm doin'. Boy, I miss you."

"Boy?"

"Come show me different."

"Oh, how I wish."

"Yeah?"

"Don't taunt me. I can't take it. It's been too long."

They talked as easily as they could with the pressure of time hanging over their every word. They discussed family and friends, and she was tempted to tell him about the possibility of buying Paradise Rock. About how Hep found out the property was a discovered 'love nest' now tied up in litigation as part of a divorce settlement. She could easily swing it solo from their savings which included Raw Cilk royalties and the money inherited from TC. Coupled with the money Qwayz was sending monthly, she'd have enough to furnish it with flare without giving up that godawful Berkeley apartment.

"I got a surprise for you." He shocked her, and she loved how much in sync they were once again; thousands of miles away. "But I'll tell you when I see you."

"OK. They do much holiday celebratin' over there?"

"They celebrate anything over here–the riots at the Democratic Convention in Chicago. They weren't too crazy about Nixon being elected, but nothing got the Bloods fired up more than the stand John Carlos and Tommie Smith took at the Olympics in Mexico City."

"That was in October."

"So? It beat the hell outta a Christmas or New Year's celebration."

"Qwayz." Jaz heard the hoots and hollers from the other room as the band ordered the chaos with Auld Lang Zyne. "It's 1969 here. Happy New Year."

"Happy New Year Jas-of-mine. This will be our year, you'll see. And we'll be together in just two short months."

"Nothing short about sixty days."

"Closer than it has been. I'm planning something very special–"

"Just being together will be special enough."

"You just wait . . ." His voice faded out then back in again. "How's Akira?"

"Horny as hell like her mistress."

"Well, her mistress better stay horny until Friday, March seventh."

"You better."

"You kidding? These women over here got stuff that thrives on penicillin and asks for more. No way Jose', not this man. Do without, before I do and die."

"Well, if the disease don't kill you, Jaz will."

"My mama didn't raise no fool. I've had to revert to taking matters into my own hands, but at least I know where they've been. That's a habit I don't need no methadone to break–"

"Qwayz, you're fading out on me!"

"Guess that's our cue from the government, huh? I love you!"

"Happy New Year, Qwayz. I love you too–" When she finished the phone was dead and Jaz didn't know how much he'd heard. She sat on the commode holding the receiver. They can send men to circle the moon on Christmas eve, but can't put an end to a war right here on earth. Shoulda sent Apollo 8 to circle Vietnam, she thought, as she hoisted herself up and looked at her reflection.

"Hang on, girlie. March seventh is D-day for you. De day you get it regular for ten days." She laughed at her own joke before opening the door on the party revelry. "These slaps don't even know there's a war on."

* * *

Jaz glided across campus, after finding her name on the roster for the Summer Surgical Program. The bounce in her step had little to do with that news, and more with her early morning call from Qwayz wishing her a Happy Anniversary and Valentine's Day, and making the final plans for their Hawaiian celebration next month. She laughed aloud recalling his saying he had a Hawaiian disease only she had the cure for, "lack-a-nookie."

Returning to the apartment she found the remnants of Mr. Sanchez's wayward key. Jaz kneeled before the huge box addressed to her and stamped with Oriental writing. She opened and flung packaging material everywhere while Akira sniffed. Inside the box was another box, then a box within a box until finally a music box.

"Is this one of Qwayz's jokes? Are snakes gonna jump out? Oh my!" Jaz held up the most exquisitely carved Oriental music box and, lifting the lid, tried to decipher the delicate tune. "Ahh," she sighed recognizing Nat King Cole's "Too Young," that had played at their wedding. "What a special man." Attached to its bottom was a tape and a letter.

"Jas-of-mine this will be the first and last anniversary we spend apart. I hope you love and treasure this gift as I love and treasure you. It wasn't easy getting Mama-San to get the tune just right but finally perfection prevailed. I'm looking forward to Hawaii, till then, here are some songs from my heart to yours. I love you, Jaz. See you soon! XXOO."

Jaz put on the tape and listened to her husband's pure voice as he accompanied himself on the piano. She only heard "Too Young," "Everlastin' Love," "I'm Glad There Is You," "Unforgettable," and "I'll Be Seeing You," before drifting off into the most restful sleep she'd had since he'd left.

* * *

Jaz brushed her teeth in the tiny bathroom, and returned in time to fasten her seatbelt as the plane made its final approach. The weather was balmy but dry; the breezes whirled her hair as she walked into the cool airport searching for that first glimpse of Qwayz. She threaded between couples, men in uniforms and women in their Sunday best. A minor panic overcame her as she realized for the first time, that she didn't know the specific arrangements, and if Qwayz weren't here due to some mix up, she'd be doomed to spend precious time in the airport until his arrival.

Then over by the wall, she saw a man clad in tan slacks and a Hawaiian-print shirt with a bouquet of peach roses hiding his face. As she inched closer there was no question it was Qwayz, and she ran to him, pushing the roses out of her way and planting a kiss born of a thousand lonely nights upon his sensuous lips.

The roses dangled across her back as he drank her in: the faint smell of Jungle Gardenia, of freshly washed hair cut with a lemon rinse tickling the back of his arms, of soft brown flesh surrendering to him, of familiar and long-wanted curves conforming to his as if there had never been any separation.

"Oh Qwayz." They finally came up for air, and she soaked up his essence. His hazel eyes were not dimmed by the war he left behind, but happy with the sight before him. A mustache shadowed his upper lip, as the hair on the sides had disappeared.

"You're bald!" She laughed.

"It'll grow back in the next ten days 'cause I don't intend to waste time shavin'."

"Don't I have anything to say about that?"

"Yes ... more Qwayz ... oh, don't stop ... oh yes Qwayz ... yes!" He teased, squeezing her even harder in an embrace.

"You feel good to me." Jaz closed her eyes to all around her, wishing that upon opening them, by magic they'd be in a hotel bedroom.

"These are for you." He presented the two dozen roses.

"I expected you to be in dress blues." She took them and his crooked arm as they sauntered off.

"Never wear a uniform unless you positively, absolutely have too."

"They'd beat that bama shirt," she joned as he hoisted her luggage into the jeep.

"You crackin' on my attire?"

"Soon, you won't be needin' any."

"Great minds ... great minds." He kissed her as they sped off to a secluded part of the island. Jaz couldn't take her eyes from him, for there was no beauty of tropical fauna that could compete with her handsome husband.

They approached the Honeymoon Cove desk and Jaz observed how everything was open, a roof but no walls.

"How long have you been here?"

"Just a few hours."

"Where is the hotel?"

"It's not a hotel, it's cottages, nosy. Maybe you should be the lawyer."

"Mr. and Mrs. Chandler? This way please." A robust native escorted them down winding paths towards a canal. "Please?" The man directed Jaz to a raft in the middle of the water. Jaz looked at him like he was crazy.

"Surprise! Remember 'Blue Hawaii?' Elvis and Joan Blackman?" He placed a ring of gardenias upon her head and a matching lei around her neck. After he kissed her Jaz noticed the bed of flowers on the raft and the strolling musicians waiting on either side.

"Oh, Qwayz."

"The stuff that memories are made of Jas-of-mine, nothing is too good for my lady."

The only other occupant of the raft steered as two young Polynesian girls tossed more flowers into the water they coursed. Then Qwayz sang "I Can't Help Falling In Love With You," which put Elvis to shame.

Qwayz carried Jaz over the threshold of the immense A framed thatched roof hut with a bed as its centerpiece.

"My kind of place," Jaz said as Qwayz dumped her on the bed, where they remained, in various stages of undress for four straight hours of unbridled love making. Qwayz scurried across the cool floor opening, then pouring champagne for them both before returning to the bed. They consumed it thirstily along with the complimentary hors d'oeuvres. Jaz pulled the white sheet about her brown body denying Qwayz any cover.

"Just looking at what's mine." She eyed Jake. "I mean I felt him but I haven't seen him for a long time."

"There he is ... still risin'."

"I can handle it ... can you?"

"You are so bad." He whipped some sheet over him, and stuffed a melon ball into her pouting mouth.

"This place is paradise on earth." Jaz snuggled against his hairy chest.

"Sorry, no fireplace."

"I like that ceiling fan. To cool our body heat, in our little grass hut in Hawaii," Jaz sang, and they fell asleep.

Qwayz stirred at sunset and they walked through the glass doors out on the lanai into their private lagoon, where they swam under the setting sun until they were just silhouettes against the fuchsia sky.

"Hungry?" Their nude bodies were intertwined as Jaz perched atop him.

"Ravenous." She drew in his bottom lip alternating licking and sucking as if she were devouring the most luscious of delicacies. Qwayz moaned as the warm water tantalized their movements.

"What do you wanna eat?" Qwayz managed without breaking the rhythm of their foreplay.

"You."

A lesser establishment may have been concerned at not seeing the Chandlers for the next three days, but the staff of Honeymoon Cove honored the Do Not Disturb sign for as long as it reigned over Hut 3. Though the staff could never clean the rooms or change sheets, an abundant supply of fresh towels always appeared sometime during the day. Only room service caught a glimpse of the male Chandler, as he cracked the door open far enough to receive and sign for a food tray, later left outside with discarded linen and three, never touched newspapers.

On the fourth day there were sightings of the Chandlers by the beach but they still relied on room service for sustenance. They had stopped the world, constructing one of their own, and refused to be invaded by any modicum of reality.

By the fifth day the Chandlers made dinner reservations for The Tiki Room which they didn't actually honor until the sixth day, causing some of the staff to lose bets that they wouldn't show at all. Reports from maid service indicated that no bags had been unpacked and everything was spotless and basically unused except for the bed and the shower.

The couple, sitting across from one another in wicker chairs made famous by Panther Huey Newton, sipped on Singapore slings, nibbled on poi poi, and vanished before the main course was served.

On the seventh day they made it all the way through the salads before they were interrupted.

"Hey, Qwayz!" A black marine slapped him on the back and Jaz's heart sank.

"Buzz! Hey man!" Qwayz stood and Jaz knew the real world had just crept in.

"This is my wife, Roberta."

"This is my wife, Jaz ... Buzz McLeish."

"Hi." Jaz tried hard to be gracious, but they could rap back in Nam. Jaz only had forty-eight more hours.

"You comin' or goin'?" Qwayz asked.

"We're 'bout to have dinner."

"Join us." If looks could kill Jaz would have been a murderer and widow.

"Buzz, maybe they want to be alone," Roberta said, and Jaz smiled at her friend for life.

"Qwayz, Mr. Popularity? Roberta, this is the guy who whipped my buns at B-Ball and wrote that love song for me."

"Really?" There goes Jaz's friend for life. "You're very talented." Roberta shrugged her shoulders at Jaz in defeat.

Jaz enjoyed the stories about Qwayz in his wartime environment but barely endured the rest.

"So how long you been here?"

"Not long enough." Qwayz took Jaz's hand.

"We've only got two days left." Jaz's comment was lost on Buzz.

"She's as pretty as your pictures, Qwayz."

"Don't I know it." Qwayz kissed her hand.

"Newlyweds huh? Roberta and I've been married six years, have two kids and another on the way."

"Congratulations!" Qwayz said.

"That's what these jaunts are for." Buzz winked at his friend, "Us lifers live for these R&R's man."

The next forty-eight hours passed like wind through a latticed porch and Jaz clung to Qwayz like a wisteria vine to a southern trellis.

"Jaz, I thought my second surprise would make you super-happy."

"It did at the time you told me and it will when you come home for good in August, but it don't do doo-doo for right now Qwayz." He looked handsome in his blue Air Force uniform though, she preferred him in the buff. She held him as the military planes readied behind him.

"Time to go Qwayz, my man. Nice meeting you Jaz," Buzz said in passing, without breaking stride.

"Jaz, I'll be home for good on an early-out in just five short months and I got big plans for the summer of '69." He embraced her again kissing her cheek. "We'll never be separated again. I promise with all my heart, soul and every fiber of my being." The engine gunned signaling the final call and Qwayz began backing away.

"Qwayz ..." Their fingertips touched until the very end and he reached down and picked up a smooth gray stone polished by some ancient volcano.

"Here ... this will be our life, Jaz, from now on ... smooth and solid as this rock. A symbol of our love. Just five funky little months ...tops." He palmed the flawless stone in his hand as if energizing it, before placing it lovingly in her hand. "Take care of that, I'll ask for it when I see you. Set it on our nightstand next to our Malibu picture, so it'll be there when we make love my first night home–providing

Mother Nature cooperates." He smiled and winked. "I love you, Mrs. Chandler."

He threw kisses and flashed his patented smile until the door closed between them. She hung onto the chain-linked fence as broken glimpses of his plane taking off, returning to Southeast Asia, could be seen. She stood there a long while, tears drenching the stylish Yves St. Laurent pantsuit Selena had sent. Opening her hand she looked at the curiously smooth textured gray-black rock, "a symbol of their love." She held it to her breast as she made way to her gate for the plane bound in the opposite direction, back to her world ... a world without her best friend, lover, husband, protector, confidant ... her rainbow's end. A world without Qwayz.

"So what'd you bring me?" The giggling voice knew better.

"Thesis Denise-es," Jaz said before continuing. "Nunca, nada, zip."

"Figures. Sure you didn't bring back a seed that will blossom in say ... nine months?"

"I wish, but your brother wants at least one full year of just me and him before we become parents."

"Selfish devil ain't he," Denny said. "And you can drop that thesis Denise-es.' I submitted my dissertation yesterday! Fifty-six pages of psychological brilliance."

"Well alright! Guess I have to call you Dr. Denny now."

"Not until that June date, thereafter I'll answer to nothing but."

"I'll be there with bells on."

"How so? You graduate the day after."

"I don't need to walk to get my degree. I'm already in med school."

"You're fooling yourself if you don't think Ma and Pa Culhane as well as Auntie and Uncle from Paris and a sister straight off the Broadway stage won't be there to see the first Culhane college graduate get her degree."

Jaz had never thought of it that way, her family was so accomplished without a college education. Her grandfather, Papa Colt, the ex-slave cowboy had founded an all-black Texas town. Her dad had risen from beat cop to President Kennedy's chief of protocol before he'd been appointed as ambassador to Italy. They had had vision and determination, but not a degree between them.

"But they were just here for two weeks at Christmas, and Dad gave up the Kentucky Derby in early May and the Indy 500 Memorial Day, for two weeks at the Cannes Film Festival in mid-May. The World Cup Soccer Championship begins in Italy for the whole month of June–"

"And they'll be here for their daughter's graduation. Get ready, girlie." Denny used Qwayz's sobriquet playfully. "Who's in that Frisco house while they're in Italy?"

"The Tennysons, Joe Virgil and Millie. I had a hell of a time getting Akira away from Millie when I came back. I thought AJ was bad."

Jaz didn't have time to consider any of that now ...it was spring, a time for rejuvenation, growth and new beginnings. She'd been energized since she'd seen Qwayz in March, and was accepted to med school. Three factors insured a perpetually blissful state– Qwayz's early out in August was official, she had settled on Paradise Rock, and accepted the honor of being godparents for Tracy's and Scoey's child expected in January.

Jaz delighted in transforming Paradise Rock from an illicit 'love nest' into a home, and remained in a constant state of euphoria. She redid the sunken couch upholstery with ecru raw silk, matching the drapes and complimenting the new carpet that lay before the fire-place. Huge pillows of muted earth tones scattered around the glass and brass coffee table finished the formal sunken living room. The parquet floors were buffed and gleamed in their natural glory. Jaz had a wall of shelves built around the archway to the bedroom's hallway for Qwayz's stereo, record collection and their books. In the bathroom she papered the walls in foiled sea shells and she found linens to match the raised aquamarine tub. The wicker bed was situated so they could lie and look out at the ebb and flow of the tides, watch sunrises, and make love in the diminishing rays of the sunsets. She knew once Qwayz got a glimpse of Paradise Rock ... the Berkeley Heights apartments would be history.

Graduation was an intrusion on her planning for her husband's homecoming. A ceremony to be endured, though the pictures, the dinners, and the gifts were more fun than she had anticipated. CC would still be around, but Sloane was going home to Atlanta University for grad school. Hep took a picture of them all, and Jaz began more painful farewells to many college friends.

Chapter Four

"Good girl," Jaz complimented Akira as she ran the sandy beach retrieving a stick and returning it to her. Jaz had already benefited from being at Paradise Rock, where she spent her weekends far away from her summer surgery program. She liked the five-foot-five brilliant Dr. Nussbaum, and avoided the Chief of Staff, Dr. Brewer, whose racist attitude was legendary.

All was well with her family and friends, she reflected dodging the cold surf. Tracy was wearing maternity clothes needlessly but proudly. Jaz threw the stick for Akira again, smiling, as she thought of Gladys Ann's pink and green letter announcing that she'd been accepted to med school. She'd joned on their exchange of graduation pictures saying "at least we both know we can look better than this!" Jaz chuckled as they began winding back up to the house, using the path Qwayz had forged past rocks and wind-swept cypress.

As her tea brewed, she rechecked the way she stocked their kitchen, ready for immediate habitation with rows of popcorn, cocoa, seasonings for blaff and callaloo, bread pudding makings and chocolate. She planned to kidnap Qwayz from the airbase and bring him directly here. He would call his Mom, while she hit the stereo already primed with Nat King Cole and Johnny Mathis, on the way to warming up the pasta with seafood sauce, and popping the cork of the 1945 Lafite-Rothschild, compliments of her Dad. They'd rush through the meal and get on to the main activity. They wouldn't eat anything hot again for a couple of days, so she had a list of cold cuts to buy the day before he arrived. The perfect reunion for the perfect couple, she thought fishing the smooth stone out of her sweater pocket. Unable to decide whether to leave it at the Berkeley apartment or at Paradise Rock, it spent most of the time in her shoulderbag. Each night she fell asleep to the anniversary tape he'd sent of him singing 'Raw Cilk' on one side and all their other favorites on the other. She drifted off to sleep looking at their picture from that Malibu summer in 1964 when Selena and Zack rented the beach house, and the photographer captured their images. Qwayz in a peach banlon setting off his deep bronze arms as they enveloped Jaz. Their smiles as bright as their love. The Malibu picture, the music box that played "Too Young," and the smooth stone, stood sentry on her nightstand–a trinity of love.

"Hi Daddy ... Happy 4th of July!" Jaz kissed her father, waved at Millie and her mother officiating on the patio outside the dining room.

"Mel and Hud here?"

"Will I do?"

"Selena!" Jaz ran half way up to embrace her aunt. "Oh it's so good to see you! Where's Zack?"

"Napping."

"What about the July 4th at Chateau Jazz?"

"Child didn't you learn nothing from me?" Selena guided her niece back downstairs. "Give the wolf a taste and leave him hungry."

"You'll be back for Qwayz's welcome home party in August?"

"My baby comin' home from the war? Wild horses and an airline strike couldn't keep me away."

The house was loaded with smiley-faced people as Hep manned the Texas barbecue, complete with apron and thongs, while Lorette played the gracious hostess. CC chatted with Selena while Hud, Jr.

ran through the flowers dodging the sculptured garden medallions, creating havoc. When everyone was full and satisfied, the guests sought the comfort of cushioned wrought iron and hushed conversations.

"I really admire you Mel, caring for a child, being a single parent," Jaz told her sister.

"You do what you gotta do. He's the joy of my life when he's asleep like this. I'm one of the lucky ones–able to be home with him during the day. Even my matinees coincide with his nap time and I'm usually home before he wakes up. I'm there to put him to bed at night before I leave for the theater. I couldn't imagine, being pregnant again now, like Mom was with me and TC, or me and you."

"Well, she did have a husband to help her."

"I'll talk to you when you have a child. Then and only then can you understand what I'm saying."

"What's this new play?"

"*The Reverend*, a black musical about a southern church with a showstopping tune for me. I'd star of course."

"Of course, Miss Thang." Jaz used Qwayz's pet name for her.

"Be doing some showstoppin' yourself in a few weeks. The Big Q comin' home. You two always had it all. While the rest of us had to run tests on a buncha triflin' dudes, you found yours from the git-go."

"I went through a few frogs before I found my prince."

"Oh, sure. Jesse Ramsey who's now Chicago Bear's star running back."

"Look at dad. Mr. Girambelli and sons must be here with the fireworks."

Jaz watched the display with mixed emotions. It wasn't like the ones she and Qwayz enjoyed in Paris at Chateau Jazz in '65, or from the boat in the Caribbean with TC before he shipped out. Last year there were no fireworks at all for her. The 4th was just another dismal day. But this 4th of July was filled with hope and new beginnings, and Jaz clapped and shouted just as much as Hud did from her lap.

"Might as well stay the night, Punkin'," Hep tempered his insistence.

"No thanks, I've said my goodbyes, and I wanna get back to the beach."

"Will I ever get an invitation out there? I flushed the address as ordered."

"Maybe, if you're good, but I want Qwayz to be the first man there."

"Coming back for dinner tomorrow? We'll only be here for two more days."

"OK, Daddy." She kissed him goodnight, leaving him in the doorway as she settled Akira safely in the front seat.

"Qwayz, we're home!" Jaz called out as she slid the door closed and turned on a light. Akira stopped in her tracks looking at Jaz then looking down the hall. "Sorry girl, just practicing. But when would I be going someplace without him, huh?"

Jaz reset the security system, a caveat from her Dad which came with the $1,000 bottle of wine. It was the only way he'd leave her alone in this secluded beach house. She surveyed the comfortable and inviting room as she turned off the light. The house that love built.

Her nocturnal ritual complete, teeth brushed, hair braided, attired in one of Qwayz's old shirts she set the tape, grabbed the stone and climbed beneath the sheets. The moonlight poured onto her face like daylight and she stared at it as Qwayz's voice filled the room. Her eyes located their star and she looked at it marveling that it was the same star that shone on Qwayz the night before and the night to follow. Soon they'd be lying in this bed together looking at the star. In many ways Qwayz was already here. It felt like he was just in the kitchen fixing cocoa, any minute he'd spring around the corner and cannonball into bed beside her. His spirit was here, and now Jaz waited for his body.

"The stars are in the heavens and all's right with the world," Jaz repeated with Qwayz at the end of his tape, and drifted off into a peaceful sleep.

On his August second birthday, Jaz shopped for his presents. He wasn't going to be here, but she wanted to be involved in the celebration on the day that brought Quinton Regis Chandler into the world. She purchased one Rolex watch inscribed ,"Till The End Of Time," and a pair of round-trip, first-class tickets to Myrtle Beach, South Carolina.

* * *

"I couldn't get a line out," Qwayz apologized over a static riddled phone line for not calling on his birthday.

"Doesn't matter," Jaz yelled into the receiver and Akira looked up. "I think I celebrated in a fashion you'd approve of." Now the voices faded in and out, some words louder than others.

"Yeah? Meet me in Hawaii and we can return to our little grass hut for a week of debriefin'."

"I got something much better planned for you right here. Guaranteed." She'd waited this long what was another week.

"Yeah? You have our rock?"

"Yep, I keep it with me most of the time along with the music box ...Qwayz?"

"I love you Jaz! See you soon–when the stars will be in the heavens and all's right with the world!"

"I love you too ... bye!"

Qwayz replaced the receiver and mopped his face with the drenched handkerchief. Jaz was his number one priority but a cool climate with hot showers, cold wine and ice cubes that didn't melt on their way to the glass was also appealing. As he sauntered across the base, dust whirled around him from a passing jeep.

"Hey Shortime! This'll all be history for you in five quick ones, huh?"

"You got it, man." Qwayz jogged over to Major Tapp in his AC-47. The tall, dark man jumped from his plane, waving off his co-pilot and crew. They'd become fast friends once Qwayz learned he was from Virginia and had summered in Myrtle Beach as a teenager.

"Paperwork?" Major Tapp noted the paraphernalia in Qwayz's hands.

"Nope, mailed a Christmas package to my wife. It's due out the 13th. I thought it would be a kick to mail stupid stuff and be there to get it together."

"I think the man loves his wife."

"You know it. You gonna make a run?"

"Just got back, running visual recon along the Laotian border. Just so Charlie knows we're interested."

"Sounds like soft time to me."

"You had the cushy job in JAG," he said, referring to Judge Advocate General's legal department of the armed services. "You gotta let me buy you a drink before you set off, Q."

"I'll be a drunk by the time I get back to the world."

"Popularity costs, man. Never did take you up in my jet."

"Hey, I've been up in Huey's, F-4 Phantom, F-105 Thunderchief, a Cessna A-37 and a Cobra–can't be any different."

"Aw, rankin' now that you're checking out? Listen, I got to go up again tomorrow, why not meet me, let me take you for a ride, then dinner."

"Deal, later."

Qwayz ate with the guys listening to Buzz still talking about how "fine" Qwayz's wife was. He turned in late, but was there bright and early, greeting a waiting Major Tapp.

"Didn't think you were gonna show, Chandler," Tapp teased. "You forcing me to rethink my assessment of you."

"Beautiful day for a flight." Qwayz sniffed the already hot, stale air squinting his eyes against the sun. "Won't be long before any of these recons are a thing of the past, huh?" He accepted the helmet and snapped it on.

"You talking about Nixon's announcing the first troop withdrawal in June? All remains to be seen, my man. Hop in," Tapp invited.

"Just us?" Qwayz's surprised eyes peered over his aviator glasses.

"Not to worry, you can't get more routine than this," spoke the seasoned pilot who'd flown over 146 missions in his five month stint. "'Sides Charlie isn't even up yet." The jet sliced the clear blue sky. "Really beautiful country from up here," Major Tapp mused.

"Reckon it would be if I could see it right side up," Qwayz cracked on his aerial displays. "Glad I didn't eat first."

"Man you haven't seen nothing yet." And the major took his pride and joy through five minutes of celestial acrobatics. "I thought you said you and your father-in-law were gonna take up flying so you can pilot your own jets?"

"If I survive this," Qwayz chuckled. "What's that?" He asked of a distant sputtering.

"Ummm Charlie's up. Myrtle Beach to control, Myrtle Beach to control we're receiving some fire from the northwest quadrant. Over."

"Fire? You mean like artillery?" Qwayz questioned as Tapp signed off.

"Not to worry just letting base know where they are. We're way outta range for that light weight action."

Before the words left his mouth a thunderous jolt hit the plane engulfing it in fire. The jet careened and exploded upon impact, belching puffs of black smoke miles back into the tranquil air that had just released it from its safe, protective grasp.

A blood curdling scream awakened Jaz and she bolted straight up. Akira was up on all fours growling. Jaz wondered if she had been the screamer. Was it a nightmare or a clap of thunder, or the crash of glass signaling an intruder? Jaz's heart raced, she couldn't catch her breath and her nightclothes were drenched. What the hell? She stared into the darkness of the quiet apartment. Her stomach cramped and churned. She slid across the bed, scurrying to the bathroom in time to vomit bile into the toilet. She hugged the porcelain bowl, recalling that she hadn't thrown up since she and Gladys Ann drank some Bali Hai, only to be discovered by Qwayz who lectured them both all the way home. She and her fifteen-year-old friend had argued over which was worse, the cheap wine or Qwayz's sermon.

Jaz brushed her teeth clean of the burning film, chasing it with a long drink of cold water straight from the spigot. She stepped over Akira to go into the kitchen, trying to remember what she had eaten that would turn on her. She eyed the front door and the balcony. All was undisturbed except for the gnawing sick feeling in her stomach and an uncontrollable shivering, as if she were cold.

"Weird." She crossed back over the canine to the bathroom where she shed her clothes, showered and returned to bed. Lying there wide awake with a knot in the pit of her abdomen she hoped she wasn't coming down with anything. Qwayz'll be home in three days, Mother Nature's cooperating, so what is this? she thought. She went from the chills to the sweats and back again. She finally fell into a fitful sleep and dragged herself to the last day on the surgical unit.

"Hallelujah! It's over. Come on, Qwayz, I'm ready for you!" She almost skipped across campus, and sang the Marvelettes, "My Baby Must Be A Magician."

Jaz hoisted the bags of munchies from the car, while Akira jumped out, relieved herself against a tree, and reached the concrete steps the same time as her mistress.

"Mrs. There was a soldier here to see you," Mr. Sanchez informed her as he returned to his hedge-clipping.

"Thanks! He's surprised us!" Jaz and Akira raced up the steps.

"Captain Bradford, United States Air Force," Jaz read the card stuck in the door. "Right branch, wrong soldier. They wouldn't even let Qwayz get home and spend time with his wife before they started looking him up, which is exactly why we have Paradise Rock."

Jaz entered the apartment and surveyed the already packed bags containing Qwayz's civvies, his birthday Rolex, the two tickets to Myrtle Beach and the Paradise Rock deed. She wouldn't have time to pack anything later. Her Dad was in from Italy to inspect the Culhane Building, and she'd promised to tour the masterpiece with him, dine with her parents, and spend the night.

As she stood wondering if she had time to drop everything off at the beach house, there was a knock at the door.

"Mrs. Jasmine Chandler? I'm Captain Bradford," the middle-aged white man informed. "May I come in?"

"Sure." Jaz scratched the looking-up-an-old-buddy scenario, and figured the Air Force must have forgotten to give Qwayz something.

"You know my husband won't be here until Thursday?"

"Yes, well, that's the reason I'm here. Ordinarily you'd be

notified in writing and you still will be, but because of his ... scheduled arrival so soon," he breathed deeply and exhaled with, "I regret to inform you that your husband, Quinton Regis Chandler IV was reported MIA-Missing In Action as of August–"

"There must be some mistake." Jaz stood and the Captain rose with her.

"The details are still sketchy," he continued, as if she hadn't spoken. "But your husband boarded an AC-47 with Major Tapp on a routine harassment run along the Laotian border. There was enemy fire ... There's been no word since the last radio contact."

Jaz let this cold distant man, the complete antithesis of her Qwayz, finish his spiel. As he droned on she thought someone other than this tactless man should be conveying such sensitive information.

"The mission covered quite a large area and the exact area where the plane went down has not been determined. It is believed from official sources that the jet was hit by a VC rocket which means they were flying pretty low. The area was swept for aerial observation but with that mountainous, jungle terrain it's almost impossible to sight anything ... even the remnants of a burned plane can be swallowed up whole and completely covered by that jungle brush in a matter of hours. The Air Force will try to locate any clues as to your husband's whereabouts," he concluded in textbook manner. "His personal effects will be sent to you shortly. We regret your lost," he almost saluted to an end.

"Captain Bradford," Jaz began. "I'm sorry you've come all this way, and equally sorry for the person for whom this information is intended. My husband was not a pilot or a co-pilot and in no way connected with any missions routine or otherwise. He was in intelligence, detailed to the Judge Advocate General stationed in Saigon. So you see there has been some military foul up."

"Mrs. Chandler, I assure you that this Quinton–"

"Captain Bradford–" Jaz cut him off by escorting him to the door. "There must be another Quinton Chandler whose family is awaiting this horrible news. My husband will be home Thursday as planned. He would have no reason to jeopardize himself or our future by taking a flight. I know how overworked the Air Force is, but a less understanding person could be quite devastated. Perhaps you should reconfirm the identity of your personnel more closely before reporting falsely on them. Now if you'll excuse me. Good day, Captain Bradford." She closed the door behind him.

Jaz pushed all the bags by the halltree near the door so when she returned from visiting her parents she could just grab them, along with Qwayz's red baseball cap and bomber jacket, and split for the airport. Showering again made her late for the meeting with her father and on her way out she yanked up the phone thinking it was him.

"Jasmine?" It was the unmistakable lilt, muffled with tears, of Qwayz's mother.

"Ma Vy, Hi ... how are you?"

"A Major Thurman just came by–"

"Ma Vy don't worry it's all a mistake–"

"But Jaz–"

"Ma Vy, don't pay them any mind they're wrong! You'll see on Thursday. They'll all see on Thursday. I don't mean to be rude but I gotta go I'm meeting my father and I'm late. Catch you later."

Ignoring the ringing phone, Jaz locked the door and proceeded down the hall. Waving to Mr. Sanchez, she let Akira hop in the car, and she headed for San Francisco.

"Oh God, Dad'll have a shit-fit." Jaz eyed her watch, as she quickly changed the radio station from "an upcoming Raw Cilk classic," and sang along with Stevie Wonder's "My Cherie Amour."

In Jaz's absolute, deep and utter denial, there was but one centimeter, in the quiet of her heart which remained noncommittal and silent against all the outer refutations; it calmly awaited more documented reality–for time to tell.

Hep's car waited in the semi-circle driveway as Jaz parked her T-Bird on the outside plaza.

"There's my Akira." Millie opened the side gate letting her in.

"Thanks," Jaz said to Mille. "Sorry Dad," Jaz apologized before her always punctual father could raze her. "Nice car."

"Needed a little something to get around in when I'm in town."

"Stylin' and profilin' Pops." Jaz teased him about the stares they received as they pulled the Rolls Royce into the driveway on Kearny Street in front of the prestigious Culhane Building.

"OOO-wee!" Jaz looked up the height of the edifice only able to see thirty stories as the last five were recessed by design. "Marble on the sidewalk?"

"Polished granite from Seattle," he said, as Jaz eyed the gold gilded 'C' in a starburst on the two plate glass doors. "On the other side of that guard kiosk will be twenty street-level executive parking spaces." He handed Jaz a hard hat as a worker opened the door to his knock.

"Good googa mooga!" Jaz's chin stretched toward the ceiling as she looked up. "It's a cathedral of rose quartz marble." She walked slowly down the colonnade pass the mammoth columns, her sneakers squeaking on the marble floor. "Holy moley!"

"You like? It has a fifty foot foyer like the old banks in New York. I want to convey strength, dependability, endurance and power. Now, over there is going be the executive elevator, mahogany paneling–an express right to the top, first stop 30th floor unless otherwise programmed. These six will be your regular elevators." They stepped into the construction elevator. "All these will be Culhane Enterprises offices. The employee cafeteria and lounge on the twenty-eighth floor. Gym on the twenty-ninth, and thirty through thirty-four will be my indispensable staff–finance offices, legal department, construction corp, my prized core of engineers, architects, interior designers and my summer intern program for talented, black college students."

"That's a real groove, Daddy."

"If not me, then who? Gotta give back and help our own. Ah! The thirty-fifth floor!" He stood proudly. "Here is the secretarial pool. Notice it's in a horseshoe shape, for luck. Surrounding it will be executive offices joined by a concealed corridor. I know it's hard to image–"

"I can dig it Dad, good use of function and design."

"Why, thank you. This way." He pointed to the left. "My office. My small conference room through here, and my washroom complete with shower and clothes closets–and here." Hep stepped outside his office and walked into another marked opening. "My right hand man's office with his own shower and closet, but not as big as mine."

"Of course not. You're the boss," not that white-man Kyle she thought.

They finished the tour by the executive elevator shaft and Jaz thought of how she preferred the smaller corner office with the two windows over them all, as Hep said, "I know you're hungry. So we'll stop by the wharf and pick up a half dozen lobsters."

"Dad, how long you staying?" Jaz curled up on the couch in front of the television after a sumptuous meal.

"Just long enough to look into the hazel eyeballs of my son-in-law and give him a welcome back bear hug," he said, as Lorette chuckled joining her husband on the couch. "Why? Were you going to invite me to the before party?"

"No way."

"But we'll be back for his welcome home party," Lorette chimed in. "Mel's flying in too." She smiled at her daughter.

"Great." Jaz turned her gaze back to Richard Pryor, who told bittersweet jokes about growing up black and poor in the ghetto.

"Mr. Culhane?" Millie handed him the receiver.

"Yes ... hello, Vilna! Yes she's here excited as all git-out about Qwayz's–" Hep listened intently to Qwayz's mother, turning his back on Jaz and her mother. He swung around answering the woman with a "Yes, she's fine," he said, looking at her laughing at the comedian, her feet tucked beneath her, a cola in her hands. "Oh my God!" Hep whispered into the phone. Hep hung up and disappeared into his officc. Jaz saw the extension light up.

Hep contacted an Air Force friend of his in Washington, General Forsythe, for information. In a matter of minutes, he returned Hep's call with the grim confirmation. Qwayz was MIA.

"Meaning what, Bill?"

"It means there's no body, no remains to ship back. In layman terms, it means that your son-in-law is either dead or a POW ... being dead is more humane. Off the record Hep, the plane was hit by a VC rocket ... he was burned to death. What wasn't incinerated on impact, the animals will finish off. Sorry, but I know you like your medicine straight."

"Is it at all possible that he escaped unharmed?"

"A fairy tale. Pray that he is dead, Hep. It's his only salvation."

Hep sank into his chair. What a hideous way for a brilliant young black man, full of promise, to end his life on earth. It was the second time he'd lost a son to that war. It was over for them both, TC and Qwayz, but it had just begun for Jaz, for his mother, sisters and all who were touched by him. Hep called Ma Vy back.

"Where's Jaz?" Hep asked Lorette shutting his office door behind him.

"You took so long, she went on to bed. Why? Something wrong?"

"It's Qwayz. He's reported missing in action."

"What!" Lorette's hand flew involuntarily to her mouth as she sank on the couch. "Oh no, no," she wailed quietly. "Not Qwayz too. Jaz?! Poor Jaz."

"She knows. She's known all day."

Hep scaled the steps, leaving his distraught wife at the newel post below. Knocking gently, he walked past Akira who stood at attention wagging her tail.

"Jaz? You awake?" He inquired, sitting on the bed.

"I'm really tired, Daddy," she said, without turning toward him. Silence hung between them, her back a barrier to any discussion.

"I know about Qwayz, Jaz."

"Oh Daddy." Jaz rose on her elbows. "You don't believe that do you?"

"Punkin' I checked with General–"

"I don't care if you spoke to the president himself. Qwayz is alive. I know it. I can feel it. You'll see on Thursday."

"Jaz–"

"I need you to believe that Daddy. I can't have any negative vibes. You're either for us or against us."

"Jaz, the facts say–"

"Don't you ever believe in feelings, things beyond facts and reports?"

"What if he isn't here on Thursday?"

"He'll be here on Thursday. If not this Thursday then the next or the next, but he is coming home ... he promised. He's never broken a promise to me." Jaz fell back on the pillows turning her back to her father once again.

"We'll talk tomorrow."

"There's nothing left to say."

Jaz intentionally slept late, rising after her father had gone off to the Culhane Building. Turning away from her mother, she told her she'd be out all today, and driving to Travis Air Force Base tomorrow.

"Qwayz and I'll pick up Akira in a few days. You know he'll have to see his dog." Jaz chuckled as she walked to the door.

"Jaz–" Lorette looked into her daughter's eyes ..."Drive carefully."

"Thanks, Ma." Honey eyes locked with ebony pools of maternal sincerity.

Jaz spent her last day alone at Paradise Rock. She walked along the beach, climbed the rocks, rechecked the house for every conceivable creature comfort. She soaked in the tub of hot bubblebath gazing at the setting sun over the ocean. Qwayz's gonna love this, she thought. On her last solo night, she slept fitfully bathed in the rays of a full moon as the waves crashed below. Tomorrow we'll be lying here together looking at our star.

* * *

Gorgeous day for a flight Jaz thought as she drove to Travis, hoping he wouldn't be upset because Akira wasn't in tow. She palmed the Hawaiian rock, and waited the ten tortuous minutes that the plane was late. Finally, it landed and taxied to a halt. The door opened and streams of uniformed men poured into the waiting arms of teary-eyed families and friends. Jaz craned her neck to focus on the last few stragglers. It was like Qwayz to be last, or to leave in a laundry sack so he could surprise her from behind. Her heart raced and her breath shortened as she looked in earnest for his distinctive, easy, street-wise swagger. C'mon Qwayz, don't dance with me now, she pleaded, absently singing The Drifters' "Some Kind Of Wonderful."

"Jaz?" Her head jerked at the sound of her name. "Buzz McLeish–from Hawaii."

"Sure ... Roberta," Jaz offered his wife's name.

"Late as usual."

"Where's Qwayz?" Jaz watched the smile drain from his brown face.

"You're not here to ... Oh, no. Damned Air Force was supposed to contact you before today."

"Is Qwayz on this plane?"

"Jaz, he isn't on this plane–"

"Have you seen him? Do you know where he is, or which one he will be on? I wasn't home yesterday so if he called I missed it." Jaz could feel her nose burn the way it did when she was going to cry. Buzz's image got wavy in the water that sprang uninvited to her eyes. Shoving the wetness from her cheeks she defiantly awaited his answer.

"I haven't seen Qwayz since he and Milton left for a flight early last week. Jaz ... they didn't come back. A bunch of us volunteered to scout the area. They were both liked alot ... but ... I was hopin' to see you, though. Qwayz gave me this to have the clasp fixed. Said you'd kill him if he showed up without it." Buzz dangled the gold ID bracelet she'd given Qwayz for his high school graduation. "First time he was without it. They'll be shipping his stuff home but I didn't wanna leave this to chance–things like this walk."

Jaz took the shiny bracelet rubbing her finger across the deep engraving, Quinton Regis Chandler IV. She'd won her battle with the tears and, now dry-eyed, she looked at her husband's name in the palm of her hand.

"This picture too," Buzz said. "It was the one he kept by his bed."

"We were just kids then ... Malibu Summer."

"I'm really sorry. He was one real special guy." The words offered to comfort caused Jaz to bolt after a quick thank you. "If you ever need anything just look me up!" Jaz heard him call to her back as she ran to her car.

Jaz drove furiously down the highway, trying to outrun reality. Her hair streamed in the wind with fleeting tears of fear and frustration. The radio betrayed her, and she flipped from "a Raw Cilk classic 'Everlastin' Love,' " smack dab in the middle of their wedding song, "Too Young." Finally she cut the radio off.

She took the turn off the main highway onto Ruidoso Road a little to fast, and sped up the driveway to a halting stop. She jumped out, turned off the alarm, slammed open the sliding door, stripping off her clothes as she went. Pulling on sweats and braiding her hair, she wound down the path to the beach, seeking the calm the ocean. High tide prevented her from venturing too far, and the ebb and flow of water began to infuse and quiet her, becoming a life support system.

She remained perched on those boulders until the dawn of a new day; remained at Paradise Rock for two more days, before calling her father to assure him that she was fine, and insisting that he please go back to Italy. Jaz returned to the apartment a day before her med school classes began, searching in earnest for any mail from the Air Force or from Qwayz himself. Instead the news Captain Bradford had extended was now in official black and white.

What do they know, Jaz thought as she lovingly placed his red cap and bomber jacket back on the halltree. She slid his still packed suitcase with his civvies, the Rolex and the tickets to Myrtle Beach into his closet. We'll be packed and ready to go when you come home.

"I'm fine," Jaz resigned herself to saying whenever anyone caught up with her to ask. She had read them all the riot act–her parents, sister, Denny, Tracy, Scoey, CC ... even Gladys Ann and AJ when she heard pity creep into their voices. If you couldn't believe he was still alive at least have the common decency to keep it to yourself.

School was a welcome distraction. Her academic reputation preceded her, and no one knew about her private life, nor cared, as long as she kept volunteering for extra Emergency Room duty so the less gifted could cram for exams or spend holidays with their families.

"You know you have family too," Hep chastised Jaz for taking another student's shift on Thanksgiving. "I know it's an honor to qualify for that ER course as a first year student but–"

"Maybe I'll come by afterwards, Dad." They both knew better.

Hep hung up from his daughter and immediately called Denny. "How's everybody down there?" Hep asked.

"Ma Vy's formidable on the outside, ripped to shreds on the in. My sister, Hanie's still pretty shaken, but AJ's destroyed. He doesn't understand why Jaz won't talk to him. I'm not a good substitute. He's beginning to close off like she has."

"I'm concerned about her. I know you said it would take time but–"

"She's not ready to accept Qwayz's loss. She's in complete and absolute denial, and we can't force her to think otherwise."

"That won't happen. She won't allow it. If you're not a believer, she cuts you off completely. You've been through this Denny, and you counsel vets and families, don't you think Jaz could use some?"

"Yes, but she isn't ready. Some people zip through the grieving stages while others take months, years even. You have to remember Mr. Culhane that Jaz and Qwayz were best friends and confidants before they became lovers or husband and wife. A lot of who Jaz is is tied up with my brother. They were very much a part of each other for so many years, and he was Jaz's first love–the kind fairy tales are made of. She hasn't begun to mourn Qwayz or their relationship ... what was ... what will never be again."

"But this isolation—"

"Her way of coping with trauma. It's classic Jaz Culhane, she did this when we were kids. She withdraws and insulates herself, during which time she nourishes and fortifies herself, then reemerges when she's ready to face the music."

"What if it takes years? She'll waste away her life."

"Healing, Mr. C. She has to reintegrate herself into a world without Qwayz."

"It just hurts to see my daughter in so much pain."

"She's not in pain yet–she's in denial. The only time she feels pain is when someone jabs her with reality. Right now she's on hold ... all her emotions and feelings. She's numb, a little angry, even sad, but hope is her strongest ally; her life preserver. Hope is what keeps her going. When she stops denying and accepts that Qwayz won't be back, then our work is cut out for us."

"An uphill climb to the bottom," Hep lamented.

Chapter Five

Jaz opened the door, and her heart stopped–for just a moment–when she spotted the large package with the Oriental writing. But she wasn't falling for it this time like she had before. In early October, Qwayz's metal locker stood in the middle of the floor, and she'd run through the apartment screaming his name, sure he was there, hiding in the shower stall, out in the hallway. She'd gone out onto the balcony looking for him when Mr. Sanchez yelled up to her, asking if she saw the package the delivery man left? The cruelest words Jaz had heard in a long time. It took her an entire day and a half to open Qwayz's things. Things he'd packed himself enshrined in the putrid smell of heat, sweat and jungle. There was military stuff on top, a jacket with the name Chandler stenciled in black, layered as if to protect treasures underneath. There were her tapes and letters, tied with red ribbon. You're such a neat freak, Jaz had thought. His composition book full of thoughts, songs titles and beginnings. Presents wrapped with his mother's, sisters', AJ's and her names on them. Letters from all his boys from Watts, even her father, and a tape recorder with a tape still in it. Jaz pressed play and the sound of his voice tore her apart.

"And lots of perfect beautiful brown babies. Rethink the four and let's go double or nothing? It'll be fun to try," his laugh filled the empty room and she cut it off before he could continue. She slammed the lid shut and shoved it into his closet, putting it under the packed suitcase with his civvies.

Now this package stood in the same place. His own handwriting could be seen amid the flurry of stamps and strange characters. She cut the twine, and unraveled the brown paper wrapping.

"I'm writing to myself 'cause I know I'm here to receive it" was scribbled in his familiar penmanship. "Lots of goodies in here for us Jas-of-mine. Another set of kimonos 'cause I know we've worn the others out!" After reading the next sentence, Jaz shut her eyes tight as if screening out a harsh painful light–"Are we pregnant yet?"

Jaz couldn't bear to look any further, and another entry was hurriedly pushed into Qwayz's bulging closet. Only then did she realize it was Christmas and she had no tree. She dressed for ER duty, refusing to think of her first season totally alone.

At her shift's end, Jaz walked back into emergency to discover a white boy lying on the cold linoleum floor, turning blue while a resident and an intern argued procedure and liability over the nonbreathing victim. In a reflexive swoop Jaz grabbed a scalpel from the tray, pushed a screaming girl out of the way, slashed open his throat and barked for the tubing she saw dangling in the resident's hand. Jaz inserted the tube amid spurts of blood as Dr. Islip rounded the corner taking charge of the just-trached young man.

"Dr. Mahler had been summoned Chandler," the resident spat at Jaz.

"But he's not here is he, Snyder?" Jaz sniped back.

"You'll hear about this!" the resident threatened as he followed Dr. Islip.

I'm sure I will, Jaz thought, washing the blood from her hands before signing out. Truth was she didn't give a fat rat's ass about Snyder or medicine. It was a scary revelation that something you had wanted for so many years all of the sudden didn't mean didley. Medicine no longer interested her. It was a way to fill her time.

"Miss Chandler!"

Good news travels fast, Jaz thought turning into the cold stare of Dr. Brewer, the chief of staff, who apparently couldn't resist an opportunity to belittle her in front of the crowd.

"The idea that a first year med student would have the audacity to think herself capable of performing an emergency tracheotomy is absurd. Your cowboy antics have surely opened us up to a multimillion dollar lawsuit and ended your short-lived medical career." He concluded self-satisfied that another darkie was put in her place.

"It's not that I even care," Jaz said to Mel as they drove down the coast. "It doesn't have as much to do with Brewer as it does with me and what I want."

"What do you want?"

"That's a Qwayz-question–'if not medicine then what?'" Jaz laughed, imagining his smiling face and warning finger.

"Who's pad is this?" Mel asked as her sister cut the engine in front of Paradise Rock.

"Ours–mine and Qwayz's."

"Aw shucks now, gimme the tour."

"I'm glad you came." Jaz served her sister tea in the sunken living room after showing her the house.

"Well, Christmas and family is important. I want Hud to be close to his grandparents the way we were. Even if it's just for two days. Lemme call Dad and tell 'em where I am." Mel rose to use the phone and returned. "Is this some coup? Dad couldn't believe I made it to Paradise Rock."

"You're our first guest." Jaz didn't notice her pronoun usage. "Got something else to show you." Jaz rose, key in hand with Mel following as she opened the garage door.

"Wow!" Mel entered the studio with one full wall removed and replaced with a glass panel and ocean view. "This equipment is first rate."

"We bought the basics and figured Qwayz could add what he wanted later."

"TC's piano."

"Everybody thought Qwayz should have it."

"Yeah." Mel agreed fingering the upright instrument that had been given to TC one Christmas by Selena and Zack.

"Here, sing your showstopper song for me." Jaz flipped on the mike and Mel obliged, singing her heart out. "Forever the ham." Jaz stood giving her sister the usual standing ovation. "Miss Thang." Qwayz's word for her hung between them.

"Now you," Mel prodded. "C'mon, you know you got a voice. I was always thankful you left singing to me, but you're just as good. TC and Qwayz agreed. You know one song I used to love to hear you sing. 'Bye Bye Baby.' For serious. You could really raunch up a song."

Jaz sang it for Mel, who took another request from Jaz and then they sang together. They emerged from the studio hours later and Mel spent the night. They talked until dawn and slept past noon.

Mel and Hud made Christmas dinner with her parents more palatable, but Jaz spent New Year's alone. She crumpled up the letter which notified her of a "change in status of Quinton Regis Chandler from MIA to KIA-Killed In Action." She threw it across the room and it bounced and landed inside his guitar, Amber. "Two points! I don't believe a word of it. They wrote off my husband but I know he is alive. I know it." That little stubborn piece of her heart wriggled and Jaz took another swig of champagne to squelch it as the revelers outside the window yelled Happy New Year!

"Know what I decided Akira. We're gonna move back to San Francisco. We'll tell Mr. Sanchez so he can tell Qwayz where to find us. Then I can get our furniture out of storage and get Qwayz's Murphy chair and hassock out." Jaz took another swig. "The love we made in that big ole chair and the things we did with that hassock. Ha!" Her laugh out loud turned to a scream, "Qwayz where are you!?" She dissolved into tears on her bed, a bottle her only company.

The next day Jaz called her father asking if he knew a good black realtor who could help her move back to San Francisco.

"Sure, what do you want?"

"I want a small building, a house with Victorian facade. I want large rooms, fireplace, beamed ceilings, sunny, bright and no trolley car tracks."

"Like Alta Vista."

"Yep, and a porch for Akira."

"Fine, if there's one in San Francisco, my people will find it."

"Thanks Daddy, remember he's got to be a brother."

"Yes Jaz, I'm well aware of your politics." Hep hung up the phone with a smile. His daughter was coming around.

* * *

"Dr. Brewer must be proud of you!" Another student and friend, Farrell, ran up to Jaz with a copy of the campus newspaper.

"Hardly. I'm on my way to see the old bastard now."

"For congrats I'm sure. It's in the paper. The guy you performed the emergency tracheotomy on was Scott Carlisle, son of the Carlisle Store chain family who was visiting a friend for the holidays. Old Papa Carlisle is so grateful he's giving a million dollar wing to the Berkeley Medical Hospital Center that saved his boy. Listen, and I quote, 'It renews my faith in the medical profession and human kind that there are some dedicated doctors who place human life over bureaucracy, hierarchy and red tape. Courage is the word I use to describe Dr. Chandler.' Ohoo, gimme your autograph girl!"

Dr. Brewer kept Jaz waiting for over twenty minutes, then joined her without apology.

"In retrospect," he began, "I suppose I should commend you for your quick action in the performance of the emergency procedure last week. There may be some hope for you yet." There was a quick insincere smile. "With a lot of hard work and my help you may become a doctor. You were lucky this time, but don't try any of that foolishness again. Dismissed." He fanned at her.

"My becoming a doctor has very little to do with any help from you. I bet the more input you have in my career, the less likely I am to succeed." Jaz rose towering above him, her honey eyes piercing cold blue. "Had it not been for my 'foolishness' you, your department, an intern and resident would have egg on their faces, a corpse in the morgue and the multimillion dollar suit you're so eager to give me credit for. What I did had nothing to do with luck. It was skill." She turned on her heels, and left his office door open as wide as his mouth.

"Damned uppity black bitch," he said.

"Racist honkey bastard," said she.

"Hello!" Jaz yanked up the receiver to answer the jangling phone.

"Hit me with your congrats! I'm a Daddy!" Scoey yelled.

"It's too early."

"She didn't think so. It's a girl, Jaz, the most perfect little black baby you ever saw."

"Oh, Scoey, congratulations. How's Tracy?"

"Sore. Won't be gettin' no nookie anytime soon."

"Typical! I'll be down there tomorrow."

"Hoping you'd say that."

"Give Tracy my love. Need anything?"

"Just your presence."

"Is that presents?"

"Them too! Gotta call her mom now. Make sure you come 'fo har." He did in his best Ma Vy imitation. "See ya tomorrow, Bucko."

Bracing herself for both Baby Girl Scofield and Tracy's mother, Jaz saw neither at the nursery window. As she tip-toed into the room, Scoey bounced over to greet her, and Jaz gave him the flowers.

"Mama and daughter are a little busy." Scoey teased as the baby suckled his wife's breast, "wish it was me."

"Aww, look at how tiny she is." Jaz bent over without touching either Tracy or the baby. "Tracy, she's beautiful."

"Weighed six-pounds six-ounces!" He forgot to whisper.

"That's your loud-mouth Daddy. Get used to it," Jaz whispered.

"Only family allowed," the nurse announced without ceremony.

"This is my sister," Tracy said. "Say hello to your Aunt Jaz, Amber."

"Amber?" Jaz stood erect.

"Yes," Tracy said quietly looking to her husband.

"We hope you don't mind. We thought it would be like her uncle Qwayz naming her. When he comes back and you two get started, well, we'll just have two Ambers."

"I think that's just ... great." Jaz smiled through tears. "Thank you for that–" She hugged them in turn, for naming their first born after a name their friend loved so, and for joining her in the hope that one day he'll come back.

* * *

Aunt Jaz stayed with Amber and her parents for a full week, watchdogging their rest, making sure visitors didn't stay too long or get too close. Tracy's mother, Mrs. Summerville, brought over meals each night, and Scoey hired a nurse.

"You done good Attorney Scofield," Jaz toasted him late one night as mother and daughter slept.

"Thanks." He looked around his barren house. "Maybe, next year we can afford furniture. The pool's got water." He sipped wine. "Thanks to your Dad throwing some major business my way, things are good. Money begets money, and as long as white folks keep making elevator music out of Raw Cilk classics, some of that kicks back to me thanks to your brother."

"Yeah," Jaz said quietly. "Couldn't happen to nicer folks."

"Everything'll be OK kiddo. Hang tuff."

"I'm hangin'."

"Talked to Ma Vy recently?"

"We had a parting of the ways." Jaz rose and stood by the fireplace.

"About Qwayz's memorial service?"

Jaz walked to the terrace door gazing at the shimmering light reflected from the pool. "How can you have a funeral without a body?"

"Maybe she needs this to put it all behind her."

"I'm not putting Qwayz behind me and I'm takin' names of those who do. I'm not letting anybody bury any part of him or my life with him. She'll look damn foolish when we drop by to see her."

"I think she'll be glad to be a 'damn fool' in that instance. That was pretty cool of you signing over Qwayz's Air Force pay to her."

"Dag, do you know everything?"

"For a change, good news traveled fast."

"Well, she's got Hanie's college tuition soon. And I got plen-tay mon-ay." Jaz sipped the wine looking up at the star she and Qwayz share.

"Denny and AJ know you're here."

"Big mouth. Maybe I'll drop by and see AJ. He graduates this year."

"I know. Denny's been given a professorship at USC."

"Time sure does fly. Just yesterday AJ would sit in the back of Reds on our way to POP or Disneyland. Now, he'll be off to college."

"He couldn't be any worse than you at that age."

"Say wha?" Jaz challenged playfully.

"Your mouth needed more rescuing than a little. I was always pulling you and Gladys Ann outta some mess your mouth started."

"Ooh you lie! It was you, Colt 45 and all them gals you were lovin' on in the backseat of that Impala. Condom city–we found enough rubber to make a pair of tires."

"Shush! Tracy thinks she married a virgin."

"And so do you." Jaz had to laugh.

"What you mean by that!?" He shot her his patented mock-angry look.

"It scared me then, only humors me now."

"As I recall nothing scared you then, that was your problem. What is so fascinating out that window?" He got up to join her.

"That star. It belongs to Qwayz and me. We declared it ours that Malibu summer. It's the same star that shines in Vietnam. You're the last one Scoey–the last of the trio." Jaz looked at her old friend.

"I can't take the weight, Jaz. Those guys were–something fierce."

"So are you. Lemme go." Jaz responded to Amber's cry. "I'll be leaving in the morning."

Jaz picked up the sweet smelling baby all swaddled in pink lace and cotton, and walked with her until the bottle warmer heated the milk to perfection.

"You're a nighthawk like your Aunt Jaz and Uncle Qwayz." She sat in the rocking chair. "Actually your Uncle Qwayz never needs much sleep. That'll be good when we have our own children. Maybe you can babysit, huh? He's gonna be crazy about you."

Tracy and Scoey watched the pair from the doorway with a bittersweet irony. Jaz and Qwayz had been the first to date, to fall in love, to marry, destined to name their first girl child, Amber. Yet Jaz was here with a child named Amber, not her own.

* * *

Jaz had found the perfect old gingerbread house perched high atop a San Francisco hill with two rentable apartments beneath hers. She'd converted the ex-hippie house into a Victorian of distinction, and with great relish, Jaz left the Berkeley Heights apartments.

"Home." She cut the engine and walked the three flights to her door, and lovingly hung Qwayz's red baseball cap and leather bomber jacket on his brass hook of the halltree. "It won't be removed until he does so himself," she vowed as Akira headed straight for the open sliding glass door.

The apartment was big enough to resurrect all their bulky antique furniture from Alta Vista, yet small enough so that Qwayz would only be a reach away. A covered porch with a spectacular view of the bay, crowned the living room which was flanked by the kitchen on the left, and the bedroom on the right. Jaz imagined she and Qwayz sipping cappuccino from their prized machine in the kitchen's bay window or rubbing derrieres in passing as they cooked.

Their wedding portrait hung over the brass bed. On the nightstand, an anniversary music box which played "Too Young," sat in front of a picture of two young people in love one Malibu summer, and a smooth volcanic rock–the last thing Qwayz handed to her. The movers had placed all of Qwayz's clothes plus his trunk, locker, Christmas package and the suitcase Jaz'd packed with his civvies into his closet. Jaz never touched them as she closed the door. All was in place. Jaz was comfortable and pleased with her new home, but all the challenge and purpose was gone. Once again she longed for more.

Well, what now Jaz? she asked herself, joining Akira on the covered porch. A Qwayz-question that needed answering, especially since she'd officially dropped out of med school. Doctors

Lochner, Williams and Islip had called her in for a conference trying to convince her to stay in med school and wanting assurance that Dr. Brewer wasn't the reason she was leaving.

"One monkey don't stop no show," came out of her mouth before realizing it. "His attitude is actually motivation for me to stay and teach him a few things about 'minority' superiority, but that would be my only reason for staying. I would never let anyone else steal my dream, but it's no longer medicine," she had told them.

"Ok, Jaz, you don't want medicine, what do you want?" Jaz asked herself aloud, and Akira looked up at her. It was June, and she didn't have a clue. "Let's go for a ride."

Jaz and Akira cruised around town, ending up across from The Culhane Building. She pulled out of the traffic to absorb all thirty-five floors of its grandeur.

"I have a B.S. degree and could get a job there when it's completed, but what'll I do now?" She asked Akira, when another Qwayz-question insinuated itself into her psyche. What would you like to do whether you got paid for it or not?

There in the midst of noise, traffic and fumes the answer shone crystal clear as it bounced off the gold steeple of the Culhane Building.

"Of course." She started her motor along with the beginning of a new challenge and life.

All the Johnny Mathis and Nat King Cole records were returned to their jackets and placed on the stereo stand. All the doors and windows secured. When he found out, AJ would have to battle Millie for custody of Akira. Jaz took one last glance at their wedding portrait and the nightstand shrine formed by the trinity–music box, rock and picture, deciding again that this was the way she wanted Qwayz to first see this room–in tact.

Europe. Paris. She had decided on the Sorbonne over the Ecole' de Beaux Arts. Her friends didn't understand why she had to go to Europe to study architecture, and Jaz couldn't articulate the razor sharp pain she felt trying to cope with life without Qwayz, no matter how temporary. She couldn't explain the anger evoked from the news, whether it reported on the war in Vietnam or the war on poverty. The shootings of her people, the urban blight, the racism, the prejudice she felt walking the streets or in the hallowed halls of the American educational system. The height of government anarchy and arrogance occurred when Governor Reagan tear gassed Berkeley students protesting at Spoul Plaza. In May she knew the entire United States was a sick society feeding upon itself, when National Guardsmen fired on students protesting the U.S. invasion of Cambodia, killing four at Kent State. Everything was reduced to race, ignorance, power or the lack thereof.

Jaz, like her aunt Selena before her, was sick of America. She longed to be treated as a human being, a break from racism at every level. Not just the sanctioned armed assassination of Fred Hampton by "law enforcement" or this crazy mess brewing with George Jackson and Angela Davis right over the bridge, but black men deemed expendable cannon fodder in Southeast Asia while the white man pull strings for his own son. Jaz needed a vacation from America.

The iron bird soared, slicing through the puffs of clouds and Jaz dared to put the headset to her ears and America gave her a farewell concert; The social commentary of the Temptations in "Ball of Confusion," the assault from Edwin Starr's, "War," and the plea of Freda Payne to "Bring The Boys Home," but it was the prayer from Stevie Wonder's "Heaven Help Us All" that pierced Jaz's heart and sent tears down her cheeks.

* * *

Jaz's leather flats clicked across the highly polished parquet floors, echoing in the faded elegance of the twenty foot ceiling in this sixteenth century Rome apartment building with the colorful past. The resident manager explained that it had gone from housing heads of state to a famed brothel and back again to an address of repute. "E' troppo grande," Jaz sighed leading the manager to the elevator.

She'd lived with her parents in the Embassy's private quarters for five days now and had less than a week before her classes at AAA, The American Architecture Academy, began. She'd fought coming to Italy because her parents were here, but it was the only place for a serious architecture student. Paris had turned on her for not bringing Qwayz back with her, had conjured him up in every nook and cranny of its being. Jaz saw them buying candy from the corner confectioner's, climbing the steps of Notre Dame, her posing for him in front of the gargoyles. She saw Qwayz coaxing her into the Eiffel Tower elevator, and sharing Berthmillion ice cream as they sauntered across Ile St. Louis. Him plucking the perfect bouquet of flowers while charming the vendor, or presenting her with a passel of helium-filled balloons as they walked through the park giving them to children. Qwayz's essence was everywhere in the parks, streets, the markets, shops, in the museums. Her heart, mind and soul ached for him in Paris, more than it ever did at home. So she had to come to Rome.

There were no imprints of Qwayz here in Italy. The world was coupled; her parents, who only bothered her on occasion, Gladys Ann had married Dr. Ulery Menair, a native of St. Barts, Sloane was engaged, and CC had run off to Maine with someone she met at Woodstock. What intelligent black woman goes to Woodstock? Jaz didn't have to ask what color he wasn't. Seems she and Denny were the last true-blues, waiting for their men to reappear. He should have called or come home by now. Qwayz was late, and Quinton Regis Chandler IV was never late. So, while she held a silent vigil for his return, she'd immerse herself in the study of architecture, take a loft apartment, and furnish it with the bare necessities, because when Qwayz called ... she was gone.

Chapter Six

In the spring of 1975, Jaz slipped back to California as quietly as she had left. All of her friends and family anticipated her return after a five year absence, but no one knew exactly when. Though anxious to see Paradise Rock, Jaz gave the cab driver her apartment's address. When they passed the street to her parents' house, she thought of how put out her father would be for not being privy to her plans. She hadn't given him an inkling during their last conversation. She'd told him she didn't have definite plans, beyond helping Tracy the month of June with her new baby. Hep warned her not to consider working any where except Culhane Enterprises. He even promised her the corner office with the two windows.

Mel and Hud Jr. had relocated to L.A., so Mel could star in her own variety show, and she'd made wedding rumblings about the show's producer. Denny, Tracy and AJ were ecstatic about Jaz's return.

Italy was less accepting of her departure. Jaz had shipped her drafting table, apothecary cabinet, three pasta machines, record collection and her "Tawny" wardrobe home before flying back.

The cab paused for a light in front of a travel agency, and Jaz caught a glimpse of an Amalfi coast advertisement. She thought of Italy and how much she missed it. Life there was as good as it got without Qwayz, who was still part of her every thought and breath. She would have given it all up in heartbeat just to feel his arms around her again, and hear him say the stars are in their heavens and all's right with the world.

She had acquired quite a lifestyle in the past five years which began when she needed to replace her bike with a car, so she could make her architectural sketch cites. Fabrizio, Selena's designer, who had hounded her about modeling during her summer visit in 1965, resumed his press. Jaz's exotic look, and bold, audacious coloring made her an instant hit. Since Jaz didn't want her architectural career or her father's position as ambassador compromised, she and Fabrizio decided on the name Tawny. No one knew her real name or identity. She never granted interviews, did no runway work, no one had ever heard her voice–she only spoke to Fabrizio. Her face graced the covers of European fashion magazines only, none distributed in America. The more reclusive she became, the more the public clamored for her. Besides Italian women imitating her look, Europe was abuzz with stories about her heritage. The most popular was that she was the daughter of a rich, South American land baron–the reason she could be so selective about her projects. Funny, when Jaz looked in the mirror all she saw was a proud black girl from Watts.

When Jaz left Italy Alonge' was paying her millions for exclusivity–working for them only twenty days a year, and no one else when she was off. This money and time allowed her to get a second masters in architecture, and lavish her friends with expensive gifts and trips. Tracy, Scoey and Amber continually received the latest fashions. When AJ visited, they did Europe, Egypt, and glacier skied in Cortina and St. Moritz. Denny came over once before marrying psychiatrist Lloyd Winslow, a truly upsetting time for Jaz, but she returned to America to be her friend's matron of honor. It was Jaz's only trip home, and it was painfully suffocating with everyone paired off and happy. Even AJ asked about Avia Checole', who was Hep's embassy assistant prior to his return to San Francisco and Culhane

Enterprises. The pretty, slim-faced girl, with coal-black hair that sprang back into curls moments after it was brushed, was the color of a wet ginger snap, compliments of her French mother and Cameroonian father, and had been AJ's constant companion when he visited Jaz.

With her parents and friends a continent away, Jaz succumbed to the charms of Crown Prince Omar Al Khalifa Sidar. The Prince romanced her with rare baubles, spirited her away to any destination she wondered about, and bought them a Nido d'Amore on Lake Como. The fact that he was married, as was she, didn't bother her until his family showed up at the Lake Como villa. Jaz would never forget the sight of his poor wife and their four children cowering beneath his ire. Despite all his princely wealth and status, he was just a lying, cheatin' man, and Jaz was raised better. Despite his pleas, she cut him loose on the spot. It was easy to do when the man only had loan of her body. The Prince hadn't touched her mind, heart or soul–they would always belong to Qwayz.

So Jaz had returned to her apartment in Rome, and began updating her portfolio when she witnessed the fall of Saigon on television. The Vietnam War was over. Jaz knew it was time to go home.

Welcome to San Francisco, Jaz muttered as the cab was caught in a rush hour traffic snarl. The plane ride home had been different from the initial one to Italy in 1970, and from the anxiety-produced, trip home for Denny's wedding. This ride held some maturity, some healing, and was full of renewed hope, of beginnings and continuing on. Jaz was ready to embrace a new career and a renewed spirit of waiting.

It was not the America she'd left, but she too had changed. The U.S. had come to its senses about some things. In 1973 on the heels of Watergate and the Agnew resignation, sanity in dealing with the armed services and human rights emerged. The draft was ended and a volunteer army begun, and Roe vs Wade gave a woman the right to determine command of her own body.

The new black cinema probably started in 1970 with "Mandingo," redeemed itself in 1971 with "Shaft," and forged on with "Lady

Sings The Blues," as Earth Wind and Fire kept their "Head To The Sky." In '74 Cicely Tyson portrayed "Miss Jane Pittman," and the Duke of Ellington left this world for the next. Jaz missed the U.S. oil crisis, Nixon's resignation, and Patty Hearst becoming a bank robber. Ali beat Foreman in Zaire, and Henry Aaron hit his 715th home run. A lot had changed in the U.S. but one thing remained constant–it will still be an existence without Qwayz. The passage of time didn't make her miss him any less.

Jaz's toes stood on her apartment threshold. She tipped the driver carrying the last of her luggage, and sighed, "Home." The apartment wasn't stuffy but she flung open her porch door welcoming the circulation of fresh San Franciscan air. Inhaling deeply she spun around noticing Johnny Mathis and Nat King Cole albums sitting on top of the component set. Without dwelling on whether she'd left them out the last time she was here, she put them away along with the opera albums she had shipped from Italy. Qwayz's Amber was still perched against the fireplace, with Papa Colt's pearl-handled guns and TC's Grammy on the mantel. Going into the kitchen, she pushed the empty apothécary chest she'd used in Italy into place at the end of the counter. She caught a glimpse of the distant ship and watery horizon through her bay window. "Home."

She crossed the kitchen threshold, walking straight past the porch to her bedroom. Then Jaz noticed its absence. Her head jerked up before she flattened her body to the floor to see if it had fallen. She searched the closets and corners for it. She called her father.

"Jaz? Where are you?"

"I'm here in San Francisco–"

"Lorette! Jaz is here," he yelled out. "I don't believe you didn't call us–"

"It's OK dad, I just got here, really–"

"Well, you almost missed me, I'm just here to pick up a few things before I fly to Houston–"

"Hello Jaz," Lorette's voice interrupted on another line. "Welcome home! Are you coming for dinner?"

"I won't be here," Hep told his wife.

"You don't have to be here for Jaz to come to dinner, Hep. My goodness if she waited for that to happen, it could be months–"

"Folks, I'm home and I'll be here for awhile," said Jaz.

"Thanks to Kyle, your father's only doing the domestic travel."

"He's aces, Jaz, you'll have to meet him, though I don't know when, he's always out of the country. He traveled with me through the Orient and they love him. He picked up some of the language and dialects. He got contracts for us to build the two luxury hotels in Hong Kong and Singapore–" Hep stopped as Tennyson informed him the limo was ready to take him to his jet.

"He must be one giant liverspot by now." Jaz's sarcasm poked at her father's continual adulation of the Great White Bwana. "How does he do it?"

"Huh? Youth I guess," Hep said, "Now Jaz—"

"Hep, let the girl relax, she just wants to be home," Lorette said.

"Dad, I called you because my wedding portrait is missing."

"What?"

"My Tretoni oil of Qwayz and me is not hanging over the headboard. I'm here and it's not."

"Where's my head, it's in the shop."

"What happened to it?"

"It fell and the frame was damaged. I forgot all about it. Don't worry it's with a reputable dealer, he did our Monet and–"

"When will it be ready?"

"Listen, Punkin', I don't have time to call right now, but I promise I'll pick it up myself when I get back."

"Thanks and congrats on making the Fortune 500 list. Unprecedented."

"You ain't seen nothin' yet. Gotta go, Punkin'."

"Have a good trip, Dad, Bye Lorette." Jaz fingered the picture of she and Qwayz in Malibu on the night table. "Guess you'll have to do till then." She opened the lid of the music box which delicately began "Too Young," and palmed their Hawaiian rock to her heart. "Home."

The ringing phone demanded attention in the empty apartment. The door flew open, and, dropping the groceries on the couch, Jaz ran to answer it. "Who knows I'm here? Hello!?!"

"It's a girl."

"Scoey?"

"And another girl."

"Wha? Twins? You and Tracy had twins!?"

"Where you been girl? I called Italy, the phone is disconnected. Couldn't find your parents number, and CE wouldn't give me squat–"

"Congratulations! They're early. Where you expecting twins?"

"Hell no, I turned around with the first baby and the nurse says 'there's something else up here' and it was another baby! Three weddings Jaz, I'm giving a bonus to the ones who elope. When you comin'? We got Ma Summerville the first week and everybody else who thinks it's so wonderful. We could really use you the second week after the cuteness has worn off and everyone has left us alone."

"I'm not waiting until then. You'll see me when you see me."

"Be like that."

"You're just the father. You've done your do, now step aside my man."

"Don't break bad with me."

"Tracy's busy I take it?"

"Both breasts."

"Bye attorney Scofield, my love to your po' wife." Twins, Jaz mused, as she put her food away and began packing for L.A.

Mrs. Summerville, bottles in tow, let Jaz in, excusing herself all at the same time. The babies yelled without shame as the uniformed nurse ran up the stairs behind the grandmother. Jaz, in no rush to join the chaos, set her overnight and shoulder bag down, and then, beyond the glass, alone by the pool, she saw her. Her feet dangled into the pool, her body wet from a recent swim, and water-logged braids hung beside her ears.

"Hi!" Jaz approached and the little brown body, deepened by the sun's kisses, straighten at the sound of a human voice.

"Hi." Her eyes darted at Jaz then away again. "They're up there."

"Who?"

"The twins, Bethany and Brittany. All they do is cry, cry, cry."

"Mind if I join you?" When Jaz rolled up her jean legs, the little girl looked at her for the first time. Big, pretty round black eyes wondered why this lady wants to sit with her instead of seeing the twins? "Later." Jaz took off her gold sandals and sat next to her goddaughter. "I'd rather talk to you. Ooo this feels good." Jaz kicked her feet lightly in the cool water. "You like to swim?"

"That's all I've been doing is swim, swim, swim, especially since they came. First my mother went to have them, then came home with them, and I don't even get to play with her or them. They just cry and eat."

"What do you like to do?" As Amber recited her likes and dislikes, Jaz absorbed the prettiness of this chocolate little girl who felt replaced and forgotten. "Maybe we can do some things while I'm here. Do you know who I am?"

"No. I've seen you sometime but I don't remember–"

"Hey Jaz!" Scoey bounded through the glass doors.

"Daddy!" Amber sprang to life jumping into her father's arms.

"Hey Ace!" He kissed his little girl. "How ya doing? Hey girl," Scoey gave Jaz a peck on the cheek.

"The twins names start with B's because my name starts with A because I was first. Right Daddy?"

"Right, you're my first big girl." He kissed her brown cheek. "You seen the babies in question yet?"

"No I been hangin' out with Amber. She's gonna show them to me later." Jaz winked at Scoey.

"Oh, good idea. Well, lemme go upstairs and say 'Hi' to Mommy, OK?"

" 'K'."

"You finished for the day?" Jaz asked.

"Naw, jury's out, gotta go back in an hour, but I thought I'd come home and see my girl, right Ace." He chucked her chin playfully. "You go on and hang out with Aunt Jaz."

"My Aunt Jaz from Italy? I talk to you all the time. You sent me Bobo. He's on the shelf in my room, Momma says I can have it when I get older."

"Well, we'll have to get you one you can use right now." Jaz never intended the mink Teddy bear to be a museum piece. "Let's go see those babies now."

For the duration, it was Amber and Jaz. As far as the five-year-old was concerned her Aunt Jaz had been sent solely for her company. They were inseparable, from breakfast in the morning until a bedtime story and prayers at night. There was no place Jaz didn't go without Amber. To buy an aquamarine, tan upholstered Jaguar sedan. To see Denny and Little Lloyd, Melie and AJ, and to see the taping of Mel's new variety show where Amber and Hud got to be students in a school scene. They went shopping, lunching, and to the movies.

"I'm heading back to Frisco tomorrow," Jaz announced to Tracy and Scoey. "And I'd like to take Amber back for a visit with me."

"Bless you," Scoey piped up sinking to one knee, "And which other one would you like to take? Two for one sale." Jaz jabbed his side playfully, but Tracy had a concerned look on her face.

"She's supposed to start camp soon," she said.

"Oh baby, she shoulda started that two weeks ago. It's June twentieth. 'Sides being with her Aunt Jaz is better than camp."

"But, she'd be home every night," Tracy said as one of the twins started up.

"C'mon baby, what's Amber gonna do once she gets home? Swim herself to death? You're asleep or busy with the babies, I'm at work. Your Mama hatted up, the nurse is just here for the twins, and Mrs. Dix for the housework. House full of folks, but none to tend to my Ace, I see it in her eyes. She's lucky to have Jaz pick up the slack. At least till we get this thing right. What do ya say, Bay-bay?"

"She has been kinda lost in the shuffle." Tracy tried to think over the wailing of first one, then both of the babies. "Alright. Thank you, Jaz."

"Don't call us we'll call you about returnin' her," Scoey joked, but Tracy didn't find it funny as she exited the room.

With the sun and the ocean on the left, almost matching the aquamarine Jag, the two brown beauties sped towards San Francisco singing "Respect Yourself" along with the Staples Singers.

Amber had done well in the front seat for about an hour until she fidgeted beneath the safety belt, and Jaz let her roam free in the back seat. She ended up where Jaz always had on those long childhood trips to Texas, right behind and in the ear of the driver. When Amber knew the words she sang along, otherwise she delighted in her aunt's voice. "You act silly just like my Daddy. Is he your brother?"

"Almost."

The pair turned into Gary's and lunched over lobster thermidor. Amber was fascinated by the stories Jaz told of her brother, TC, who used to take her out somewhere different every May, and they often came here to Gary's sitting right at this very table.

"I wanted a brother, but I got two sisters."

"Well he was my big brother, just like you are a big sister. Mel is my big sister and I'm a little sister like Brit and Beth." Jaz had fallen into Amber's nicknames for them.

"Mel is nice." She had enjoyed her visit to the studio and her house. "Where is your brother now?"

Jaz explained enough about the Vietnam war to satisfy a five-year-old's curiosity and not get all caught up into herself.

"Do you miss him?"

"Very much. I think about him all the time."

Amber napped after lunch allowing Jaz quiet for the last few miles.

"Ah, this is nice, Aunt Jaz." Amber surveyed the apartment as Jaz shuffled through her mail. "Where's my bedroom?"

"I only have one bedroom and we can share, if you're not a squirmer, or we can toss for the couch."

"Oh, wow, look, a guitar." She ran towards Qwayz's treasure hoisting it awkwardly.

"Lemme help you. Here, sit on the couch." Jaz arranged the instrument and they strummed out "Tom Dooley." "Is this yours?"

"No, its Qwayz's and guess what its name is? Same as yours; in fact your Uncle Qwayz named you." Jaz relayed the story of Qwayz, her Dad and TC and how she was named.

"Is he still in Italy?"

"I wish . . ." Jaz shared the less gruesome details. "So I'm still waiting for him to come back."

"Can I wait with you?"

"Sure."

"I hope he comes soon 'cause we aren't getting any younger you know."

"Out of the mouths of babes." Jaz fished out the crumbled piece of paper in the hole of the guitar, and read "the change in status" paper declaring Quinton Regis Chandler IV dead.

"Oh, who is that, Aunt Jaz?" Amber stood in the bedroom pointing to the wedding portrait.

"That's me and Qwayz on our wedding day."

"Oh boy, he's some good looking dude, just like Prince Charming."

"Well, he's my Prince Charming ... always will be."

Over the next few days the pair did girl things. They washed their hair, did their nails, played dress-up, made each other up and had tea parties with the new black doll Jaz bought, which Amber named Lucretia. They baked brownies, went shopping and sightseeing, and stayed up late watching old movies with a bowl of popcorn between them. They did whatever struck their fancy, which for Amber was riding the ferry and eating strawberries at every possible hour.

"Amber!?" Jaz searched for her pigtailed niece across the stalls of the Farmer's Market. Walking down where two aisles intersected, she caught a rear glimpse of Amber's blouse as the little girl stooped to pick up dropped strawberries. "Ah!" Jaz gasped as a tall black man stretched to his full six feet, and offered Amber her last berry.

"Sorry. Didn't mean to startle you." His handsome face split into a wide, warm grin.

"I think that's all of them, now I have to weigh them, right?" Amber looked between the two adults, neither of whom was looking at her.

"Allow me." The man whisked her up toward the scale before Jaz could object. "One pound and three quarters."

"Is that OK?" Amber looked back at Jaz for approval.

"Fine."

"You gonna eat all those by yourself?" He asked placing the little girl back on the floor.

"I sure can. All by myself unless you want to come over and help?"

"Maybe some other time," he said after an awkward pause.

"Oh, good, corn on the cob." Amber saw the ears in Jaz's basket."That's my favorite," Amber told the gentleman.

"Looks like you might have a little problem with that." He stooped momentarily to her eye level, to look at her mouth.

"I've been hearing alot about that lately." She smiled to show her snaggled-teeth, and the two of them laughed.

"Well, I hate to break this up but we better get our goods home, Amber," Jaz suggested, nudging her niece in the opposite direction.

"Bye," Amber looked around her aunt to the man. "Thank you." She returned his wave. "We have to get some whipped cream too." She peeked around her aunt again. The man was standing in the cashier's line, but he saw her and waved again.

"You're a flirt," Jaz said.

"Isn't he dreamy?"

"Sounds like a Sandra Dee word."

"A what? Ooh we need some cake cups."

"We'll get them at the bakery with the bread on the way home."

"He's gone!"

"Who?"

"My Prince Charming." She checked the aisles and other lines. "Do you think we'll see him again?"

"If fate wills you to, Cinderella."

"I'm not cleaning behind nobody, ever–especially Brit and Beth."

As Jaz opened her front door, balancing a brown bag of groceries on her knee, she heard Amber say "Hi."

"Hello!" a male voice replied. Jaz looked over the bannister to the downstairs apartment. "Welcome back, neighbor." The blond haired, blue-eyed man said from the apartment below.

"Hello," Jaz said ushering Amber through the door. I must tell all my friends who claim they can't meet men to rent-a-kid and go for it.

"Amber, didn't your parents tell you not to talk to strangers?" She sat the bags on the kitchen table.

"Who?" Amber climbed on the stool to get the colander so she could pick and wash the strawberries.

"The man in the market and the guy downstairs."

"The man in the store was my Prince Charming, and the one downstairs is your neighbor, like our neighbors the Ebersoles, but they don't have anyone for me to play with, their children are grown. But they give good treats for Halloween."

"How many Prince Charmings can you have? You have the one from the market, that's enough. So you shouldn't talk to any more."

"I don't know, I really like AJ. I haven't decided if I want him as a big brother or Prince Charming. Is he coming back over today?" Amber asked, remembering the last time he came over they had made pasta, played records, danced, then taken Akira for a long walk.

"I don't think so, but you'll see him on the fourth of July."

"Oh goodie! Maybe I'll decide by then."

"It's no press, Amber, but you shouldn't go around speaking to every man you see. What about the guy downstairs, could he be a Prince Charming?"

"No, he's not tall, dark and handsome. My Dad said only guys who are tall, dark and handsome are good enough for me."

"He's a real smart man, your Dad." Jaz grinned knowingly.

"Yeah, I like him alot."

Chapter Seven

Hep's yacht jockeyed in the bay for the choicest position for firework viewing. He'd sent his captain out early with most of the guests, and joined them later by motorboat.

"Where's Kyle?" Lorette asked as her husband came aboard.

"He and a lady-friend are entertaining on his boat, thought he'd bypass the boss and his friends this year."

"Haven't seen much of him at all," Lorette complained.

"I got him traveling so much now, I give him his space when he's here. Can't have a disgruntled employee who's not having his needs met. Hello Punkin'." He kissed Jaz before slapping five with Hud, now a cool seven-year-old, and asking where Mel was.

"In the air-condition, of course," Jaz said as she watched her father circulate among his other guests, thankful at being spared from meeting that old coot Kyle. Loyalty. Dad must be holding on to Kyle because he brought the man out of retirement in 1963 to help manage Culhane properties in New York while Hep was in Washington as chief of protocol, and later, while ambassador to Italy. But imagine that old guy having a date, can't be doing much but remembering, Jaz thought.

"Jaz, look what AJ brought me, squirrel nuts!" Amber said.

"Yeah, I used to love them when I was your age, and a certain guy and gal kept me supplied." AJ winked at Jaz, as Amber scurried off to show someone else.

"You could bring her a handful of dirt, AJ, and she'd be elated." Jaz sipped her ice tea.

"Yeah, well, I been there too." His mouth cut a wide smile, recalling the crush he had on Jaz.

"And you outgrew it."

"Had no choice. So will she." He looked out over the bay. "Fourth of July ... so how ya doing?"

"Not bad actually as long as I got that little spitfire to keep me busy, not alot of time for thinking." Jaz knew this would be her life if she and Qwayz had had a child.

"Did I tell you I was going to Europe for six weeks?"

"No, Melie did. But I've been waiting for the details."

"I was asked to be part of a consortium to study European surgery wards."

"I'm proud of you. One of those stops Italy?" Jaz already knew the answer, Avia had written her that AJ was coming for a visit.

"Matter of fact it is. I've talked to Avia. I hope she's free when I come through," he said, casually.

"That'll be nice seeing her again." Jaz couldn't contain a smile.

"What? See ...you always think that–" He fidgeted like a school boy.

"What? I didn't say a word."

Jaz and Amber spent the night sharing a stateroom, and the next afternoon returned to the apartment.

Despite Jaz's attempts to win her niece over to her favorite, Ghiradelli Square, Amber preferred Pier 39, near the water and the ferry, with its cotton candy, balloons and the Doll Shoppe.

"Look." Amber pointed to a crowd, and began elbowing and twisting her way to the front pulling Jaz along. "What is it?" Amber asked, not seeing a clown or a movie star.

"I dunno, a car. Let's go."

"Not just a car lady, a Bugatti Royale 1931," an impressed man said as the female pair skipped toward the wooden pier.

Armed with popcorn in one hand and cotton candy in the other, Amber roamed away from Jaz who was on a quest for a Bon Voyage gift for AJ.

"Hi!" Amber jerked at the gentleman's jacket, her cotton candy settling against his companion's skirt. "Remember me?"

"Well, hi there, Amber." He stooped down. "This is my friend, Amber," he introduced her to the woman beside him.

"Want some?" She offered some of the pink fluff, which he took.

"Thanks, where's your mommy?" He eyed the crowd.

"My Mommy!?" Amber giggled at his mistake.

"Uh-oh, here she comes." He stood confused by her amusement.

"Amber." Jaz spotted her and stood firm until the laughing girl joined her. "You are not suppose to wander away from me."

"Someone's in trouble," the gentleman said to his disinterested date. "Aren't kids adorable?"

"As long as they belong to some one else," his date said, taking hold of his arm, and leading him away.

"Aunt Jaz, PC thinks you're my Mommy." She was still giggling.

"Who's PC?"

"Prince Charming. He said 'where's your Mommy?'" She laughed without stopping until they entered the Doll Shoppe.

As usual, they lingered at Pier 39, then visited Akira, and had dinner at Jaz's parents before returning home.

"It's late, call your Mom, Amber," Jaz directed, going into the kitchen for Amber's vitamins.

"Aunt Jaz look–it's her." Amber pointed to the television.

"Who?"

"The prince's wife!"

"... As the first black woman anchor for San Francisco I know you understand." The male commentator was remarking about a colleague's marriage and move.

"We wish you hardy congratulations, and the best of luck at the New York network, Phil," she offered a semi-frigid smile before continuing, "Back to you, Jim."

"That's PC's wife! She's a movie star."

"You've got a good memory, Amber."

"She's pretty, but not a pretty as you Aunt Jaz or him," she giggled.

"Call your Mama, girl!" Jaz laughed with her.

Jaz's hair billowed in the wind as she aimed her car towards Ruidoso Canyon Road. She missed her little shadow talking in her ear, but the time had come for Amber to go home. Jaz smiled remembering Amber's amazement at how the twins had grown. She was allowed to hold them and decided they weren't so bad.

The Jag maneuvered the hairpin turn like it was a straight away, frothing up dirt as if it was as light as air. Jaz paused on the bluff, the expanse of the ocean welcoming her back to Paradise Rock, a beaconing charm on the coastline. She turned right up the gravel driveway, the crunch of her tires rivaling the beating of the ocean against the granite. Jaz switched off the engine, and soaked up the sights, smells and sounds of the familiar. It was as if she'd never left. Of all the places she's been or seen in this world, this is where Qwayz's spirit lives. Not in Watts, not in Vietnam, not with Ma Vy's memorabilia of medals and flags over her fireplace. This is where Qwayz is, and she couldn't wait to be with him.

She flung open the sliding door, rendering the alarm inactive, and she simply stood there, watching the light and shadow play on the fireplace facade. "Qwayz I'm home!" She couldn't resist, her heart, body, mind ached to be free to acknowledge him, to talk with him in a way no other human would understand. She closed and locked the screen and walked around the rooms, opening the terrace door in the bedroom breathing in the circulating air. And there Jaz remained, just enjoying the freedom that only Paradise Rock afforded; the cleansing and the sanity.

She stood on the terrace awaiting the moon and the stars and when they came, she studied them for hours more. Finally when positioned just so, Jaz climbed into bed, her face basking in the moonlight as breezes flowed over her body. "Qwayz are you here?" There was no voice as he drew her to his chest, his lips touched hers, and they matched the rhythms of their being, as she felt his unconditional and everlasting love.

Jaz remained in the cocoon of Paradise Rock for days, much to the chagrin of her father who feared a psychological relapse in his daughter. Only Denny's coming to Frisco for a conference drew Jaz away from the "land of the dead," as Hep referred to it. Jaz's reentry back into the 1970's usually took a few hours.

Denny, there for the weekend, presented her paper early on Saturday. So the pair was free to tool around San Francisco, eating and acting-up, and going to see "Cooley High." Both women related so easily to the context; it was set in Chicago, but could have been Watts. The mood, the method, and characters were all folks they'd grown up with. At the movie's end, they cried, remembering Qwayz and Yudi and how hard it was to say goodbye to yesterday.

"When you coming back down to L.A. girlfriend?" Denny asked at the airport.

"I best get my hindparts to working before I forget everything I ever learned. When I come you'll know."

"You have to stay with us sometime. Tracy and Scoey aren't the only ones with guest rooms you know. Thank your Dad, again. I've never been on a private jet before. Love you." She kissed her friend.

Jaz saw "Cooley High," three more times and spent two more weeks at Paradise Rock before she called her father. "OK, Dad, I'm ready to work," she announced. It was music to Hep's ears.

The corner office her father had saved for her had never been used. A smaller version of Hep's grand mahogany desk sat in front of one window facing the door. Jaz placed a drafting table at the other window; a couch, chairs, and coffee table had also been provided. An original Tretoni of the Amalfi coast, hanging over the sofa, always caught her eye as she looked up.

Jaz's work attire was carefully orchestrated to project the right corporate image. Her coppery tresses slicked back into a severe chignon with only the ripple of waves suggesting latent wildness. She wore coatdresses and suits. Her jewelry, always gold, was as simple and straightforward as her professional approach. Her ears adorned with gold earrings, her wedding band crowned by her circle of diamonds, a watch forever tangled with her interlocking hearts bracelet, and on her other wrist, the gold cuff bracelet her father had given her for her 18th birthday.

Her blouses were made of the finest silk, never a ruffle, bow or any hint of cleavage. Her wardrobe reflected the professional person she was, no frivolity, nothing to divert the attention from what she was presenting; no room for misinterpretation or an opening for anything more than a business relationship.

As Jaz poured over CE perspectus, corporate profiles, financial analysis, current projects and California building codes, she hadn't time to notice the subtle change in hairstyles among the female support staff. Every length of hair had been neatly brushed into a chic chignon knotted at the neck; those who could did, those who could not improvised with a wig shop purchase. As the top professional woman in the executive suite, she set the style. When Jaz breezed in in the mornings she had no idea that her entrance and what she wore was the talk of that floor and those below. The other women took great pride in attempting to duplicate, trying to outdo one another at least, but when Jaz came in one day with attache', shoes and handbag that had little bumps on it all bets were off. Thanks to her boss, Addie had learned the subtle difference between crocodile and alligator, but this pimply "leather" was odd. Addie finally asked Jaz what the material was and returned to the pool with the answer. "Ostriche. The girl can rag."

"Jaz, got a minute?" Hep walked into her office.

"Sure Dad," her lips said, but her hands and eyes kept working.

"It's about the elevator man."

"What?" Jaz looked at him unbelievingly.

"There's been a bit of a mutiny among the staff. I guess it's been brewing for awhile but they've finally approached me about it."

"Dad–"

"Bear with me. Many think he makes folks coming to the building uncomfortable. No one wants to ride with him and they wait for one of the other elevators. So what's say we put the old WWII vet on the executive elevator. Could keep his job and some dignity."

"Fine," Jaz said.

"Great."

"Dad," Jaz said, as Hep was leaving, "You done good." Jaz thought of the camaraderie that old World War II vets have that Vietnam's don't.

"There but for the grace of God go I." Hep sauntered from the room and Jaz returned to her work.

"Jaz?" Addie stuck her head in, it was the first time she'd called her by her first name. "Got a minute?"

"Sure." Jaz didn't, it was like a social club around here, if you wanted to work, you'd have to go home.

"I just wanted to thank you for Zeke," Addie began as Jaz tried to search her brain on personnel; Marc and Derek were the young, crack architects, graduates of Hep's intern program. Dory was the landscape architect. Tre' was in Finance. Zeke–who the hell was–

"The elevator guy," Addie answered Jaz's curious eyes. "You were the most important vote, Kyle said yes from the Orient and you were the last one polled. Face it, if you or Kyle had said no, Zeke would be out of a job."

Jaz was no angel, she recalled herself tensing at the sight of the grotesque figure of a man holding the door open. She was one of those who often opted to wait for the executive elevator, but she had seen Addie talking with him at her desk, seen her wait for his elevator.

"There are too many around here who don't understand or care how hard it must be for an old man alone like that–"

"Why do you care, Addie?"

"I had a retarded brother and saw how everybody treated him. Zeke isn't retarded, but he suffered those wounds defending us in a war. My brother had a good soul, but all people saw was his outside, and I used to worry about how he'd be treated when he grew up. Well, he died in a car accident. I'd give just about anything to have him back, to take care of him myself, and I can't do for him, but I can for others." She began to tear and stopped. "So thanks," she left.

Jaz was at work by ten and never left before seven, often after eight. She usually ate lunch in and avoided dinner meetings of any kind. On Fridays, she left CE for Paradise Rock, returning from there on Monday mornings–her weekend inaccessibility was legendary. It was dark when Jaz walked to the elevator saying goodnight to the cleaning staff.

"Ahh," she gasped at the sight of the attendant. "Zeke! I didn't know you'd still be here." She tried to cover as she slowly inched into the small chamber.

"No reason for me to rush home."

Jaz stood behind him, his voice didn't come from his lips but from his neck region. She tried not to think about him, but there was nowhere else to look but the back of his head. She'd never noticed how small this elevator was; how dark and close, or how long the ride down was. There was a smell of decaying innards, an oldness, and liniment like Papa Colt kept in his barn for the horses. She watched his arm labor to work the controls, and noticed the cane over his stool. He was in complete uniform, purple with gold epaulets that didn't sit right. One shoulder up, one down, gloves covering his hands. You couldn't tell whether he was black or white except for his voice.

"Workin' kind of late."

"Yes, it's quieter." She clutched her bag as if he were a robber. "Umm-humm." He touched his hat, as crooked as his uniform. One side sat over a patch of pinkish-brown hairless skull intended to hide a malformed ear, probably the result of grafting. "Here you go." He stiff-legged shifted to the right, his breathing uneven and labored.

"Thank you." Jaz eased past him, as if by touching him, she'd be similarly inflicted. "Goodnight." She threw over her shoulder. He didn't respond.

The next morning she arrived preoccupied with the newspaper, she'd forgotten all about him until the elevator door slid open, forcing her to look directly at his face before she realized it.

"Thank you." He presented her with a single pink rose.

"Oh, you didn't have to–"

"I know I didn't 'have to,' but I wanted to. Thank you for saving my job," he stated simply before closing the door.

She stared at the rose in an attempt to obliterate the vision of his face. It was more horrid than anything one could imagine happening to a human being. The right side of it was of the same smooth pinkish-brown, looking as if it melted and was sliding from its position had it not been caught by the chin. Every feature on that side was deformed, his eye, a hole–his nose, non-existent. His lips fused together with just a small opening on the left through which he spoke. His left side of the same color was not as severely deformed; the left eye shrouded with extra skin and rheumy. There was no hair on his face, no eyebrows or lashes and only patches of hair sprouting from beneath his cap on the left. He began coughing, first just rumbles in his chest, then convulsively, until he took a tablet and drank some medicine. He seemed composed by the thirty-fifth floor.

"You have a good one." He had intended to tip his hat, but his arm didn't reach that high.

"Thank you ... thanks again for the rose."

Jaz stood there staring at the closed elevator door thinking that this was far more than she bargained for.

"Hey Punkin', change your mind?" Hep asked about the mutilated vet.

"No. Anyone who wants to work as bad as he does–should. Gave me this rose. Kinda ironic, a man so hideously disfigured still sees the beauty in a flower."

"Dad." Jaz barged into Hep's office waving a folder. "When are you going to let me have a project of my own, from the ground up?"

"When you're ready."

"I'm ready. I've done additions to a library, a school, a wing on a hospital and collaborated on two homes. I'm ready to step out on my own."

"Kyle and I–"

"Kyle?" she interrupted letting his name drip like venom from her lips.

"Yes, he's my architectural authority and I concur with his decision."

"It's Kyle's project to begin with–he did the original house. Why can't he do the addition?"

"Would you have me call him back from Singapore to build onto his award-winning beach house? It won't be long Punkin'," he placated recalling how he and Kyle noticed the kind of work Jaz elicited and inspired from the builders and contractors she supervised; they loved her. When warranted she was as free with her compliments as she was with her criticisms. "We're both very impressed so far," he soothed as his daughter rolled her eyes which landed on the Tretoni oil painting of them as children.

"Daddy, when are you going to replace that?"

"Are you kidding? My favorite picture. Gives me great inspiration."

"I'm ten years old in this one." Jaz perused the framed pictures on his desk. "A current one of me please Dad."

"When you give me one, like your sister did ...I'll proudly display it." He rounded his desk. "Now have you decided what you'll wear and who'll you'll take to the awards banquet?"

"I don't understand why I have to go."

"You're a part of this firm."

"Can't I accompany you and Mom?"

"It would be nicer if you had a date."

"Goodbye, Mr. Culhane." Jaz snatched the plans for the Santucci addition off the desk.

As Jaz left her father's office, she passed Kyle's on the way to her own, and decided to look in out of curiosity. Pushing the slightly ajar door open she ventured inside unseen. It was highly masculine with polished leathers smelling of rubbed oil. African masks watched her from the paneled walls as animal skins complimented the beige carpeting.

"The Great Bwana," Jaz scoffed leaving the office of the old white guy fixated with the dark continent. "Figures."

"Hey, Dory," she spoke, reentering her office.

"Oh, I was just leaving you a note."

"What is the big deal with this banquet?"

"CE purchases a table for ten each year, twice a year, at $1,000 a pop. The AIA, American Institute of Architects, in the fall and the ASA, American Society of Architects, in the spring." He stopped pondering. "Or is it AIA in the spring and ASA in the fall? Anyway we garner most of the awards for innovation."

"Why the big press for me to attend. It's not my bag."

"Besides a proud father wanting to show off his gorgeous daughter? He always freaks out when Kyle's away–leaves two vacant seats, not good."

"So now I'm Kyle's damned replacement. Are they joined at the hip or something?"

"Practically, Hep relies heavily on his expertise. He's well-respected in his field."

"Spare me." Jaz wasn't interested in more accolades for her father's idol. "Expects me to have an escort."

"He likes neat perfection and balance. His people aren't only brilliant, they're normal too, and have time for relationships. I enjoyed the banquets when Carol and I would go. We'd make a big event out of it ... limo, flowers–the works." His voice drifted off.

Over the past few weeks of their collaboration, they'd shared the stories of their mutual losses and how difficult and unaccepting the world was around them. Dory had lost his wife only two years ago, and the emptiness and pain remained acute. Hep had left him alone about the banquet the past two years, but expected him to attend this year.

"I suppose I could ask Tre', Marc or Derek." She thought of the handsome, gifted young trio who hung together, made big bucks and enjoyed themselves to the max. "But I'm iggin' them. Left me on the dance floor at Tramps."

"As I heard it, you were Le Freaking with Chic so fierce, for so long they couldn't get to you to tell you they were leaving," Dory chuckled. "Hear you can really 'get down.'"

"That disco stuff isn't my thing. They gave me this, gift wrapped." Jaz held up a mood ring. "So they'd know when I wasn't pissed off at 'em anymore." Jaz laughed at their sense of humor. "They have it made don't they?" she pondered, top graduates of their colleges, landing plum jobs. "The world on a string."

"Listen, why not go together?" Dory said. "He wants us there, we'll be there. Have a great time and go home."

"Sounds ideal to me. Then we won't end up with a date we'd spend weeks getting rid of."

"Aw Sweat!" Jaz glanced at her watch, gathered papers and stuffed them in her attache' and headed for the elevator. She was always surprised at the late hours Zeke worked.

"Working late?" He slid a little to the side.

"You too."

"Going to the disco? It's Friday night?"

"Nope. I can't abide by those disco's, and the music. I prefer my music of the Sixties to the stuff out there now."

"I know what you mean," he finally said, after his chuckle turned into a rumble then back again.

She had gotten used to Zeke, seeing beyond his grotesqueness, to his soul. He had an inner spirit which allowed him to live past his disfigurement. He still had medical problems that forced him to remain home on damp days, and caused him to compensate with the stifling heater in the elevator. But it was short ride compared to the one he'd taken from WWII to here.

"You all had some good music, too," Jaz said.

"Yeah, 'If You Gonna Walk All Over My Love Baby, At Least Take Off Your Shoes.'"

"I was thinking more of 'I'll Be Seeing You,' and 'Unforgettable.'"

"What a youngin' like you know about those old songs?"

"My husband and I loved those old songs, old movies ... we used to have our own concerts out on the beach just singing them to each other." Jaz's eyes glazed over remembering.

"Husband? I didn't know you had no husband."

"We're ... separated." Jaz stiffened.

"Man's a dang fool wherever he is. Here you go young lady." The elevator door eased open. "You have a nice weekend Miss Jaz."

"Thanks, you too." Jaz threw over her shoulder as she walked toward the door and her Jag beyond, thinking that his voice sounded like a weary, old jazzman.

Jaz didn't like going to Paradise Rock if she couldn't stay the entire weekend and since she had the opera tomorrow night, she stayed in town. She rarely accepted a client's invitation but she hadn't seen *Donizetti's Lucia Di Lammermoor* since she left Italy.

Saturday night, Jaz wore Tawny's grand opera cape under which a Tawny gown of bronze sequins hung to the curves of her body. Her hosts' seats were close to her parents' box but Jaz couldn't tell who sat in the Culhane's seat. During the intermission Jaz strolled into the outer lobby with her flute of champagne, and spotted Amber's Prince Charming holding court with fans of Mrs. Charming, the news celebrity. Jaz watched until the lights flickered and she returned to her seat. Jaz bowed out at the Conover's after-opera soiree and as she waited for her car she noticed PC joining the crowd as it marveled over that old Bugatti Royale. Jaz would have to tell Amber she saw her PC.

Jaz flipped through the Vanderpool specs that she hadn't had a chance to review yet, since she salvaged a Sunday at Paradise Rock.

"The Vanderpools said 10:30 tomorrow is fine," Addie informed her as she laid a portfolio on her desk.

"Thanks. How's Zeke?" Jaz not only missed her daily pink rose but knew that Addie called him when he was out.

"He says 'fair to middlin'' which translates into 'not so good.' He'll probably be out another day or so."

"He sure loves to work." Jaz thought about the elevator without him. His metal stool, folded up against the panel, his crate in which he held all his paraphernalia, turned toward the wall, the bud vase he uses to keep Jaz's rose fresh until she arrives, empty.

"Old guys like him measure themselves by their ability to hold a job. If they don't work, they feel useless. My Daddy was that way," Addie said.

"Mine sure is." Jaz chuckled. "We could use some of those old work values for today's guys. Does Zeke have family?"

"Not here, in St. Louie where he's from."

"Seems he could go back there and live alot easier."

"Zeke don't fly and Zeke don't want easy. He's an independent old coot, and I'm sure he couldn't find another job like this with all the perks and leave your Dad gives."

"True. Is your beau Bob ever jealous of you and Zeke?" Jaz teased.

"Naa. If Zeke's out a week or is hospitalized, guess who takes me to see him?"

"Sure, he's protecting his woman."

"I got no complaints."

* * *

On Dory's arm, Jaz strolled into the awards banquet, a vision of copper in Tawny's long, off the shoulder gown which resembled poured gold. Her hair was twisted in a topknot with tendrils spilling around her face. Jaz took her seat, along with the interest of every male and female in the large ballroom. Her presence added flair to an otherwise staid dinner, awards presentation and acceptance speeches. After the banquet, Jaz and Dory went to the local Whitetower for hamburgers and a milkshake before calling it a night.

Later at home, Jaz removed her make-up, washed her face, brushed her teeth, sat cross-legged on the bed as she braided her hair and flicked on the news.

"... First Phil, now you," the anchorman said.

"And now marriage is breaking up that old gang of mine," Mrs. Charming said.

"You ought to try it sometime Bev," the weatherman added.

"Maybe I will." She swiveled her chair towards the camera. "Well this is Beverly Nash ... Goodnight." Her smile froze on the screen.

"Well, won't Amber be pleased. PC isn't married after all." She switched channels to Susan Hayward in "I Want To Live."

Jaz pulled off the road onto a concrete slab designed for parking and cut the ignition. The award-winning beach house stood several feet away like an island in the sand, hoisted upon stilts, underneath its belly was the outline of a sports car. She closed the car door, and stood studying the exterior facade. Other than the door, there were three staggered rectangular windows ascending the first flight of steps, a circular window probably at the landing, then a set of two other slim rectangular windows. There were no other windows. "A damned fortress."

Jaz cursed as her lizard-skinned heels sank in the sand. Removing them, she walked to the door, then replaced them before she rang the bell. The door swung open, and Jaz's heart leapt into her throat, stealing her breath. Nowhere in the old specs or the new, in the portfolio or in any info on Nick Santucci did it mention that he was drop-dead gorgeous.

"Mr. Santucci?" Jaz didn't know where she gathered the wits to ask. She was obviously operating on professional reflexes. What she wanted to say was, "Good God almighty ... Hello handsome ... goodbye heart."

"Miss Chandler?"

"Mrs," she corrected.

"Please come in." He stepped back allowing her what little space there was to maneuver the turn that led upstairs.

Jaz walked up the dozen steep steps fighting for her composure. In her adult wisdom she wasn't naive enough to think it was love-at-first-sight, there was no such a thing. But lust at first sight? She's got it. She couldn't remember ever being so turned on by the sheer physical presence of a man.

She reached the first floor and to her amazement it was a spectacular design, which stole her attention from Mr. Santucci. While the outer facade appeared a fortress, the back was entirely glass, revealing an uncomparable view of the ocean and the beginning of a beautiful sunset. The flight of steps continued on up to the top floor, but the open pathway where she now stood divided the sunken living room with its grand fireplace reaching to the cathedral ceiling, and a platformed dining room on the left. There were no walls and the room was as open as Mr. Santucci's waiting smile.

"May I?" Jaz resisted his easy charm as she crossed a glass bridge into the kitchen. He was uncommonly good-looking, a tan more natural then worked upon, with deep blue eyes the color of the Mediterranean, an aquiline nose, brown hair cut just enough to calm the curl and inspire the wave, sensuous inviting lips, and a cleft in his chin you could get lost in.

"Kyle does good work." He flashed a smile, just the right amount of charm and sincerity.

"As I understand it you want a study?" She almost expected him to have an accent, he looked so authentically Roman.

"And a powder room and laundry room. We bachelors need to wash clothes too." He leaned casually against the doorjamb, with his arms folded, and that same inviting smile dancing on those gorgeous lips.

"May I see the upstairs?" She hated to ask.

"My pleasure." His arms extended in an "after you" fashion.

They walked back to the circled window and climbed the other flight of steps. Jaz was surprised to see it was one big loft-like bedroom, the bed immediately in front of her. So she meandered to the right where a built-in dresser was crowned by giant louvered shutters. Mr. Santucci flung them open flooding the room with light, and a perfect view of the dining room directly below.

"Kyle's big on ventilation and light," he explained.

"Mr. Jagger regrets he cannot follow up on your addition himself, but he is in the Orient. I'm here to discuss your requirements." Jaz had the nerve to look directly into his eyes for the first time. Lawd have mercy, she prayed. "So Mr. Santucci–"

"Nick," he corrected.

"Do you want your office up here or downstairs?"

"Downstairs, definitely."

Jaz followed him down the steps, and watched his back field in motion. Not bad for a non-brother, she critiqued as he excused himself.

Jaz tried to determine his accent as she jotted down notes. There was a staccato abruptness and regional enunciation to it like vintage New York, first or second generation Italian. "He's too cool to be whitebread," Jaz chuckled at the way she and Gladys Ann used to talk about Paul Newman. Nick didn't walk, talk, dress or look like a California white boy.

"Oh!" Jaz was startled by the appearance of a friendly, fluffy shaggy dog. "Hey!" Jaz petted the soft hairy animal.

"That's my roomie, Beau." He pushed up the sleeves of his sweater. "You have pets Mrs. Chandler?"

"No." Jaz rose and returned to her professionalism.

"He doesn't usually take to strangers." Nick flirted unabashedly.

"Right." Jaz cooled that shit fast, and he chuckled as he escorted her to the door. "Well, Mr. Santucci–"

"Nick." A smile splitting his handsome face.

"I'll draw up some plans for your approval and get back to you."

"Any ideas off the top of your head?"

"Well, you have only a few options so as not to destroy the integrity of the existing house. A simple plan would be to add your study to the other side of the fireplace, open it up so both rooms could enjoy it and extend your terrace. Another option would be to place the study right next to the living room, but you'd give up some of your light and compromise the catwalk–"

"Tell me the one you like," he said.

"A silo addition– a semi-circular attachment built onto your kitchen, giving you the office, a den/guest room and laundry room."

"I like that. I'm interested in seeing what you come up with." Nick paused, asking with a glint in his eye. "Will you be working on this project until completion or until Kyle comes back?"

"Completion."

"Good, so you'll be in touch?"

"Yes. I'll call you for an appointment."

"No need, I'm always here or on the beach, just Beau and me."

Sure, a handsome stud like you couldn't pick up a loaf of bread at the corner store without causing a riot, and you expect me to believe that "boy and his dog" are here all alone. Yeah, right, Jaz thought.

"You know Kyle pulled some long hours," he said as he guided her down to the front door. "Night and day." He opened it and leaned against it with a boyish, devilish grin. "I don't want to cause any problems between you and Mr. Chandler." He was obviously fishing to see if she was really married, or if the rings were a protective ruse.

"You can't." Jaz watched a pleased smile stretch into a wide grin. "He's MIA in Vietnam." His face dropped.

"Oh, I'm sorry."

"So am I. If you don't mind I'll walk around to see the back of the house before I leave."

"Fine." He was still stunned when Jaz stuck out her hand.

"Thank you Mr. Santucci."

"Yeah, sure ... Mrs. Chandler. Thank you."

"Bye, Beau." Jaz removed her shoes, and walked in the warm sand, passing underneath the house by his all-black Porsche.

As she viewed the house from the ocean side she thought of Qwayz, not knowing whether she had said what she did out of habit or necessity. The wind whipped her hair and the hem of her dress, as she surveyed the magnificent beach house. Perhaps she should give the Great White Bwana more credit, it was a magnificent house. With her back to the beautiful fuchsia strewn sunset, she saw neither it, nor the man of the house with the aquamarine eyes, the brown hair and the clefted chin who looked down upon her.

"Hello Zeke, welcome back," Jaz sang brightly, as she entered the elevator.

"Sounds like someone had a good weekend," the old man pried as he handed her her daily pink rose.

"I missed these and you. How are you feelin'?"

"Fair to middlin'." He sighed, cranking up the controls.

Jaz spoke to everyone as she went to her office and her secretary followed. "Addie! Tell me what you know about Nick Santucci?"

"Oh, he called you today. Haven't you read any of his books? He's a best selling author who writes novels about love and romance, with strong women and lots of sex. Three have been made into movies, *Distant Rhapsody* was the best. Fine for a white boy. But I don't have to tell you that, you lucky dog."

Jaz spread out the designs for the Santucci addition on her drafting table. She had worked on them Sunday, thinking about him in the process, and wondering what he did. At lunch she sauntered into the bookstore to buy *To Catch The Wind.* As she stood in line to pay for the item, she tried not to look at his picture on the back cover with his penetrating eyes. She told herself this purchase was merely to get an understanding of her client.

Jaz swung by the Vanderpools to check the progress on their in-house gym, before going on to the Santucci beach house.

"Right on time." He opened the door as wide as his smile and Jaz sashayed up the steps in the quilted multicolored Chinese jacket that Claire Vanderpool had drooled over. "How was your Thanksgiving?" he asked casually as Jaz spread out the blueprints on the dining room table for his inspection.

"Fine–quiet." He didn't need to know that Mel and Hud flew up for the big dinner with her at her folks. Or that she spent the weekend reading *To Catch The Wind,* and was both surprised and moved to tears by his sensitivity. "How about yours?" She tried hard not to notice how his sweater hung over his body.

"Quiet–just me, Beau and Tom turkey. I talked to the family on the east coast though."

They poured over the plans and he asked questions about structure and integrity before deciding on the silo.

"I'll be in touch," Jaz said when they finished, and she turned to go out the door.

"Mrs. Chandler?"

"Yes." Jaz looked directly into his eyes, fighting the urge to look away as if the intensity of his gaze hurt hers.

"Do you ever wear your hair down?" Their eyes held each other's for a moment.

"Sometimes. Goodnight, Mr. Santucci."

"Nick." He corrected her with a smile.

Jaz undid the buttons to her Chinese jacket as she opened up the sunroof and the engine of her car. Suddenly she was hot. Though it had been nearly a year since Prince Omar, Jaz hadn't truly missed the sex at all. Her life was so full and exhausting, she hadn't the time or inclination to think about it and rarely did until she saw a couple so in love that they didn't see her. How wonderful, she'd think and dismiss it. Jaz hadn't wanted sex, didn't know where to find it, couldn't get it if she did and wouldn't know what to do with it after she finished it. It was clearly a non-priority then–Whammo! One day you open a door and there it is–SEX in a 5'10", healthy, living, breathing, gorgeous package reminding you of what you're missing. That was Nick Santucci whose presence pushed past her cool veneer, aloof facade and labyrinth of career and personal obligations to family and friends. Just by being, he screamed and dared her to deny her basic animal urges and desires.

"Well, Nick," she chuckled, "we'll have to give you extra time and get this project over ASAP. That's my only salvation."

"I don't believe I left them in my desk drawer," Jaz lamented as AJ turned the corner in front of CE, and stopped.

"I do. You spend your life there," AJ teased.

"Can I go too?" Amber piped up from the back seat, her Shirley Temple curls already unraveling.

"No, I'll be right back," Jaz said, opening the car door.

"You'd better," AJ agreed to the little girl's glee. "Or she'll start working and forget all about us."

"I'm going, too." Amber grabbed Jaz's hand and walked toward the elevator.

Their collective heels tapped on the marble flooring. The pretty brown women, dressed in red velvet–Jaz's off the shoulder with a sweetheart neckline, and Amber's adorned in bib of cream French lace with matching tights.

"Hello Zeke." Jaz climbed aboard the elevator. "You still here?"

"Ooow!" Amber screamed.

"Amber, what's the matter?" Jaz ran out to get the petrified little girl.

"It's a monster!" She cried tears of terror, cowering in the folds of Jaz's soft red gown. "He'll eat me!"

"Amber." Jaz was amazed and embarrassed. "This is Zeke. He's my friend and a very nice man." She coaxed her into the small chamber.

"He's going to kill us!"

"Amber!?"

"That's a mighty pretty name," Zeke commented closing the door.

"She's not acting very pretty. I'm sorry–"

"Aw, guess I'm kinda scary to children. You all are mighty pretty, dressed up and all." He spoke facing the closed doors.

"Yes, we're going to see *The Nutcracker* at The Opera House." Jaz wiped Amber's face of salty tears, as the little girl whimpered and stood on the bench clinging to Jaz. "I left the tickets in my drawer."

Amber wouldn't let go of Jaz's hand, but she snuck peeks at the man's back, when they descended to the ground floor. Once Zeke opened the door Amber bolted straight into the arms of AJ a few feet away.

"AJ, there's a monster in that elevator!" She pointed as he walked toward her and Jaz fanned them back.

"I'm really sorry Zeke." Jaz apologized, knowing it must have hurt him despite his brave front.

"Have a nice time at the ballet, Miss Jaz," he said, but when she turned to join the pair, he wiped a single tear from his one eye.

Amber had forgotten all about "the monster in the elevator," as her attention was captured by the music, costumes and dancing of the troupe. But Jaz couldn't stop feeling sorry for the lonely old operator. By intermission, however, in the cacophony of children, orangeade and excitement, even Jaz had pushed Zeke into the back of her mind.

"Aunt Jaz." Amber pulled on her gown interrupting her adult conversation. "I saw him! Prince Charming. He was right over there." Amber pointed. "He said we looked really pretty, like Princesses, and he was glad my Daddy was back," she giggled. "He thinks AJ is my Daddy." She loved when adults were wrong.

"What? What's this?" AJ asked.

"It's Amber's Prince Charming." Jaz acknowledged the flashing lights by taking Amber's hand. "She's Tracy's child, I'll explain later.."

"I'm her father?" AJ was confused and amused.

At the ballet's end, Prince Charming on the arm of his anchorwoman princess, watched the reunited family leave. He recalled seeing Amber away from her mother on the ferry, asking about her father when the little girl stated that they "were waiting for him to come back." What a nice Christmas gift – reuniting a family for the holidays. As he watched the profile of the lucky man escort his two ladies outside to the waiting Jaguar, he was happy and envious at the same time.

"Take care of them, my brother," he advised sotto voce.

"What?" The princess anchorwoman inquired.

Chapter Eight

"Jaz are you coming to Kyle's later?" Addie breezed in from the Christmas party.

"No." Jaz looked up. "I've got to finish this and I'm outta here. Besides I wasn't invited."

"No invite required. He has an open house once a year when he's here and does all the cooking. We thought we'd miss it this year with him traveling so much, but he's here and we'll all be there."

"That's nice." Jaz wasn't even listening.

"Everybody loved your bread pudding."

Jaz paused biting the eraser of the pencil remembering Qwayz and that bread pudding. "My mother-in-law's recipe. My husband loved–"

"And thanks for my belt, it is bad. Well, Merry Christmas. Don't work too late."

"Bye Addie." Jaz realized her secretary had a Yuletide buzz.

Finishing up the final review and approval on the Santucci addition, she felt a presence darken the doorway, but it was the liniment smell that caused her to look up.

"Hi Zeke. C'mon in," Jaz put down her pencil.

"You wanted to see me, Miss Jaz." He shuffled, negotiating the threshold with care. "I've never been in here before." He talked to pass the time it took for him to reach her desk.

"Lemme turn on the overhead light."

"I'd rather you not," he said quietly.

"Alright."

"Lotta little doodads." He eyed her picture frames, music box, rock and desk clock, breathing heavily and catching his breath.

"Want to sit down?" He shook his head no.

"Might–never–get–up." He managed with some difficulty.

Jaz never realized how overexerted he got with the simplest of tasks. "Merry Christmas, Zeke." She presented him with a large box, and cleared a space on the desk since he couldn't hold it with both hands.

"Oh Miss Jaz, that bread pudding was gift enough. Everybody likes it, even the young folks."

Zeke began scratching at the box, not denting the foil paper, so Jaz opened it for him, pulling from the tissue paper a raincoat.

"Oh-my. Isn't that nice."

"It's got a lining for those cool days." She had noticed he didn't have one.

He held onto a nearby chair for support. "I don't have a thing for you, Miss Jaz."

"Oh Zeke, I don't give to get. 'Sides you give to me everyday, not just the rose but your optimistic spirit."

"Aw, thank you, Miss Jaz."

For him, even talking seemed labor intensive, but he wanted to, so Jaz let him tell her of his plans to call his family in St. Louie. Of friends he had in his apartment building who were also alone. Jaz shared her plans, before he said he was returning to the party, but she suspected he was so exhausted he'd just go home.

* * *

Jaz made her Yuletide circuit in L.A., eating and visiting from home to home, often with Amber in tow. She could be found at one of three places; Tracy's and Scoey's, Denny's and Lloyd's or Mel's. She returned to San Francisco in time for her parents' New Year's

Eve bash, and then, with eagerness, back to work. Another year without Qwayz.

Jaz gathered her files together on the Vanderpool and Santucci additions, placing them in her briefcase.

"Fixin' to leave?" Addie swung in, fluttering her hand about like a bad impersonation of The Inkspots.

"Yeah, I'm going out for the final inspection of the Vanderpool's and the Santucci addition if the engineers followed my instructions."

"Why would you want that to end?" Addie held her hand out. "Your father wants to see you first."

"OK."

"Jaz!" Addie scolded, and stuck her third finger left hand right under Jaz's nose.

"Addie–you and Bob?"

"Yes! I want a May wedding. Everybody gets hitched in June."

"Congratulations! You two have renewed my faith in true love." They hugged, and Jaz left a giggling Addie for her father's office.

"Hey Dad." She stuck her face in, and he invited in the rest.

"Well, how about a late Christmas and Happy New Year gift? Your very own project from the ground up."

"No lie? It's not a bowling alley or a waste refuse plant, is it?"

"No. It's luxury homes on prime real estate. We think you're ready. Of course, Kyle will continue to oversee your projects."

"I'm sure he's real good at overseeing."

"What is it with you and him? He's really a very nice–"

"Spare me. Gimme the lowdown–the location and preliminary surveys."

"I knew you'd ask." He whipped out the waiting portfolio.

"Hot damn, near the bridge? I'm going out to do the finals on the Vanderpools and Santucci, but I'm checking this out on my way. You won't be sorry."

The project's terrain was roughly hewed from mountains overlooking the bay with Sausalito in the distance. Jaz envisioned houses spilling down the cliffs Amalfi coast style, but knowing the California codes would never permit such a design, and people wouldn't buy them in this earthquake prone area, she regrouped. Every home would be situated so it had spectacular views of the bay and she would incorporate as many European features as were feasible and cost effective. The Cliffs, she'd call it. Glancing at her watch she jetted to the Vanderpools where the gym and the lap pool passed inspection.

Jaz then led the way for the final walk-through at the Santucci addition, and Nick had already moved into his office.

"How do you like it?" Jaz asked.

"I love it, can't you tell? Like it was always here," he smiled. "Kyle couldn't have done better." He crossed his hands over his chest in a stance he'd come to own.

"Well, Nick Santucci, it's been a pleasure." She stuck out her hand for a final shake.

"Hey, we gotta celebrate. What I gotta do, build onto my house to get to see you again? C'mon we can celebrate up the road–a little place only us locals know about."

"Can I go like this?" Jaz asked of her jeans.

"Required dress, ponytail and all. Hold on a sec." He went to let Beau in, and get his wallet and keys.

"My Dad would love this car." Jaz thought of TC but decided not to mention him as they sped down the highway.

"It's a 1954 three fifty-six Speedster in premium shape. Your Dad into classic cars?"

"Is water wet? He has my grandfather's Doozy and a–"

"A Duesenberg? He's a serious collector." They turned off the road and went a mile or so to Pancho's Hideaway.

"Little Italian place I like," he said as he opened her door and took her arm escorting her as if she were dripping in diamonds and furs.

Jaz and Nick exchanged family histories over chicken cacciatore and fettucine Alfredo. They talked about their current work, his *Shadow In The Sky* and her Cliffs project until they closed the restaurant and drove back to his house.

"I really enjoyed myself." Jaz stood with her car door opened between them. He was leaning dangerously close. She warded off the urge to taste his lips drenched in the same wine as hers.

"I'm glad," he answered simply, only the tension of desire radiated between them.

"Well, bye," Jaz said, weakly, not wanting to go, but afraid to stay.

"Wait!" He almost shouted like a little boy with a line in the Christmas pageant. "Forgive me, I'm sorry, but I just can't let you leave like this." Jaz stood only inches away, she could feel his breathe on her face as he spoke. "I know you'll think me terrible, self-centered and I'm not really, but I'd like to kiss you if I may. I've wanted to since the day I first saw you. I know about your husband and I'm truly sorry, I really am," he added quickly, his eyes unable to look directly into hers until now. "But if you leave tonight I'll never see you again, no matter how many additions I put on this house. I'll call, and you won't return them. It's now or never–and I want it to be now. I couldn't take never."

Jaz was surprised by his openness, his lack of game-playing. He was like the character he created in *To Catch The Wind.* "Don't think I'm a sleaze. If your husband comes back, I'm outta the picture in a flash, I respect and accept that even if–"

"Shut-up and kiss me," Jaz directed, fortified with Chianti and desire. Nick grabbed her hand and pulled her into the house.

Once the door was closed, Nick took her in his arms and brushed his lips gently across hers, as if he were savoring the taste of a fine vintage before devouring the red liquid. His hands caressed her back and she sank into him feeling the urgency of his maleness even though his lips spelled patience. The faint smell of the garlic and wine they'd just consumed, mingled with a hint of cologne from earlier that day. His taste was urbane; sweet and salt, tinged with burgeoning sweat that their body heat produced. He suckled her lips first gently, then more deliberate tracking more territory than the wave before, and his hands, now beneath her blouse, were pure heat upon her naked back. Her eyes opened at the rhythm established by the kissing, and caught glimpses of his dark hair, curling in the heat, his fabulous eyes hooded by long lashes. The sound of the distant ocean gave way to throaty moans, his or hers–soon she didn't care. Swept up in the tide of passion, she'd seen him towering over her, removing his shirt, baring his muscled chest. Her hands ran up his moist flesh, as she encircled his neck pulling him down upon her. Sure, she'd be taken on the steps, so she was surprised when he swept her up to the landing under the circle window, beneath the skylit cathedral ceilings. As if his reserve gave out and he could resist no longer, he entered her deeply, fluidly, insatiably as her pulsating orifice accepted him willingly, continually, hungrily, with such fierceness she shocked herself.

They lay in their exhausted nakedness, the moon peeking in on the contours of two exquisite bodies. Nick carried her the few feet more into the living room, where they stretched out in front of an unlit fireplace, covered by a throw he retrieved from the couch.

"I guess you could tell this wasn't planned," he said, offering that same infectious smile.

"I would have worn better underwear," Jaz said, trying to sound worldly.

"Where is it?" He smiled looking about.

"We left it on the steps." In their mutual awkwardness they began to chuckle. "I'm new at this," Jaz admitted, thinking he was only the second man in nearly thirty years of life, she'd ever slept with besides Qwayz.

"We'll get better with time." He brushed her nose with his, and she thought him the most handsome of men.

"I gotta go." Jaz tried to raise herself against him.

"Oh, I was just going to offer you some wine–something to eat."

"I think we've covered that." She reared up on her elbows in time to catch Nick blush momentarily. She wanted to go. She wanted to stay and maybe do it once more, enough to last her awhile, or in case she'd never have him again.

"Do you really want to go?" He rubbed her arm gently and felt himself rise against her thigh. "Maybe we could make it up the stairs to the bedroom this time." He smiled, his hand crossing her shoulderblade and inching down to her erect breasts.

They had made it to the bed this time, barely, and afterwards, fell into a deep sleep. Jaz awoke at the first hint of distant light. She lay in the crevice of his arm. The beginnings of a hairy shadow played about his sensuous lips, cleft, and Roman jawline. He was almost too gorgeous to be real. Without removing her gaze from him, she tried to untangle his legs from hers. In the process, his eyes flew open.

"Good morning! Gosh you're an early riser." He reached for his dead arm and shook some life back into it.

"I gotta go." This time Jaz rose, gathering the sheet about her like a robe, and descended the stairs to her clothes.

"Hey, what about breakfast?" Nick had wrapped himself in the spread, not fully understanding this false modesty.

"I'm sorry. I thought I could–but I can't." She had jumped into her panties and jeans, pulled on her blouse and reached for the front door.

Heading toward Paradise Rock as if it were her one salvation, Jaz recognized in affairs of the heart she was still lost without Qwayz. Not that this or any other liaison could approximate what she had with her husband, but she was unnerved by it. Prince Omar had been pure fantasy, but Nick was reality, here on domestic soil and more importantly it was the first time she'd run into someone whose style of loving approached her one true love. It scared her soul. But she could loan Nick her body, never getting in so deep she couldn't pull out at a moments notice; that was her protection. The stage was set and Nick understood, so what's the harm?

"Damn!" she shouted hitting the steering wheel. If Qwayz were here, there wouldn't have been a Prince Omar or a Nick Santucci–she would have never needed them.

Sitting for awhile, she absorbed the sounds and rhythms of her surroundings; the crash of the sea below, the smell of the salt air and she purged herself of all thoughts because when she entered Paradise Rock, she entered alone–with no thoughts other than her beloved husband. For in Paradise Rock, Qwayz reigned supreme. This was his house and she respected him and it.

As if repenting impure thoughts and deeds, Jaz cut off the alarm, slid back the door and stepped into the cathedral ceilings of natural light and presence.

"Qwayz ... I'm home!"

* * *

"I hate when she goes to that beach house," Hep said redoing his tie. "It's a goddamned mausoleum to a dead man." He finally turned to let his wife work her magic.

"It's a place for her to relax and get away," Lorette said.

"It's a place for her to remember. It's not natural. She should have been over this years ago." He yanked his jacket from the stationary valet. "Then she drags that music box and rock with her everywhere. Puts them out on her desk every Monday morning. It's been nearly ten years–the girl's almost thirty. AJ's marrying Avia, for christsakes. Jaz ought to get on with her life."

"Maybe this is her life Hep and we have to accept it. She's happy–"

"She is not happy."

"You're not happy that she's missing this dinner meeting. She gives you twelve hour days in the office, she doesn't owe you her weekends too."

"Is it wrong to want what we have for our daughters?"

"No. And Jaz had it with Qwayz. I wouldn't want the impossible task of finding your replacement."

"You couldn't!" Hep boomed and Lorette smiled.

"Hi, how are you?" Jaz could hear Nick smile.

"Hey! I was just thinking about you." He'd thought of nothing else for the pass five days. "I was going to call and invite you to Beau's birthday party." He'd picked up the phone 1,000 times but decided that this relationship had to be her call or not at all. "Made a big pot of marinara, even got a cake."

"Sounds good." She fanned Addie in. "What time?"

"Seven-ish."

"Can I bring anything?" Jaz watched Addie's approving smile. "Great! See you then." She hung up. "Wipe that grin off your face."

"I don't know who, where or when, but I'm happy for you." Addie set the papers on the desk.

"Nothing from Kyle yet?" Jaz rifled through the papers looking for his approval of her specs for The Cliffs. He was tap dancing on her last nerve. She'd assembled her team, Marc and Derek as collaborating architects, Dory for landscaping, Tre' for finance, and they were ready to proceed to the next step.

"He hasn't returned my call? No overseas communique? Damn! He's holding up production."

"Nothing yet."

Jaz waited until afternoon and still no return call or word from the Great Bwana. Her guys had inquired about the final approval, and Addie had asked if Jaz wanted her to wait around after five.

"No, you and your fiancé have a wedding to finish planning."

"About that–I was wondering if you'd do a big favor for me. In lieu of a gift even. Bring Zeke for me." Addie read her reluctance. "I want him there and you are the only one I would dare ask besides Kyle, but he'll still be in Hong Kong. It'll be our last goodbye since I'll be leaving for our honeymoon and then we'll be in Atlanta for good."

"Don't remind me." Jaz stroked the bridge of her nose, thinking of the headache it will be to replace her and break in a new secretary.

"One of those days, huh?"

"One of those months." Jaz picked through the papers on her desk.

"Well, will you be Zeke's date so to speak?"

"Yeah, yeah."

"If you have to leave early with him or something, I'll understand."

"Great."

"I wouldn't go in there if I were you," Addie warned Marc on her way out.

"Hey boss, wanna go boogie at the disco tonight?" He did a twisty movement.

"Have a nice weekend, Marc." Jaz waved him off playfully. She recalled how hard her team had worked, giving up a Saturday afternoon for The Cliffs when Jaz enticed them with a home cooked lunch and a celebratory dinner at Guiseppe's. The session produced the flawless plans on which Kyle now sat in Hong Kong. Jaz snatched up the phone.

"Kyle Jagger of Culhane Enterprises, please," Jaz sounded as official as possible.

"Sorree," the heavily accented woman apologized. "He in meeting now, no disturb."

"I'm calling for his boss, Hepburn Culhane." Her information and tone caused the secretary to think better of Mr. Jagger's instructions.

"Hold on please." Jaz wasn't lying, Hep too wanted to get on building the luxury homes.

"Yeah boss?" A male voice spoke after two expensive minutes.

"This is Jasmine Chandler and we're waiting for the final approval and specs on The Cliffs." There was a long pause. "Hello?"

"Mrs. Chandler." He began tightly in a lethally low tone. "The information you request is on its way. I can neither do anything to expedite that process nor communicate the changes to you over the phone. Therefore, you will have to exercise some professional patience." There was a brief pause before he continued. "Never. I repeat, never call me out of a conference again." The slam of the phone caused Jaz to jump, the sound of the dial tone infuriated her.

"Bastard!" She retaliated in kind. "Arrogant shriveled up old honky."

Across the continent Kyle had thoughts of his own on the boss's spoiled daughter. While he personified "grace under pressure," and maintained the outer presence of cool, calm, control, underneath, he seethed at her audacity. She'd irked him to distraction with her demands, as if expert work could be rushed. She was a young, pampered, indulged brat whose father probably bought her the degrees here and abroad. He admired and respected Hep's business acumen and vision, but the man had a blind spot when it came to his daughters, both of them ... the star and this one, for whom he actually saved an office for three years until she was ready to go to work. He'd heard she was drop-dead gorgeous and, knowing her type, was sure she'd be onto something else soon when architecture bored her. She was special to her Daddy, but was nothing to him ... except a nuisance. If he never met the woman it would be too soon.

"Now gentlemen." Kyle reentered the room, unbuttoning his jacket. "Where were we?" An easy smile claimed his face as he spoke to his Hong Kong investors.

* * *

"How was Miss Checolé's wedding to that handsome son-of-a-gun?" Zeke asked Jaz as she returned from the weekend.

"It was gorgeous," Jaz said. She had stood in as Avia's "family" as well as AJ's aunt. "I feel a certain amount of responsibility for that one. Hope St. Theresa's has a Christening soon."

"Not too soon," Zeke said, his chuckle leading to a phlegmy cough.

"You okay?" Jaz asked once he caught his breath.

"Fine, Miss Jaz. Have a nice day." Zeke closed the elevator doors between them, and Jaz proceeded to her office.

As Jaz entered her office, Addie danced in and closed the door.

"Here ya go!" Addie slapped the overseas mailer from Kyle on Jaz's desk.

"It's 'bout time."

She undid the tie, thinking of the compromises she'd made to Kyle–adding the skylight in the master bedroom and making the industrial kitchen appliances optional instead of standard. She'd bumped heads with him, and won, over the adjoining European courtyards, the tri-level master bedroom, fireplace and picture window; the first floor atrium, and the number of houses to be constructed.

"Yes!" She yelled when she saw his chicken scratch, "*OK. Good job, may buy one myself. KJ,*" written before her overseas call. "So was I, but rather than have you as a neighbor ... hey, it's yours."

She hoisted the mark-ups on the board. It was pure genius. A big outer courtyard with flower beds and trees secured by wrought iron gates and three huge configurations, each with two detached houses sharing an open marble vestibule with a fountain. There were six houses per outer courtyard construction and Jaz had put in four making a twenty-four house project. And it was ready to go!

"The Cliffs!" Nick had toasted at Pancho's Hideaway. "*Shadow In The Sky!*" Jaz countered, and their glasses clinked in unison. "We done Little Italy and Watts proud."

"Yeah, we're pretty damned lucky," Nick said later, groaning and stretching in satisfaction after an arduous lovemaking session.

"Shower?" Jaz asked, kissing him on the nose and climbing off him.

"Let's just lie and bask for awhile." He caught her and rolled her onto her back. "Maybe the goodtime fairy will call again."

"Somehow fairy and Santucci just don't belong in the same sentence. Besides I have a wedding to go to."

Their time together went too fast for Nick. They'd settled into a comfortable existence even though he never had enough time with Jaz. He understood her reluctance with going public, but he was tired of getting reports, not invitations to important events in her life. The anniversary party for Denny and Lloyd, the twins, Brittany and Bethany's first birthday party, the AIA banquets, her sister Mel's engagement soiree. He knew he'd never win over AJ, but he could melt Amber's little heart. So Nick showed her the way, gave her a key to his house, had her speak to his mother in New York, they had even dined with his sister when she visited. He had told Jaz how he felt about her, but she ignored him. Patience. Slowly, she would have to come around.

"Mama wants me to bring you out for Christmas," he said when she returned dressed in an exquisite peach suit. "You look great. Comin' back after the wedding?"

"Probably not. I've got that business brunch on Sunday, and work to make up 'cause I'm here today. You understand." She kissed him goodbye. "I'll call."

"What about Christmas at Mama's?" He yelled after her.

"Sure–Bye." Jaz walked out to the car and started it up. Christmas, dag, she thought, anything can happen between now and then.

Jaz sat beside Zeke in the church, and teared as Addie, having spoken her vows, stopped at Zeke and touched his hand. At the reception, while Jaz was worried about the stares Zeke would get, she found that the acorn doesn't fall far from the tree. Addie's family filed by Zeke as if he were the guest of honor, and it warmed her heart. She recalled picking him up earlier. Entering his stark, brightly lit, squeaky clean one-room apartment, with no rugs so the wheelchair and oxygen tank could move freely. The radiators puffed steam into the stale, hot room, and mixed with the hospital smell of antiseptics, alcohol and liniments–making Jaz just as nauseous and lightheaded as riding in the elevator. As he strapped on his leg from behind a curtain, she studied the clean kitchenette, with its one plate, one fork, one spoon and cup neatly draining near the sink next to a row of pill bottles.

When the wedding was over, it seemed a shame to return Zeke to that mean little room, so he popped a few more pills and consented to take a ride with her to her beach house. He wasn't much company as he slept going, and coming, though she looked up after getting her papers from Paradise Rock and saw him standing there. "Not much to it," he'd said, before Jaz helped him back into the car.

Jaz returned to her apartment, eyed Qwayz's red baseball cap and stroked his bomber jacket hanging on the halltree. She braided her hair, climbed into bed, and touched Qwayz's face on the Malibu picture by the lamp before cutting it off. She was exhausted, yet her mind was full of thoughts of him. The wedding ceremony of Addie and Bob and their new beginnings, only screamed at Jaz's lack thereof. Jaz balled up a pillow, and fell asleep.

Most of Jaz's time was spent in an on-site trailer at The Cliffs, where things were progressing with such ease it was scary. She chastised herself for resenting the break when she flew to L.A. for fittings for the matron of honor dress she was to wear in Mel's wedding to Lee Harker Fontaine; the only black executive for NBC, the executive producer of her show, and time enough for her. Using the company jet enabled Jaz to slip in and out of L.A. undetected by Amber, although Jaz felt guilty. Things with Nick were status quo–good loving and companionship.

"Did you hear me?" Nick asked as they caught their breath from the recent love tryst. "I love you and want to marry you."

"C'mon Nick, don't get intense."

"Intense? Loving someone is about as intense as you can get. What is it Jaz, you let me make love to you but won't let me touch you?"

"What do you know about Ronnie Dyson?" Jaz tried to tease him.

"I grew up with the Tops, Temps and Raw Cilk. Ah, you're sensitive about what we don't have in common, instead of what we do."

Oh cheeze, Jaz thought, there is no winning with him today. Maybe she'd leave and come back when he's in a better mood.

"If that's all–I assure you my family doesn't care."

"I care. Or doesn't that count?"

"No one's saying for you to forget your people."

"Hold up. I suggest you don't say anything more about 'my people'."

"Santucci's didn't come here until 1908, so you can't lay any of that slavery stuff on—" He watched the frozen amazement on her face. "It's about us, Jaz; I love you, you love me." She shook her head no. "You do love me."

"No, I care for you. I enjoy your company–"

"Jaz, I'm on your side. I know how hard it is being black in America–"

"You don't *know*. You can read, empathize and sympathize but you don't *know*." Jaz moved across the bed. "That's an arrogant statement, and therein lies the difference between your race and mine."

"I don't want to get into a whole discussion on race relations–"

"We do that every time we open our mouths. Look, I am going to marry someone like me. Who shares the same past and heritage–"

"You're a bigot."

"Why is it that when an Italian, Jew or Vanderpool wants to marry their own–they're applauded. Let a black person show a little racial pride–"

"Why can't two people in love of different races marry and–

"Many do, but not this lady. I have a wonderful responsibility to the ancestors before me, and my children to come."

"They'll be both."

"No, my children will be black–no cultural treason here." Nick was very quiet. "Listen, I want a man like my daddy, my granddaddy, my brother. Of all the things you can give me, Nick. You can't give me that." She stood by the dresser. "So this is as good as it gets, and as far as it goes for us. You knew the deal when we started. I have a husband."

"Here we go with the sainted husband routine," Nick wailed out of hurt and rejection. "You know he's not coming back Jaz. He's not MIA–he's dead." He heard the irrevocable rip of their relationship.

"You bastard." Jaz cut her eyes, pulled out her suitcase and filled it with her belongings.

"Jaz–" He was immediately sorry as he watched her pack her things to take the trip out of his life. He wondered how a simple marriage proposal had turned into the end of a spectacular love affair.

Chapter Nine

The rest of the year sped by catching Jaz in a whirlwind of activity. Mostly trips to L.A. for Mel's gorgeous wedding to Lee Harker, attending Denny's surprise birthday party for her husband, Lloyd, and trips to see Amber. In San Francisco, The Cliffs was completed and fully occupied, and Hep promised her a multimillion dollar project in New Orleans. Jaz helped Avia adjust to becoming an interpreter and executive assistant at Culhane Enterprises as AJ completed his third year of med school in June. Life was chuggin' along.

The American Institute of Architects Award Banquet was extra special this year. Not because of the absence of Kyle for yet another year. Not because she was escorted by the handsome "Doc AJ," as Amber called him. Not because she wore the brand new Russian lynx that she had treated herself to, but because Jasmine Bianca Culhane Chandler received the design award for The Cliffs. Hep was ecstatic and had to be quieted so Jaz could make her acceptance speech.

When Jaz went home she placed the award on her mantel beside TC's Grammy, and underneath Papa Colt's pearl handled guns and

Stetson hat. Finally something she'd achieved and can display. Her professional career progressed at warp speed, even if romantically she was still stalled in 1968.

The presenter's words still rang in her ears about the "innovative design." Maybe Kyle should have flown in from Japan just to see her get her due. She'd bought a house in The Cliffs since Kyle had not. It'd be fun decorating and having a larger place in which to entertain. Amber and Hud would relish having their own room when they visited, and the ten thousand dollar appreciation since breaking ground was a bonus.

* * *

Jaz arrived early for the lunch meeting with her father and the Great Bwana. Her luck had finally run out, and she had to 'share' the New Orleans project with him. She perched on the corner of the sofa in the elegant lobby of The Fairmont, impeccably dressed feeling like a natural child about to meet an adopted, "preferred" one. Glancing out the window, she observed a small crowd admiring that Bugatti Royale she and Amber had seen when they'd been at the pier. Haven't seen Amber's prince since then. No sooner did the thought enter Jaz's mind than she spotted him gliding pass the doorman. Her reflex propelled her to the lobby door where she coyly dropped a glove which was retrieved by a man, as the prince was stopped by a hotel attendant.

"Thanks," Jaz snapped, jerking her glove from the clutches of the man. I was never any good at this game-playing crap, Jaz sighed.

"Hello!" Jaz jumped at the greeting. "Didn't mean to startle you." A slow easy grin spread across the prince's face. "But I thought it was you."

"Hello." Jaz couldn't suppress her grin, noticing for the first time deep parenthetical dimples framing his smile.

"How's Amber?"

"Fine."

"Tell her hello. So, are you here for lunch?"

"Yes, business meeting actually. And you?"

"Same. We must be a couple of workaholics to be here on a Saturday."

"What business are you in?" They asked each other simultaneously, and laughed, just as Hep approached, his booming voice proceeding his body.

"I love punctuality in my people." As Hep came between them, he called to a man coming in, "Charlie Barnes!" and went off to greet an old friend, leaving the gap mouthed couple there.

"You're Kyle Jagger?"

"You're Jaz Chandler?"

"But I thought you were an old white man–"

"What?" Kyle joined her in laughter as Hep rejoined them.

"Ready?" Hep walked between them, ushering them towards the elevator. "I knew Charlie Barnes at Fisk, haven't seen him in years."

As Hep went on about Charlie Barnes, Jaz and Kyle were absorbed in thoughts about each other. Seeing him now explained his house in Africa, his office motif, his voice not matching that of an old codger, as well as why the female student interns always wanted Mr. Jagger and why the secretaries were so protective and enamored of him.

Kyle stood on the other side of Hep racking his brain for the discarded details Hep had given about his two daughters. Topaz eyes was Hep's daughter and Amber's mother. She wasn't the one who just got married, that was the star – or was it? Topaz had wedding rings, she was married to Amber's father. Someone had a husband who died in Vietnam, was that Hud's or Amber's father? No, they never had children ....

The three discussed the plans for the New Orleans project, which was to convert the old railway station into a pricey luxury hotel and shops. As Hep reviewed the project, he noticed the preoccupation between the two.

"Is there something going on here?" He asked abruptly as a teacher would accost two mischievous pupils.

"No Daddy."

"It's just so ironic that we've seen each other around all this time and never–"

"Well, of course you've seen each other around. You've worked together for almost two years."

"This is our first meeting," Kyle said.

"I've never seen him in the office before Dad, only around San Francisco."

"But your offices are right next to each other. The Cliffs–"

"All memo and specs sent from the Orient. And a very nasty phone call."

"Believe me I didn't know," Kyle apologized with a smile. "May I drop you somewhere?" Kyle asked Jaz, while Hep paid the bill.

"No I have my car."

"An aquamarine Jag."

"Right, how do you know that?"

"Ahh, didn't your father tell you I was the best."

"Best male."

"So I'll guess we'll be seeing more of each other."

"Speck so. Enjoy the rest of your weekend."

Jaz surprised her parents by accepting their dinner invitation on Sunday.

"It was great Millie," Jaz said as she removed the dishes. "I thought Kyle might be here today." She tried to sound casual.

"Kyle doesn't hang out with us old folks anymore than you do. On a day like today you'll find him on his boat," Hep said. "Did you know that they didn't know each other before yesterday?"

"Yes dear, you told me," Lorette drawled.

"I guess I had him traveling more than I realized."

"Told you so. Kyle is a sweetie." Lorette sipped her coffee.

"Why did I think Kyle was an old white man who managed your assets before you went to Italy?"

"You're on your own with that one," Hep said.

"You know who she means, Hep?" Lorette said, "Tippy ... Kylerton. He ran things while we were in Italy. He is old and white and retired when we came back."

"Oh no. I met Kyle Jagger at an antique car show in Scottsdale, Arizona. Then I saw him in Cannes, baited and lured him away from New York with big bucks and complete autonomy. Comes from a good family with solid values, morals and pride. Jeremiah Jagger, a Texan, moved his family to Chicago in the 1900's and started 'The Negro Voice' which became 'The Negro Gazette' in the twenties. His son, Buck, Kyle's father, parlayed it into the highly successful, nationally distributed 'Chicago Journal;' the only black owned paper of its status in the United States."

"His mother, Dallas, is the most genuine woman; you'd never suspect she grew up filthy rich," Lorette said.

"Her daddy was a Texas wild catter who struck it rich before the federal regulations," said Hep.

"And they have the nicest children–"

"Six of them, two boys and four girls," Hep interrupted again as Jaz's head volleyed back and forth between the two old married people who slipped in and out of each other's conversations.

"You know them?" Jaz asked.

"Sure, they have a big Texas BBQ every summer at their Winnetka estate outside Chicago."

"All their children are as accomplished as mine," Lorette beamed.

"A great big old house with its own lake where all the kids grew up–full of pictures, trophies and awards . . . real homey and strong."

"Sounds like a house I know about in Colt, Texas," Jaz smiled. "The kind Grandma Canary created."

"The woman sets the tone of a home. Remember that," Hep instructed.

"Sounds like a Hep-ism to me," Jaz told her mother and they giggled.

"Oh Lawd, am I old enough to create 'isms?'" Hep joined in the fun.

Over the next several weeks, staff began noticing the path worn between the offices of Kyle and Jaz. They worked long hours on the New Orleans project, often lunching in, hunched over a drafting table. Hep had been right, Kyle was brilliant, innovative and knowledgeable about everything from budget considerations to stresses of materials. Despite his proven genius, he was always open to Marc's and Derek's suggestions, accepting the plausible ones, discarding the others after he explained why.

Only Zeke was treated to the after-work conversation, and the nosy man strained his one "good" ear to hear the end-of-the-week invites.

"Do you like boating?" Kyle would ask on a Friday.

"Not especially. Have a good weekend!" Jaz would pop off toward the parking lot.

"Hang in there Kyle," Zeke said.

"I dunno man. I ask the lady if she wants to go out for a drink. She doesn't drink. Dinner? She's not hungry. I don't think she's interested in a personal relationship. We get along great in the office, but once I suggest something after five. Boom . . . the shield." Kyle caught himself wondering why he was telling the elevator man.

"She's scared."

"Scared? She doesn't strike me as a lady who's scared of a thing."

"Take it from me. I hear it all in here. You'd be surprised. You gotta slow walk her. It's that first husband, he still got a hold on her, but she ain't dealing with nobody. Wait till you get her to New Orleans. Nice and easy does it. Have a nice weekend." Zeke dismissed him.

"Yeah." Kyle looked at the sad old man. "You too."

The following Friday as they finished up, Kyle mentioned having a brainstorming session aboard his boat. Intentionally waiting until the last minute so Jaz couldn't make up an excuse, he thought he would make it more comfortable by having her guys out with them, while easing Jaz out of the office setting.

"Sorry, Mel's coming up for the weekend." Her eyes locked with his as she went off to answer her telephone. He didn't pull rank.

The relationship had jelled into a wonderful working one Monday through Friday, but when the sun went down, her defenses went up. Nice and easy does it, Kyle kept singing the jazzy song suggested by Zeke. It hadn't taken Kyle Rawlings Jagger long to decide that Jasmine Bianca Culhane Chandler was the woman for him. He hadn't been so sure about any female since his last year at Princeton. Every time he saw her, his heart went aflutter: A whiff of her perfume as they worked, the way her hair curled around her neck in coppery swirls, the turn of her head when she asked a question, those glasses perched on her nose or worn across her head like a headband. He saw in her qualities missing in his other friends. Jaz enjoyed her job, but she didn't have the blind ambition of Beverly Nash for instance. Jaz wanted more than a career at the top at the end of her days. She had an interest beyond working, which he'd seen with her care for Amber and Hud.

Kyle decided that Jaz was the prize of his life, the reason he hadn't married. He determined not only to ride the course out, but to manipulate it. To have her think it was her idea to fall for him. It wasn't going to be easy but nothing worth having ever was. He visualized them as a couple. It was the image he wanted and would get. Kyle Rawlings Jagger always got what he went after.

When Kyle combined an on-site inspection review with a Rawlings family reunion down in New Orleans, Jaz scheduled a session with her team at her apartment.

"Well, if we augment this here." Jaz drew a line on one side, as Marc held the blueprint in place. The doorbell rang. Jaz jumped up from the floor, her ponytail swinging in the breeze. "Ahh!" she gasped. Kyle was leaning against the doorjamb, wearing a short tan leather jacket, pair of brown slacks with a matching shirt and his patented smile. "You've cancelled your trip?"

"No, the wonderful world of private jetting gets you where you want to go and back in hours. Hope you don't mind." He knew she did.

"Not at all." She opened the door wide, and saw the Bugatti parked below. "That old car is yours?"

"Bugatti Royale," he said, hanging his jacket on the halltree next to Qwayz's, not noticing Jaz's expression. "Gentlemen, help has arrived." He slapped his hands eagerly, but Jaz's eyes were riveted to his jacket hanging next to Qwayz's. She removed it and put it in the closet with the others. She returned to the floor with Marc and the specs. Towards the end, Dory led Kyle through the buffet while Jaz accepted over-the-shoulder compliments.

"Dessert time!" Jaz jumped up once the last pencil mark was accurate.

"Reward time!" Derek said, slapping five with Marc.

"That's quite a machine you've got there," Kyle said as Jaz allowed the expresso to flow from its brass recesses.

"Thanks." Jaz ignored the fact that he was there. She hoped to conjure up the camaraderie they enjoyed in the office here, but it wouldn't translate. Everyone had spread out to enjoy the delectable homemade sweets, and when Jaz didn't see Kyle, she relaxed. Good, he's gone, she thought. Then he emerged from her bedroom, and it rattled her to the core. "Get a grip girlie, he only used the bathroom."

The younger guys were leaving to go to the 'Screw and Family Love' concert, and Jaz teased them for not asking her.

"You said you'd never go with us to a concert again," Marc reminded her.

"Except an 'Earth Wind And Fire'," Derek said.

"You got it. Well I hope they show," Jaz said.

"It's their hometown, they'd better show," said Marc.

"Good luck, have fun guys." Jaz waved them off, returning to face Kyle and Dory. "Well, you two got big plans?" she said brightly.

"May I have another cup of coffee?" Kyle asked relaxed, crossing his legs. "Do you have any cardamom?"

"Cardamon ... the spice?"

"Yeah. I kinda picked up the taste for it in Kuwait."

"Make that two, Jaz," Dory said.

"Two cardamom-laced coffees coming up."

"How's your coffee plantation in Kenya doing?" Jaz could hear Dory ask Kyle. Why not go visit it right now? Jaz thought.

The three chit-chatted until Kyle offered to help Jaz clean up, which she declined. He asked if she had any plans this evening. As he could have predicted, she begged off, being tired.

"Maybe some other time," Kyle smiled, reaching for his missing jacket.

"Enjoy your reunion tomorrow." Jaz whipped the jacket out of the closet.

"You alright?" Dory asked, as Kyle jogged down the steps, aware of the unnerving effect Kyle had on her.

"Sure. See you Monday."

Armed with all the recent information on the New Orleans project, Kyle scheduled a meeting at his house the next weekend, and Jaz could not refuse. She and Dory came together. Dory was a wonderful ally, noting how The Chief disturbed her but never saying anything about it directly.

Parking in the visitors lot for Secret Harbor guests, the two traversed one of many footbridges perched over a canal full of quacking ducks.

"This is quaint," Jaz said, of the section of town she didn't know existed.

"Built in the twenties by a millionaire who fell in love with Venice," Dory said as they approached the foliage-hidden homes. "There're only about fifteen houses along here ... all different."

"I know Kyle doesn't park that Bugatti out there."

"Oh no, he has a two-car garage under his house, one for it and one for his Ferrari."

"A Ferrari? Figures." As Jaz followed Dory up the winding stone steps, she noticed that the homes were situated on a peninsula with a canal on one side and the San Francisco Bay on the other.

"There's an access road back there for homeowners complete with guard and gate," Dory told her. "All the people have boat garages in the bay for their yachts."

Jaz followed the stone walkway past explosions of colorful flowers to a richly-hewed door with a Tiffany inset of beveled glass. Once inside, she was dwarfed by the cavernous A-frame structure with exposed beams and a mammoth stone fireplace stretching from the ceiling to the floor. Arranged around it were leather sofas, chairs, and smooth slabs of wood nailed together as a table. The floors, with a rug only under the conversation area, were buffed to slipperiness. Opposite the fireplace was a twenty-foot African print hung on the wall from the rafters, stopped by another conversation area of more leather chairs, and divided by a long table, currently laden with all sorts of goodies.

Dory followed Kyle into the kitchen and Jaz could see Kyle's sleeves were rolled up to the elbow. She walked toward the African print, and looked beyond a set of double French doors which led out to a spacious wooden-floored terrace with built-in stone seats. On the other side of the French doors, near the fireplace wall, was a built-in etagere housing an elaborate component system and record collection.

"Jazz," she scoffed as she read the titles. "Figures." She read the selections in The Wurlitzer jukebox as well. The doorbell rang and she went to answer the door.

"Hi Jaz." Kyle's greeting stopped her. "Would you get that for me?" he asked as easy and unhurried as you please.

"Sure."

The rest of the crew was familiar with their environs, and Jaz watched Derek open cabinets she'd overlooked that hid the bar. "I aspire to be just like Kyle Jagger when I grow up. To live in a million-dollar one bedroom lodge with two cars, one boat and security to keep all you triflin's folks out," he said.

As Kyle ushered Marc out of his kitchen, Jaz sauntered through the first set of French doors into Kyle's office–a long, organized space with a desk, matching cabinets, all his awards and a drafting table. Traipsing through the second set of French doors brought her to the terrace, where she couldn't see the bay for the trees, but she could hear the lapping waves and smell the wet saltiness.

Despite its uncomfortable beginning for Jaz, the day proved productive and relaxing.

"Jaz, you wanna help me clean up a bit?" Kyle asked casually.

"No I don't. You only asked me because I'm the only woman here, you chauvinist pig." She kidded him and the guys loved it. "I'm the guest, you're the host."

"Coming here once makes you a guest, next time you're not," Kyle said as he brought out the coffee.

"Might I have a little cardamom with that?" she asked as Kyle and Dory laughed.

"Must be an over thirty joke," Tré said.

"Watch it. I'm not there yet. Can't speak for these two fossils," Jaz said.

"Since this is your first visit here, you're entitled to the fifty-cent tour." Kyle extended his hand to Jaz who grew immediately uncomfortable. "It's not as comfy as yours but my life hasn't been as full," Kylc said when they reached the bedroom.

Jaz stepped into the large room with a huge fireplace, and the sight of two curious rocks on its mantel.

"Amber?" She asked, picking up the rough rock.

"In its natural ore state," Kyle informed as she picked up the deep gold transparent rock. "Topaz." He decided not to tell Jaz that Topaz was the pet name he'd given her when he'd seen her about town, before he knew who she was.

"Nice view." Jaz was stopped by the sight of the bay with boats bobbing in the distance beyond the terrace.

"Would you like to go out and sit?"

"No, the tour."

"Sure. Closets on either side, bathroom through there." He pointed and Jaz tried not to look at the four-post antique Chinese bed.

"Make-out city!" Marc walked in and looked around.

"When you get to be my age you'll find quality far exceeds quantity," he spoke directly to Jaz.

"Then I hope I never reach your age man," Marc joked as they returned to the living room.

"What can we do to entice you to take out the 'Golden Lady' for a quick spin in the bay?" Tré asked.

"Alright, lemme get my jacket and keys."

"Well I'm off," Jaz announced.

"No ride on the bay?" Kyle's smile slid from his face.

"Not this time, I'm going to LA. I'll be back in the office by Tuesday."

"You'll be missed." Kyle's easy smile returned.

"I can see why you haven't lost any weight," Jaz teased her friend as she sliced a hunk of cheesecake.

"That is so cold." Denny twirled the knife playfully. "Lloyd likes it."

"That's who counts girl." As if on cue, Denny's husband, Lloyd, walked in carrying a tired Little Lloyd. "Hey cutie." Jaz jumped up to hold him, but he shrugged away.

"What's the matter, Champ?" his father asked him. "I'm going to put him to bed and I'll be right behind him." He kissed his wife, then Jaz. "See you next time, Jaz." Father and son disappeared.

"You done good, Denny. Give him a daughter."

"Not in this life, girl I'm too old. So what's on you wee little?"

"Just stopped by to see my old ace boon coon."

"Umhum. Just spit it out girl."

"OK. There's this guy–"

"Really!?"

"It's not what you think so don't get happy," Jaz warned. "He bothers me."

"What do you mean 'bothers' you?"

"I mean he gets under my skin." She stabbed the cheesecake with the fork. "He works at CE, my father's right-hand man and we have to work closely together. We work very well together, he's brilliant, quick and we relate to the music, dances and the times. We have lunch in, usually in my office. We've been out on a couple of dinner meetings with the clients, I drove and he drove so–"

"So what's the problem?"

"He won't stay put." Jaz looked at her friend. "Our relationship is a working one, and he keeps trying to move it to another level. He asks me out for dinner or a concert or a movie or to go out on his boat–"

"So did you put this offensive slime ball in his place?" Denny asked with a laugh knowing Jaz wouldn't have any problem telling him where to get off if she so desired.

"He's very nice, gentlemanly. Amber calls him her Prince Charmin'–"

"Amber?"

"We used to see him around Frisco before I knew who he was, and Amber called him her 'Prince Charming.'"

"Outta the mouths of babes. So what is it, Jaz?"

"I feel out of control, like I can't keep him where I want him."

"He doesn't sound like a man who lets anyone put limits on him."

"When he came to the session at my house, he put his jacket on the halltree right next to Qwayz's. I was appalled. And he used my personal bathroom when the powder room was occupied. He was in my bedroom with my things, commenting on my antiques and–"

"Well Lloyd, Scoey and AJ use that bathroom all the time–"

"Not the same thing," Jaz snapped.

"Do other team members use your personal bath."

"Yes, but I know them."

And they're no threat, Denny thought, and asked "Is this guy married?"

"No, no time, with all the traveling he does." Jaz walked to the window.

"So what's wrong Jaz?"

"Intellectually I know Qwayz is not coming back to me. The only way he could is if he'd been a POW with years of torture, but emotionally I haven't let go. I don't think I ever can or will. But if I did, Kyle would be the *type* I'd think about dating."

And there it was. After all these years Jaz was letting go. Denny's eyes brimmed with tears of joy she wouldn't let fall. After all these years, Jasmine Bianca Culhane Chandler was moving on, accepting, instead of denying, and it warmed her heart. This Kyle guy may not be the one, but he was a start, a rung on the ladder to ultimate happiness, and Denny welcomed him.

"He's not Qwayz," Jaz spoke of the first man who threatened his memory. "Not even close. He eats blood red meat, can't carry a tune in a bucket, drinks scotch on the rocks, and loves buttermilk, boating, skiing and jazz."

"Can he dance?" Denny got up to freshen their coffee.

"I dunno. I guess he can waltz–"

"Jaz, I was just kidding."

"I won't be out of control again."

"You think you were out of control with Qwayz?"

"I think we were both out of control," she smiled.

"You were both young and in love—it was allowed."

"He was my spirit in the dark. All I wanted was to love and be loved by him, but life beat us up like two doves in a hurricane. I could never be in love like that again. Never."

"You know why? 'Cause you'll never be sixteen or twenty-one again."

"I tell you Denny, the idea of reservations for two scares the shit outta me. I'm not ready for a friendship with a future."

"Take it slow, this will be your first since Qwayz." Jaz thought of Prince Omar and Nick, but she had felt in control of those situations. "Go out with Kyle. He might be lame, dufuss or gay, then you went through all this for nothing." Denny hunched her friend with a wink. "It's almost the '80s, you can sleep with men and still be a good girl."

"I'll never forget your brother. Never stop loving him."

"No one's asking you too, Sweetie."

Chapter Ten

"Man you know this is not my thing." Kyle took his chair under the thatched cabana out of the sun. "If I'm in the sun, I want to be on my boat."

"Bitch, bitch," his cousin and best friend, Cass, answered catching a glimpse of a scantily-clad beige beauty. "Look cuz, it's more than your environs. You don't want to be in beautiful St. Kitts because your mind is elsewhere. Rap to me brother. Lawd have mercy!" He fanned himself as two natives sashayed by.

"Grow up, Cass."

"And be a stick-in-the-mud like you? No thanks. I'm young and single and ready to mingle."

"Two out of three ain't bad." Kyle sipped his tropical drink.

"OK man, who is she? This babe that's got your nose? I don't remember you being this bad off since Marisa Margeaux at Tulane."

"Ancient history."

"You know she's divorced, no children."

"How nice."

"Who is this lady of yours man?" Cass watched the familiar smile glide across his cousin's features.

"Let's say I think you'd approve."

"You in love or what?"

"Yes I am."

"Aw man, I'm happy for you." Cass slapped him five pivoting off to pour a toast of Chivas Regal. "Here's to you and her man."

"Thanks." The gold liquid slid down his throat easy as you please.

"So, who is she, man, and when can I meet her?"

"Gotta bide my time. I'm the one with love jones, I gotta convince her before I speak her name–especially to you."

"Aw man, I'm the one from New Orleans who should believe in jinxes, voodoo and shit."

"You'll be the first to find out, if it works out."

"And I'll be the first to find out if it doesn't. You did the right thing man, waiting till the right one," Cass said, reflecting on his own two failed marriages and two children. The cousins talked until the sun came up. "Timing is everything, man. Raina and I were too young to get married."

"You're a good daddy, Cass."

"Yeah, meant to be a father and not a husband."

"I think your lifestyle might have something to do with finding a good woman."

"Man, I can't give up my night spots in Houston–goldmines."

"All depends on what you want man. I know what I want, and I'm gonna get it. The whole shabang."

"I wish you luck, my brother."

The CE team's arrival in New Orleans garnered the kind of fanfare usually reserved for Mardi Gras, but that was months off and the party people wanted an excuse now. The restoration and conversion of the old railway station into a luxury waterfront hotel and shops in the French Quarter had been the Commerce and Tourism department's coup, and contracting the prestigious Culhane Enterprises was celebration enough. The Harbor View Groundbreaking-Ribboncutting Ceremony in the afternoon and Gala Banquet the same night had been sold out for months, as were all the promotional weekend activities.

The Culhane entourage flew in for the festivities, occupying the three bedroom suite at the small elegant Chalfonte, where Kyle joined them. Hep's and Lorette's room was at the immediate left of the entrance, Jaz's a few steps into the living room on the right, and Kyle's past the fireplace and conversation area in the far left corner.

The Mayor of New Orleans and major financier, Mr. Ribauld, and the Culhanes were the most photographed folks at the morning groundbreaking ceremony. Hep and Kyle stood shoulder to shoulder like a pair of black Adonises, looking cool in the sweltering New Orleans heat. Lorette was refined and elegant in a coral St. Laurent suit, and Jaz wore an impeccable Giani alabaster linen suit with the embroidered lapels. The crowd cheered as the first shovel of dirt was pitched by Hep, and again when Lorette cut the red ribbon releasing thousands of colorful balloons into the steamy blue sky.

Having gotten wind of Lorette's heritage, the tabloids almost ignored the Harbor View project in its headlines: "Return of the Native Daughter." As a result, Lorette was to be the guest of honor at a luncheon hosted by the Creole Daughters of Fine Lineage.

"Jaz the invitation includes you," Lorette said.

"Kyle offered to show me around."

"Sure did," he agreed, trying to hide his surprise.

"Just don't be late for the banquet tonight." Lorette threw over her shoulder as she went to her room to change. "We'll meet here at six."

"I owe you one Jagger." Jaz stepped out of her heels. "Not since D.C. have I felt hot like this."

"New Orleans hot. I suggest you wear shorts," he said, backing into his room.

"Listen I was only kidding. I thought I'd just stay in here and cool out until–"

"Uh-huh. You're not making a liar outta me. Get dressed and wear comfortable shoes." He wasn't about to pass up private time with his newest project–slow-walking Jaz Chandler. "That's quite a hat," he joned on her wide straw bowler as they climbed into the air-conditioned cab. With relish, Kyle escorted Jaz around the hallowed halls of Tulane University, his old alma mater and stomping grounds.

"Then, you went to Princeton. Impressive for a black guy in the Sixties."

"Ain't no thang."

Jaz chuckled at his slang. Despite the Ivy League grooming, Kyle knew who and what he was, where he'd come from and where he was going, and she was impressed.

"You know I'm at a disadvantage." She took off her hat and fanned herself. "You're used to this heat."

"No one gets used to New Orleans hot, you just learn to respect it." They walked by the small shops, hotels and restaurants of the French Quarter. "This is why Harbor View is going to be so successful. We need a large, first class luxury hotel. We'll have time to check out all of these," he mused, as they passed the jazz clubs, which would be jumping tonight.

"You know my aunt Selena started down here at The Onyx, after a short stint at Chez Armour. That's where she met Zack."

"It's a romantic city." Kyle smiled as they crossed over to look at an overgrown, abandoned house.

"Just like in 'A Streetcar Named Desire.'" Jaz pulled some of the vine off the gate making space enough to look inside.

"Suppose the owners just wanted to keep nosy voyeurs out?"

"No one's lived here for eons. I bet it was something in its day."

They both marveled at the classic French motif. The two-story building had louvered doors on the second floor that opened onto the terraced galleries. Downstairs the French doors stood sentry, beyond a magnificent stone courtyard complete with fountain, statues and the remnants of manicured gardens.

"The people who must have visited this place in the 1800's." Kyle didn't remove his eyes from the structure.

"You think it's that old?"

"Easily. It would make a fine small hotel or restaurant. Look at these gold J's on the gate. That alone cost a fortune in those days. 'J' for Jagger."

"Negro please. Javier is more likely. Javier, I wonder if this could be my mother's people?"

"Were they rich?"

"Filthy. But my grandfather J's folks cut him off when he married a brown-skinned woman from Tennessee."

"Sounds 'bout right."

"Imagine stumbling over your roots like that?"

"That's the way we have to do it most times. Right now we gotta head back. It's showtime."

Jaz and Kyle returned before Lorette, and Hep was busy on the phone, so Jaz went in to bathe and dress. When she emerged hours later, their restful living room had been converted into a hospitality suite.

As the guests began filing out for the big bash, Jaz fell back.

"C'mon Punkin'." Hep stopped to hurry her up.

"Aren't you waiting for Kyle?"

"He's not here, he went on with his aunt, uncle and cousins."

If Jaz felt self-conscious accompanying her parents to the Gala, she felt even more so when all the attention was focused upon her. She remained aloof, distantly friendly, shimmering in a halter topped gown, which dipped low to the small of her back, as the split rose up, treating spectators to a glimpse of stately bronze leg.

"Holy moley." Cass slapped Kyle on the arm. "Lookit there. She is one F-I-N-E fox–" before Cass could finish, Kyle had strutted to her side, much to his cousin's amazement. "Well excuse the hell outta me!"

"You look like a million bucks," Kyle said, escorting Jaz to her seat.

"I know," she said without looking at him, though she heard him chuckle.

"Won't you save me a dance, Mrs. Chandler." Kyle inclined his head as he slid the chair up behind her.

"I can't make any promises." She tossed her wild coppery mane, which, by design, fell right back over her eye.

The evening progressed nicely, with Kyle paying the right amount of discreet attention to Jaz. When the dancing commenced, Jaz danced first with the mayor and assortment of his staffers until her father rescued her, then Kyle cut in.

"What took you so long, Jagger?"

"I thought I'd give everyone their chance up front, because I don't plan to give you up without a fight." He swirled her around on the dance floor, and Jaz made a mental note to tell Denny that the brother could dance.

"You kids coming back to the hotel now?" Hep asked.

"I thought we'd go on down and catch a few sets. Why don't you two come?" Kyle said.

"Ah no," Lorette said.

"The boss has spoken." Hep followed his wife into the sleek black limo.

"You know you have fine bone structure." Kyle's eyes followed Jaz's bare back down to her waist, and back up.

"And you have exquisite taste." She sashayed ahead of him.

The next morning, when Jaz emerged from her room clad in shorts and a T, no make-up, her hair combed to one side in a lopsided pony tail, Kyle bellowed.

"Oh Cinderella! What happened?" He was dapper even in casual clothes.

"The ball is over." Jaz reached for juice.

"This is the real Jaz," Hep said. "Not pleasant until noon. In fact she doesn't usually rise until noon. What's the occasion?"

"Gladys Ann is here for a medical conference. I'm meeting her for lunch before she catches a plane back to D.C."

"So you'll be back by, say three?" Kyle asked, and Jaz looked at him as if he were daft. "I have a surprise for you and your mom. Hep you're welcomed too. I managed to get keys to the old Javier mansion."

"I'm sorry, but I meet Ribald at two-thirty." Hep chowed-down on a piece of French toast. "Then I'm taking the company jet back at about seven."

Jaz and Lorette followed Kyle as he used a key to open the wrought iron gates of the mansion. It was a surprise for Lorette, so it took longer for her to register the significance of this house. When she did, her hand flew to her mouth and she approached the inner courtyard, mustering old memories of being here in her father's house years ago. She looked up at the open galleries, at the faded elegance, perhaps hearing sounds, seeing sights that Kyle and Jaz were not privy too.

As they were leaving the mansion, Lorette thanked Kyle for bringing her face-to-face with part of her past. "Got rid of some bigoted old ghosts," she told Jaz.

Jaz stood perplexed by the bellmen who were loading her parents' luggage and leaving hers. Hep was explaining that he thought she knew she would be staying in New Orleans for the duration of the project–that's what it means to have a Culhane contract.

"Kyle you didn't tell her?"

"Hey, Hep, I don't make that kind of money."

"But Dad, I have a few things on my agenda and I'm not prepared for this wardrobe wise. I still have to go home and pack for–"

"Is it alright if she comes back tomorrow Kyle?"

"What the hell are you asking him for?"

"It's his baby, Jaz."

"Sure, tomorrow will be fine." Kyle grinned knowingly.

"You already closed up your houses and your Jag is in my garage. You can buy clothes and clear your calendar from here," Hep said, and Jaz decided to stay.

But once her parents departed, and she was ensconced, bag and baggage, with Kyle here in New Orleans, she realized the implications of this project. It had been fun and games, flirter and flirtee, but never had she focused on the fact that it would be the two of them, alone in a suite for months. Her mouth had written a check her body couldn't cash.

The law of propinquity was in full effect as the talented architectural duo spent mornings, noons and nights in one another's company. Kyle and Jaz accepted but essentially bypassed the offices offered by the Mayor, working mostly from the on-site trailer, and their three bedroom suite. They preferred to work hard all day, dine at one of the local cafes in the evening and, walking the meal off, catch a little jazz before heading back to the hotel. It was over those quiet dinners that self-revelations unfolded. Jaz listened as Kyle told the story of his grandparents and parents, of his Tulane college days, Princeton, and the trials and victories of his career in New York before he was lured away by Hep Culhane.

Over the next few weeks, Jaz shared her Watts upbringing, all her friends, of Roosevelt High, Berkeley, Paris, Italy and back again. She spoke easily of Qwayz without realizing it. Kyle was the first male she'd confided in who didn't know her history with her husband. It felt good to sing Qwayz's praises to someone new. It was like keeping him alive and passing him on.

"Do you think he's coming back?" Kyle asked after one such conversation.

"Yes I do." It was the first time she'd lied to Kyle, and intentionally lied about Qwayz. She thought the inner turmoil was all over, but the lump of untruth stuck in her throat and she couldn't swallow. Kyle touched her hand reassuringly, and suggested they get some air. He didn't press her for conversation as they strolled back to the hotel.

"Can I get you anything before I turn in?" he asked, once in the suite.

"No thanks."

"Goodnight then." He went into his room and left Jaz standing by her door like a date without a goodnight kiss. Once inside her room she realized why she felt so bad. She'd used Qwayz's memory to keep Kyle at a distance, neither of which she wanted to do.

During their dinners, Kyle enjoyed hearing about Jaz's studies in Italy, while Jaz was intrigued with the descriptions of his retreat in Kenya, his coffee plantation and its operation. As they sipped cappuccino at The Black Dove, Kyle spoke of the investments Hep had roped him into; An Australian vineyard which they sold for a Hawaiian coffee plantation, and olive and avocado oil in Napa Valley. Kyle had stuck to his vanilla and cloves in Madagascar, oil in Nigeria, cocoa on the Ivory Coast and ginger in Australia, which were lucrative on their own. Jaz mentioned her real estate holdings.

"Lemme guess. The San Francisco apartment you live in, The Cliffs and the beach house."

Jaz was startled by his referral to Paradise Rock, but added, "And those my brother left me."

"I suppose you'll meet my brother sooner or later. I'll be forever grateful to him for going into business with my father at the paper, allowing me to become an architect."

"When did you know that's what you wanted to do?"

"When my grandpa gave me Lincoln logs and an erector set one Christmas, that was all she wrote. I still made excellent grades in English, more for my Dad's benefit–couldn't have the son of the only successful, nationally distributed black daily paper getting C's. My father worked so hard, he was seldom home before we went to bed and always gone when we got up in the morning." He twirled the swizzle stick around the ice. "Then when I was about eight, my folks gave up three upstairs bedrooms to create the Great Room, which would double as a den for the family and an office for my Dad, so he could always see us when he worked at home. Funny, it takes being a grown man to understand why my father missed all the scout meetings, track meets and basketball games. Not because he wanted to. Anyway, I followed that work crew around, forever, and knew I wanted to build and create spaces for work and leisure."

"You any good at B-ball?"

"One of the best." The easy smile stole his face.

They walked pass small houses toward their home away from home.

"You grow up in a big house, Jagger?"

"No, at least it didn't seem big to me at the time. You think that everyone grows up the way you do, regardless. I suppose it would be considered large by some, all of us had our own rooms with adjoining baths, but my Mom made it feel cozy. We're all close." He smiled at her as they reached the suite door. He wasn't used to talking about his growing up, people weren't interested in that. He was constantly dealing with tomorrow.

Over the next month, Jaz watched Kyle's close friends rotate in and out of the suite. His crazy cousin Cass, and his "boys" from college, who, with Kyle, had constituted "the wild bunch" when they partied at Dillard and Xavier, showing out in their crimson and cream. Kyle had met Jaz's aunts and cousins, as well as Sloane and Gladys Ann when they came through for their sororit's Boule'.

As the pair drove to his Aunt's and Uncle's Saturday night house party for Cass's birthday, Jaz felt a little trepidation, which was quickly allayed once she was greeted by the family. It was Kyle who set her back, introducing her as "his colleague on the Harbor View project." "Friend" would have described their relationship nicely, but colleague suggested she didn't have anything to do, so he brought her along. The food was decadently sinful, good and fattening; the room full of old anecdotes, lots of laughter, music and the news of Marisa Margeaux's return.

"Who is Marisa?" Jaz asked Genna, Cass's equally crazy sister.

"She and Kyle were an item back in the day when he was at Tulane and she at Dillard. Against her wishes, Kyle took the scholarship to Princeton, and Miss Lady, invited to come along, decided not to, so she stayed back here." Genna spooned more of the reddish brown gumbo into the serving kettle that Jaz held. "So while he's up there studying, she up and marries a doctor and moves to–guess where?"

"New Jersey?"

"Bingo girl, Montclair. Kyle pays her no never mind, graduates, works in New York then on to California. Close chapter. These romantic voodoo who-doo fools should let sleeping dogs lie. My cousin is not interested in and is too good for her. Ass-backwards, Marisa decides letting Kyle go was her big mistake. Look again, he was the one who did the letting and the leavin'. The sorry heffa. Now I suppose she thinks her divorced butt is just gonna stroll in and capture his heart again." She replaced the lid. "Nothin' you have to worry about."

"Me?"

"You. My money's on you." Genna winked and carried the streaming delicacy to the waiting guests.

Marisa Margeaux never showed. Jaz didn't ask about her. She wasn't even curious–so she told herself.

Chapter Eleven

"Hello!" Jaz ran into the suite to catch the telephone. "Hey, Amber." Jaz perched herself on the back of the sofa, Kyle removed his jacket and disappeared into his room. "Of course, I'll be there for your dance recital. Wouldn't miss it for the world."

"Is Prince Charming coming?"

"I don't think so Amber, and his name is not Prince Charming."

"Is she talking about me?" Kyle reentered the living room.

"Is he there?" Amber asked.

"Yes." Jaz gave Kyle the phone.

"She says she'll see us next Thursday night," Kyle said as he hung up.

"You're going?"

"Why not? I was invited by the Sun and Rainbow herself." He watched Jaz go into her act now. He'd become used to it, whenever he mentioned their being together somewhere outside the New Orleans city limits. "Told her we'd be in early, about four, and maybe we could take her for ice cream–"

"She has parents you know," Jaz snapped. "I won't be ready to catch the plane that early. I speak at St. Gabriel's of the Sacred Heart

Girls School that morning."

"OK." He came up close to her, in a stance she'd never seen him take before. "Tell you what, Jaz. I'll take one plane and you can take another, even though we're going the same place. I'll take one cab and you take another. Maybe we can trade our seats so we sit on opposite sides of the auditorium." He cut his eyes and turned away from her, disappearing into his room, where he remained the night.

The following day Kyle's attitude wasn't much improved, he was cordial, but curt. At the end of the work day, Jaz returned to the suite alone, since Kyle had told her to "go on," he'd be busy on-site for awhile. So she ordered up room service, and settled in to watch "South Pacific" on the smaller set in her room.

Later, Jaz heard Kyle come in and go directly to his room. Shortly thereafter, when the telephone rang, Jaz decided to let Kyle answer it. But he didn't, so she went out into the living room to find his door closed. She picked up.

"Kyle Jagger please," the female voice requested.

"May I ask who's calling?"

"Marisa."

"Hold on. Who does she think she is, Cher?" Jaz knocked on the door, then buzzed his bathroom. "I'm sorry Marisa, he's not available. Is there a message?"

"Just tell him I called. My number is–" Jaz smiled like a Cheshire cat as she took her number, which meant he didn't already have it.

"Alright I'll see that he gets it." Jaz taped it on his door.

She'd fallen asleep after the movie, and when she got up to turn the television off, she noticed the telephone light was lit. Opening her door a crack, she checked Kyle's door. The message was gone, and now Jaz was pissed.

The next morning Kyle's attitude was much improved, but by then Tracy called reporting that Amber and half of Ms. Terrell's dance class had chicken pox, so the show was off.

"Well, how lucky for you," he said.

"I'm going up to see her if you can spare me for a couple of days."

"No sweat. Tell her they'll be other Suns and Rainbows." He smiled, and Jaz seethed beneath her facade.

* * *

Aunt Jaz soothed Amber as much as possible, then, seeking babyless and more adult conversation, she visited Denny ready to discuss her feelings about Kyle.

"Well now, as the Dragons used to say, 'not gonna give me any grass and gonna tell me where to graze?'" Denny said, and Jaz laughed. "Lemme get this straight, for the record. He hasn't, that is, has *not* made any advances towards you?" Jaz shook her head. "Not a rub of the arm, a kiss on the cheek, a hand slipped around the waist? Well, congratulations you've gotten just what you wanted from him. A nice platonic relationship. That *is* what you wanted?" Denny's dark ebony eyes pierced Jaz's.

"I'm not sure," Jaz said slowly.

"Well, if you don't know what you want, then how can you go about getting it? It's obvious that if you want the relationship to change, you're gonna have to be the one to make the first move. He's not going to do anything to mess it up. The ball is in your court."

"Enter player number two ... Marisa, an old college sweetheart."

"Ooh, the plot thickens. Anything you have to worry about?"

"Probably screwing their brains out in all three bedrooms as we speak."

"First, you have to decide if you want this guy, and then have at it–if it's not too late." Denny watched the panic in Jaz's face. "Well, you said there was this old gal come back."

"I just dunno." Jaz stood and began pacing. "I don't want him right now, maybe later."

"So you're going to be another Marisa? Years later realize that you missed the boat and try to come back to the pier, only to find the ship has sailed."

"I'll decide soon. We're going to the AIA next week. He asked. Let me rephrase that. What he said was 'since we've both got to attend, we might as well go together.'"

"He said it that way because of your ornery attitude." Denny wanted her friend to pursue this man so badly. "The man's no fool."

"Well, if he hasn't announced his engagement when I get back, I'll consider this thing more seriously." The idea of his being "engaged" to someone else struck her as weird. She didn't see him with anyone else, yet she didn't see herself with him.

Cass and Jaz came into the suite laughing as Kyle rose from the drafting table.

"What have you two been up too?" he asked of his cousin and his colleague.

"Jaz is teaching me what classy women want in their men?" Cass said, placing some of Jaz's purchases on the sofa.

"Can't teach an old dog new tricks," Kyle said and Cass barked on cue.

"Dory will be down tomorrow," Kyle told Jaz as she went into her bedroom.

"I like her," Cass said to his cousin quietly. "She's good peeps."

"What you doin' with my woman ... huh?" They started sparing like they were kids.

"OK, boys." Jaz reentered like a scolding mother. "Are we gonna eat?"

"Cheeze, I'd hate to be the man who feeds you," Cass quipped.

"I feed myself. In fact, I'll feed you both. My treat. Let's book," Jaz said.

Kyle had tried backing off, distancing himself from her, but when he did that, Cass was flying in routinely to fill the void. He was glad she got along with his friends and their wives, even his cousin, Genna, who didn't take a liking to anybody. His parents were now curious about Hep and Lorette Culhane's daughter. Kyle kept reassuring them they were only friends. He wanted their relationship made or broken just between the two of them, not the in- or the out-laws. Knowing what a private person he was, everyone respected his wishes and kept their hopes to themselves, not so much regarding Jaz but anyone. It was time for the boy to settle down and make a family.

Kyle and Jaz flew to San Francisco for the AIA Banquet. CE had four tables and garnered eight of the twenty-six awards–Kyle's Seattle restoration project being the most notable. They danced, went past the Culhanes for the after party celebration, danced and ate some more, before Kyle saw her home.

"I had a really good time. It's good to be back where you can breathe easy." Jaz fished for her apartment keys.

"New Orleans is not that bad." Kyle defended his second home.

"You wanna come in?" was out before she realized it, an invitation made of wine and good feelings.

"I'd better not." He wanted to, waited for the day when they both could go in together, slip off their clothes together, slip underneath the covers together, and stay there until death do them part. "We've got to get back to the real world tomorrow."

"It's really going well."

"We should be finished by January-February, if the weather doesn't mess us up."

"Then we'll be back here for good." Jaz hoped her disappointment didn't register on her face.

"Hey, let's not get maudlin, we got a few more months in Nawlings. See you tomorrow. Need a ride to the plane?" Wanting to kiss her, he backed away.

"Yep. Bye." She wanted to kiss him, just on the cheek, like she did AJ, she told herself before admitting, Naw I want to bust some slobs.

She watched him drive off and closed her door. Turning to the halltree she looked at her fedora and buckskin jacket and stroked Qwayz's brown leather bomber and his red baseball cap out of habit.

"You'd like him Qwayz. You two coulda been friends," she said aloud, leaving her shoes where she'd stepped from them. We did make a striking couple, she thought undressing, washing her face and brushing her teeth and falling into bed. She reached for the picture of Qwayz and her, kissed him, and decided to let the music box put her to sleep before remembering it was on her desk at CE along with her Hawaiian Rock. She sighed and rolled onto her side in the darkness. The phone jangled in the quiet.

"Hello!" She hoped it was Kyle.

"Are you alone? Is he there with you?" Denny whispered into the phone.

"I am all by myself. Thanks for pointing that out."

"Good, gimme the details."

The line was busy, so Kyle returned the phone to its receiver. He'd gotten used to telling Jaz goodnight, but he'd see her in a few hours anyway. He unwrapped the thick plush-piled paisley robe Jaz had given him as a birthday gift, and got into bed wondering who she was talking to this time of morning.

* * *

"I'll ask her, Mom." Kyle invited Jaz to Winnetka for Thanksgiving, but he knew better.

"Thank your mother, but I have plans," was her reply.

"You know Moms. No matter how old you are–"

"I got one too."

"I think that's really a nice idea, you all going back to the Evelyn, Tennessee homestead for the holiday."

"I haven't been there since I was a kid. We always went to Colt, Texas, 'cause there was more to do. Then my maternal grandparents died, and my aunt and her husband took over the place. I've only seen my Aunt Coke and Vashti. I can't wait to see my other aunts again, to meet all my cousins." She settled down on the couch to watch an old movie. "In a way, we have you to thank for it. Getting us into that old Javier place started Lorette thinking about lost time. The reunion was her idea."

"I couldn't figure out her reaction at the time," Kyle said.

"Well, I'm still naming my daughter after the bigoted old bat, Lorette's grandmere."

"A known racist. Why?"

"I fell in love with the name before I knew anything about the woman. A rose by any other name."

"What's the name?"

"Gabrielle Giselle," Jaz said, and Kyle repeated it.

"It's lyrical. Does your husband have anything to say about this?"

"If I have one, he can name the boy, which will probably be a junior. You guys have no imagination."

Kyle left Jaz watching "Back Street," mentally retaliating that he had more imagination than she thought. Gabrielle Giselle Jagger sounded almost as good as Mrs. Jasmine Jagger.

As wonderful as the separate Thanksgivings were, the two

couldn't wait to get back to the suite at the Chalfonte, with their respective reports on their families. They eagerly fell into their former routines, relishing their time together. Kyle invited Jaz to accompany him and Cass skiing.

"I hate cold weather. Genna and I may go to the Caribbean."

"What? Oh no," he'd answered before realizing.

"It's no different than you and Cass going skiing," she said, pleased by his reaction. She and Genna had discussed no such thing.

"We're only going to Gstaad, and may I add, that you wear a lotta clothes when you go skiing."

"Which come off when you dine at the lodge."

"They won't be bikinis."

"How do you know what I wear?"

"I can imagine." He smiled. Then the suite door flew open, with Marc and Derek, lugging their own bags.

"Oops, did we interrupt something?"

"No!" Jaz and Kyle answered in unison. "This place is like Grand Central," Kyle said.

"Too cheap to tip a bellman?" Jaz teased from her desk.

"Speaking of cheap," Kyle began, "only you two are to come up here to this suite. No girls, women or members of the opposite sex."

"He covered all the bases, didn't he?" Marc asked Derek. "Where to?"

"Straight down the hall," Kyle said.

"Oh, Wow! get aload of this crib!" Derek said loudly.

"For you," Kyle said, handing Jaz a wrapped gift. "Happy Birthday."

"Why, thank you." She opened it. "You're early."

"That didn't stop you from opening it." He had thought about replacing the gold star she wore, but had learned it was a gift from her husband, which she never removed.

"Earth Wind and Fire tickets! You do listen. Thank you!" She kissed and hugged him. "In San Francisco?"

"No problem, you can fly up to catch the concert, then come back.

"Oh no sir, Buster." She leaned over his back to say, "You gave

them to me. You take me. Besides you need the cultural exposure."
"I was afraid of that." He looked at her with a grin.

Jaz sang with the group, and Kyle was awed by the prim, proper professional sophisticate, partying hardy with the concert audience. "Ah! I had the best time!" she enthused, skipping with excitement to the car, holding his hand as she would have AJ's or Scoey's. "It was the perfect gift. Have you changed your mind about their talents?"

"I must say I was pleasantly surprised. I like that song about needing a woman like the air you breathe, and the other one, making love till you're satisfied."

"You would. Stick with me Jagger, there's hope for you yet." She stood with the car door between them. "Thank you," she said, and at that very moment, if she could spirit them into bed by magic, she would have.

She was so wound up. Kyle listened as she spoke of Qwayz's and TC's group. "EWF reminds me of Raw Cilk's instrumental roots–innovative, relevant and ahead of their time. I'm hungry. You hungry?"

"Hungry?" Kyle said with a chuckle.

"We have time to eat, don't we?"

"Just so we're back in time for our A.M. meeting with Ribauld."

"You're joking aren't you?" The idea of your place or mine evaporated with the moon. "A Saturday morning meeting? In Nawlings? Surely you jest?"

"Couldn't be helped. That reminds me." He snapped his fingers. "I gotta go past Hep's to pick up something." He U-turned in the middle of the block.

"At this time of night?" She checked her watch. "Good luck, Lorette's been in bed for hours, and so have Tennyson and Millie. Dad might be working in his downstairs office, but he won't hear the bell."

"I better call." He pulled over to a pay phone, used it and returned. "He says to use your key, he'll put it by the door."

At the house, Jaz opened the door feeling around for the light switch. "Surprise!" The lights came on as folks shouted and, in reaction, Jaz slammed the door shut.

"Good reflexes for a thirty year old," Kyle teased from behind.

"C'mon Punkin'." Hep reopened the door. "We've seen you now." He pulled his daughter into the house as the group sang "Happy Birthday."

"See, I can keep a secret." Selena and Zack were the first to catch her in a hug.

"I just talked to you!"

"Happy Birthday, Sugar." Zack kissed her cheek.

Jaz was filled with an indescribable sense of pride as all her friends from various stages of her life gathered to help celebrate this milestone. They mingled in comfortable groups holding mini-reunions. Qwayz would have loved this, she thought.

As usual, Selena was fiddlin' on the ivories, and a group of music lovers gathered around her to sing old songs. But when Hep cut up the volume on the oldies tape, the dancing antics started. They formed Madison and Stroll lines, and started reproducing dance steps from the pony, hitchhike, monkey, cool jerk, Philly dog and boogaloo. When Jr. Walker's "Road-runner" came on, Jaz and Gladys Ann cut loose like they were teens outside Studio #3 again.

Jaz, Gladys Ann, Mel and Selena blew guests away with four-part harmony on a few acapella songs, then Jaz said to her aunt. "C'mon, let's do 'Dr. Feelgood.'"

"You sure?" Selena asked.

Finishing that song signified the end of the singing, none could top the aunt/niece rendition of that bluesy, funky finale. Jaz saw Zeke, the elevator man, way off in the distance, and she went over to him.

"You're leavin'?"

"Yes, Addie and I are going to lunch tomorrow so I gotta rest up," Zeke said in his scratchy voice.

"Did you get enough to eat?"

"Aplenty, although there wasn't no bread puddin'," he joked.

"Well, my mother planned this one." Jaz winked. "Wait." She went and cut a piece of cake for him, even though they hadn't officially sung Happy Birthday yet.

"Oh Miss Jaz, you didn't have to do that." He was so touched a tear threatened to fall from his one good eye.

"I never do what I don't want to Zeke. Take care," Jaz said as Mel pulled her away.

"She's a fine woman," AJ sidled up to Kyle.

"Yes she is."

"She's very special to all of us," AJ continued, as they watched her mingling. "We'd hate to see anything or anybody hurt her." AJ's cold stare penetrated Kyle's causal gaze.

"I can understand that, Doc." He knew this little punk wasn't threatening him. "I don't think anyone would intentionally hurt her."

"Haven't I seen you someplace before?" AJ couldn't remember where, but thought it had something to do with basketball.

"Anything's possible," Kyle said, and turned to join Jaz.

"Kyle, this is Denny," Jaz introduced, eager to see what she thought of him.

"Hello Kyle?" Denny said, sticking out her hand for a shake.

"Dr. Denise Winslow."

"Don't believe a word Jaz says about me."

"It's all been good, 'a brilliant psychologist married to a handsome psychiatrist who have one cute little 'big-head boy.'" They shared a laugh and Jaz relaxed.

The party broke up around four, with the last of the revelers bidding adieu as the sun peeked over the garden wall.

"He really is a Prince Charming," Denny whispered to her friend. "You didn't tell me he was fine with those cute dimples. From the mouth of babes." As Kyle turned toward her, Denny said, "it was so nice to have met you Kyle, I hope to see you again, soon." She purposely didn't look at Jaz's scolding eyes.

"That was great, thanks Dad, Mom." Jaz hugged her parents.

"We had co-conspirators; Kyle was one of them."

"I suppose there's no meeting with Ribald this morning?" Jaz asked Kyle.

"Would I do that to you on your thirtieth birthday?"

"You know if you never mention my exact age to me ever again in life, I wouldn't mind."

"Thirty? That was an excellent year wasn't it Hep?"

"Too long gone for me to remember," Hep passed.

"How many birthdays since, for you Jagger?"

"A few."

"Ooo! You are old. Here." Jaz handed him an Earth Wind and Fire tape. "A little positive reinforcement for your ride home ... and thanks again."

"My pleasure." A smile split his face. "See ya, Hep."

"What's this?" Kyle entered the New Orleans suite to find Jaz decorating a tree.

"Now that my birthday is over, it is officially Christmas. Ta-dah." She turned on the lights.

"Nice touch." He placed his briefcase by the drafting table. "The food's all arranged. We better get dressed."

Kyle was adjusting the music on the stereo as Jaz emerged, dressed for the Christmas party they were hosting together. The ebony pair had been on the party circuit as a couple; one seldom invited without the other, but their friends were never part of that inner circle, so they decided to throw this one for them.

They met in the middle of the room. Kyle bowed and held out his hands for a slow dance, and Jaz fit comfortably in his arms. At the song's end, she looked up at him. He brushed a tendril from her face and their lips drew closer.

"Saved by the bell," Jaz taunted as Kyle went to answer the door.

The party was a huge success, with excesses in the food, drink and merriment. Cass passed out and slept on the couch. In the morning, when each emerged from their separate rooms, Cass sat up puzzled.

"You guys are unreal. Live together and don't ... aren't–"

"Can I drop you somewhere?" Jaz asked, picking up her purse.

"On his head," Kyle suggested.

"Oh, no please, I've been through enough." Cass massaged his temples and followed Jaz from the room.

Jaz relaxed in her comfys, preparing to watch "Pocket Full of Miracles," with Chinese, when Kyle bounded in. With a quick "Hi," he disappeared into his bedroom. There were only a couple more social obligations; one was The Grand Ball, then the CE couple was off duty until Mardi Gras time, and perhaps they'd be gone by then. Jaz was considering taking the St. Gabriel's church project gratis since she liked the all-girl parochial school.

"Oh God, what did I forget?" Jaz questioned as Kyle emerged from his room tuxed down.

"Relax. It's just me." He was inserting a cuff link as the phone rang.

"Your limo is downstairs." Jaz hung up the phone. "Where to?"

"Just a soiree Courtney wanted me to escort her to. I envy you." He almost started to kiss her goodbye, but headed for the door. "Enjoy!"

She threw her moo shu pork across the room as Glenn Ford bought an apple from Bette Davis in front of the swank hotel. She thought of hurling the pancakes and plum sauce too, but tossed the chopsticks she'd formerly reserved for Kyle, instead. So Courtney, the Mayor's assistant, asked him to escort her to a soiree! Jaz thought. "So you say thanks, but no thanks. You don't go ...you–man you!"

Jaz recalled a brief conversation with the girl, when she'd asked if Jaz and Kyle were dating. "We're just colleagues," Jaz had answered, ala Kyle.

"So he's a free agent? Great. 'Cause there are so few good black men around here, you wouldn't believe it," Courtney said, and Jaz hadn't thought any more about it until now. I can't win for losing, Jaz thought.

Kyle returned to the dark suite about two. Jaz heard him come to her door and leave. The next morning he was up and eating breakfast as usual, sitting next to the Christmas tree.

"Mornin'." He folded the paper and laid it down.

"How was the party?" Jaz poured juice and slathered apricot marmalade onto a waiting croissant.

"Great, it was at the governor's mansion, made a few new

contacts. Everybody asked about you." He offered with that infectious smile.

"You tell them I was partyin' with Bette Davis?"

"Not exactly. Listen, since you won't go to Gstaad with Cass and me and won't invite me to the Caribbean, why don't you consider coming to Kenya when we have a longer break? You'd love it, Jaz. It's as wild, untamed, earthy and as natural as you."

"Won't your staff get me mixed up with all your other Afro-American women guests?"

"No." He stood and placed his napkin beside his plate. "You'd be the first." His sincere ebony eyes caused her topaz pools to look away.

"You ready?" Kyle asked returning from his room and putting on his suit jacket.

"Yep." Jaz stood, gathering her attaché.

"We're ready for Ribald in every sense of the word. Madame," he said, holding the door for her. She looked so fresh and professional in her chocolate wrap dress accented by the ecru lapels and matching French cuffs. "We're still on for the Grand Ball aren't we?"

"Yeah. But I'll be coming in from L.A.," she told him, as they waited for the elevator.

"L.A.?"

"Yeah, Amber and I are doing our traditional 'Nutcracker' in San Fran. Then I have to take her home."

"That's right. Just don't be tired."

"Me tired? I'm a nighthawk." Jaz winced as the strong New Orleans sun assaulted her eyes. "It's the mornings I have problems with." She nodded a greeting to the chauffeur.

"Lemme know if you want tickets to The Dance Theatre of Harlem, my sister dances with them–"

"What! Avia and I saw them at the Festival of Two Worlds in Italy in Seventy-one, then in Milan in Seventy-two. Yes, I want tickets whenever they're within a two-state radius. What else don't I know about you?"

"Plenty." That easy smile spread across his handsome face like a wet spot on a thirsty paper towel.

While in L.A., Jaz found herself in front of Ma Vy's house. The front door was wide open with the screen locked, as usual. She could see Qwayz's mom taking down clothes from the line in the backyard. Jaz was glad she'd dropped Amber off, or the nosy girl would have asked a thousand questions by now. Instead Jaz had the leisure of remembering, alone.

"Jaz?" The woman came to the door, where Jaz waited, almost unaware that she had walked up the path and rung the bell. "Jaz," Ma Vy soothed at the sight of her daughter-in-law.

"Hello, Ma Vy, Merry Christmas."

"Come in, child."

Jaz hesitated midway across the threshold, knowing that to step back into that living room was to step back in time. Seeing the staircase up to the second floor, she recalled how Qwayz used to jump the last four steps, to the chagrin of his mother. Jaz imagined his room upstairs, just as he'd left it on his way to Stanford. Full of basketballs and athletic trophies; academic certificates on the wall, next to a blown-up picture of Jaz and her new car. A cherished varsity jacket of three years, and the All-American one he gave up to wear the brown bomber jacket, which now hung on her halltree next to his red baseball cap.

"Come, please." Ma Vy smiled and Jaz sighed loudly.

The place hadn't changed at all; the same furniture, the same impeccable cleanliness and order. Jaz looked at the mantel, seeing again the pictures of all three Chandler children at various stages of development with snaggle-teeth and braids. Jaz looked away, but her gaze was drawn back. Qwayz's trophies from swimming, track, football and basketball–so many they spilled off the high perch onto the floor around the fireplace. Then there were medals from Vietnam, a dog tag with his name engraved on cheap metal, and a heavy bronze urn. Jaz held onto the mantel for support and cried, as she should have years ago.

"He never did like the idea of being put into the ground." Ma Vy had taken the silent journey with her.

"This is all that's left of him?" Jaz sobbed, and Ma Vy held her. "How can that be? We were so happy. So in love–"

"I know child."

"I still miss him." And her body shook as she wept.

Hours later Jaz's face was swollen with puffiness from yielded tears, her eyes red, but finally seeing.

"I still talk to him, Ma Vy."

"Me too. I talk to father and son–they are together." They fell into comfortable silence.

"And Akira. He is never coming back to me, and I'm so tired of being alone, but I can't move on."

"You must."

"I just can't."

"Who is holding you back? Certainly not Qwayz. If he were here, just for a split second, what would he tell you? Not to keep on as you have, Jaz. He loved you and he would want you happy, not sad."

"But you didn't, Ma Vy."

"And now I am alone." She stroked the girl's brow. "I had children, which was my gift, and now I have a grandson. There is still time for you Jasmine, and for the children you have to bear. No one can say you didn't grieve for my son. It's been ten years. It's time, just like I told Denny when it was time. Profit from my mistakes. He was my only son who is gone now, but you are here."

During the return flight to New Orleans, Jaz recognized that it may have been ten years since Qwayz's death, but it had only been months since she accepted it. Ma Vy was right. But the realization was a far cry from the action, Jaz thought as the plane banked and landed.

The Governor's Grand Ball evoked all the high drama and theatrics of a Hollywood premiere. In the center of the action was an ebony couple; a handsome man in exquisite tails and a dashing red tie, cummerbund and boutonniere. The woman, a symphony in a dripping-gold ball gown, plucked from an Italian opera.

"You better give that dress back to Deborah Kerr in 'The King and I,'" Cass said.

"Don't tease her, she feels like Scarlett O'Hara as it is," Kyle warned him.

"Well it is the south," Cass conceded winking at Jaz. "But you outdo them all. Belle of the Ball."

"Who let you in here?" Kyle joked.

"I just told them I was a friend of Jaz's. In like Flint." Cass snapped his finger. "Shall we dance?" He crooked his arm, Jaz took it, and they waltzed on the huge dance floor, ignoring the swooshing rhythms of hooped gowns fighting for territory.

"You know my cousin's in love." Cass tested her, during a turn.

"Is that right?" Jaz didn't want to know "who with," in case it wasn't her, and she didn't want it to be her–not yet. She wasn't ready for him. She wanted to try her shaky freedom out on a couple of guys first, and then come back and marry Kyle, after all her excess baggage had been launched overboard. He deserved that.

"Aren't you curious?" Cass pressed.

"Nope."

"Speak of the devil." Cass allowed Kyle to cut in.

"What's he jawjackin' about?"

"Nothing special. You know Cass."

"He really likes you."

"Am I breathing?" Jaz said, insinuating Cass's only requisite for females.

"He's not that bad. Just a little scared."

Aren't we all, Jaz wanted to say but asked instead, "Of another failed marriage? It takes two to tango."

"He's still in love with Raina, his first wife." Kyle double-spun her. "Some people don't know what they have until it's gone."

"That was a wonderful Grand Ball!" Jaz whirled around the suite, kicking off her gold sequined shoes. "I could have danced all night." She flipped on the stereo switching the dial from his jazz to her soul station.

"You did." Kyle removed his tails, loosened his tie, stoked the fire the hotel built on winter weekends, and plopped on the sofa to watch Jaz sway to the mellow sounds.

He loved her in those slinky knock-out gowns which invited attention but denied access. The ones with high slits and backless halters, spun from fine fabrics. But in this Cinderella extravaganza, she looked magical. The gigantic puffed sleeves decorated with gold braid that resembled beveled glass. The same braid bordered the plunging sweetheart neckline, challenging the right side of propriety. She was gorgeous.

"C'mon Jagger." Jaz pulled him up from the couch. "You're not that old. Let's see if you've perfected the D.C. bop yet. I love this tempo. You know I was quite a party animal in my day." He whirled her around. "Very good."

"You're a good teacher." He held her close, his hands on her back, before releasing her for another volley of fancy footwork. Then they were groin-close again.

Jaz held her breath at the nearness of him, her champagne buzz evaporating as his hand ever so gently touched bare skin. This wasn't the governor's ball. This was one-on-one in a top floor hotel suite dancing in a fire's glow.

He spun her twice in a row and her head reeled and, though it was a mid-tempo song, Jaz felt swept away as they swayed cheek-to-cheek, heartbeat-to-heartbeat, with the intermittent rustle of her gown masking her breathlessness.

Kyle's dip coincided with the last note of the song and the last bobby pins fell from her French roll. As he pulled Jaz back up to him, her hair fell wildly about her shoulders.

Jaz wanted to say something flippant and witty, but the words stuck in her throat, and her eyes couldn't bear to pull away from his. She melted into Kyle's body, as his arms encircled her even tighter, his lips brushed the side of her cheeks, and the DJ from heaven spun right into the next slow jam.

Jaz just knew she'd stopped breathing and only the sight of Kyle sustained her in this world. The warm, sweet wind from his parted lips landed on her own, but she turned hers in upon themselves like a child resisting spoonfuls of cod liver oil. Then an Earth Wind and Fire song from the concert played, and Jaz's lips sprang loose like the tight blossoms of some deprived plant responding to the sun; Opening, and ready to accept the rain. And, finally, Kyle Jagger and Jasmine Chandler kissed.

Still locked in an embrace Jaz attempted to unfasten the zipper of her ball gown, but Kyle stopped her, his eyes questioning her readiness. She reassured him with a kiss, and began unbuttoning his tux shirt while he unzipped and peeled the gold fabric from her body.

Leaving her $4,000 ball gown collapsed in the middle of the floor, Jaz's breasts grew taut with desire. Kyle rolled her hot pink panties over her flat abdomen down to her feet, and scooped her up in his arms to lie with her on the sofa, as they basked in the glow of the fireplace. Jaz fingered his chest, her eyes exploring the wonders of his lean body and the projectile just within her reach. He leaned over her, kissing, prolonging the delicious inevitability of events.

Jaz awakened in Kyle's bed, not knowing when they'd moved from the couch, but remembering every spectacular movement. She felt energized and alive again–all silly and giddy.

"Good morning." His stretch included her in an embrace.

"Morning." She smile-smirked as she watched his nature rise.

"What's say we freshen up, and I meet you back here in ten minutes?"

"Sounds like heaven to me."

They did, making love more deliberately but just as satisfying. "Ah Topaz, you are–"

"Topaz!" Jaz shot up and was out of bed with a robe like a bullet. "Who the hell is Topaz?"

"Oh Jaz, lemme explain–"

"There's nothing to explain." She gathered her pantyhose. "You're a free agent, neither of us are kids. You have your–"

"Jaz." He surprised her by grabbing her wrists.

"Let go of me!" She jerked away.

"You are Topaz."

"Nice try, but I'm from Watts. You can't pull that bullshit on me."

"Jaz, you are Topaz. That's what I called you when I thought you were Amber's mother. Get it Amber, Topaz ...your eyes. I had to call you something, you kept creeping into my dreams." He watched her eyes zero in on him as if she could tell if he was lying just by looking at him. "Remember the two chunks on my bedroom mantel? You and Amber." Confident he'd calmed her down some, he climbed back into bed. "You'll never guess who I thought your husband was."

"Who?" She wanted to believe him, had to believe him, because if she didn't she would have been totally wrong about him.

"AJ. I see this pretty little girl with a woman she tells me is her mom. Then I ask her about her father and she says you two are 'waiting for him to come back.' Then I see you three at the ballet, and in the park flying kites, and I figure, Dad's back." Jaz, giggling down deep in her stomach, began climbing toward him from the foot of the bed like a cat on all fours. He tackled her and playfully pinned her down. "We're gonna have to talk to that girl about her imagination." He kissed her.

"Oh, I dunno." She kissed him back. "She was right about you, Prince Charming."

"Ah, Topi–my variation on Topaz," he explained hastily, and they made love all over again. Prince Charming and Topi.

Chapter Twelve

There were two more uninterrupted days of glorious lovemaking, before they went their separate ways. Despite Kyle's plea that Jaz join him for a Jagger Christmas and skiing in Gstaad, she stuck to her usual California plans.

"You have your obligations and I have mine," Jaz said.

"You don't want to go public with this just yet?"

Jaz was amazed and relieved at his refreshing honesty. "Yeah, it's been awhile for me, and well, I haven't even gotten used to it."

"I have, but I respect what you're going through."

Jaz pirouetted through her usual Christmas visits and rituals in San Francisco and L.A. These festivities which had been so satisfying, were now lacking. They were Kyle-less, though the smell, sight and sound of him accompanied her everywhere. Although he called her from the Jagger estate and Gstaad, it wasn't the same as seeing someone daily, sharing events at a day's end, or lounging lazily in bed in fluffy robes with the paper and a breakfast tray on a Sunday morning.

Kyle had snuck up on her, whisking her away to a new horizon. It was only in retrospect that Jaz convinced herself she was in complete control of the situation. But that gnawing, quiet, respectful portion of her inner voice told her she was kidding herself, and she was already in too deep to pull out.

In L.A., Denny noticed Jaz's preoccupation, and at her parents' annual New Year's Eve party, Selena, tickling the ivories as the guests sang, caught a glimpse of her thoughtful niece. Jaz had one more stop, to see Mel and Lee Harker's baby girl, Star, before she could get back to New Orleans, and Kyle.

* * *

"Hello handsome." Jaz entered the Chalfonte suite, and hurried to him.

"Hello Auntie Jaz." Kyle put down his papers in time to accept her embrace. "Why didn't you call and lemme know you were coming, I'd sent a car. I missed you."

"Me too." She returned the kiss, before he swooped her up.

"How are mother and baby, Daddy and Hud?"

"All are fine. They loved your flowers but the diaper service really hit it big with Mel. How'd you get so smart?"

"I've got sisters remember?"

"Ah yes." She bent her head way back so he could kiss her neck. "Keep going," she moaned.

Their relationship bloomed and flourished. Kyle brought music back into her dreary life. After Qwayz, Jaz had shunned listening to the radio, new songs of longing made her feel empty, old songs made her cry. With Kyle she danced and sang again. He was almost everything Qwayz wasn't. There were obvious differences in personality and demeanor, musical ability and taste, and their packaging was different, yet there were similarities. They both possessed a confidence and a coolness, an intelligence, pride and honesty. But she didn't know how Qwayz would have been at thirty or how Kyle was at twenty. But Kyle's slow deliberate speech, was as much of a turn on, as his smile flanked by canyon-deep dimples. She never compared Kyle to Qwayz the way she had Prince Omar and Nick. Kyle stood on his own. She didn't know why, but she didn't feel as if she were cheating on Qwayz with Kyle.

* * *

"That went well," Jaz said of the Grand Opening of Harbor View, dropping her purse on the table, as Kyle stole a kiss. "Kyle!" Jaz reprimanded him, eyeing the door waiting for her parents to return from the celebration.

"We're not teenagers. Meet me in my room after they go to bed."

"No way."

"OK. The Rousseau served us well the last time they were here."

The Rousseau Hotel served them well again, until Hep and Lorette left, and they were free to roam the Chalfonte suite again.

"It feels strange making love in the bed my parents did," Jaz mused, as Kyle went for clean champagne flutes.

"You so sure they did?" Kyle jumped back in.

"I know my Daddy." She licked her lips at the sight of chocolate-covered strawberries.

"Think we'll be like that?" Kyle held a succulent red ball above her mouth before he let her devour it, then licked the chocolate from her lips.

"Humm, just as good as the berry," Jaz moaned. "I bet the maid service thinks we're demented, hopping from bed to bed."

"They're paid well, besides, we'll be gone in a couple of weeks." Kyle settled back on the mountains of pillows as Jaz joined him. " I was thinking, why don't we do something super special for Valentine's Day. We can go to Acapulco or the Caribbean–your choice."

Jaz soberly sat up in bed. "No, I have something else to do."

"What?" Kyle sat up with her. He knew her schedule as well as she knew his.

"I can't do anything on the fourteenth," she said, climbing out of bed.

"Jaz?" Kyle grabbed her arm. "What is it?" He walked her around to his side of the bed. "Ah–your anniversary, no problem, we can do it later. OK?"

"OK." She lay on his chest, overwhelmed by his understanding.

"We're still on for Mardi Gras right?"

"Right." She accepted his kiss on her forehead. As she drifted off to sleep, she thought it appropriate that the carnival celebration would mark the end of their New Orleans closeness. She missed him already.

* * *

Kyle turned to his panoramic view of San Francisco trying to find the answer to Jaz's abrupt change of temperament in its skyline. They'd returned from New Orleans three weeks ago, and she offered him only vagueness, indifference and preoccupation. They hadn't dined together for lunch or dinner, and hadn't made love. His mind, body and soul ached for the nearness of her but he was left famished.

On one weekend, she was off to AJ and Avia's, the next, flying down in Hep's sleek new Harker 800 to see Amber in a recital. He wondered what she'd let come between them this weekend. She informed him of her activities as if he was her secretary, not the man who'd become her lover. He swiveled around with a sigh, just as Maxine came into the office with finished contracts.

"Thanks, Maxi." He hoped everything between them would be straightened out next week, when they were flying to Hawaii for the botanical garden project. It was the reason he'd been so patient.

"Hep wants to see you," Maxine said.

"Thanks." Kyle used the private passage linking the two offices. "Yeah, Hep."

"Ready for Hawaii, my tireless wonder?" Hep asked, slapping him on the back. "New Orleans was a charm."

"That it was." Kyle's grin spread for different reasons. "But I'm looking forward to this smaller project," *in a romantic setting with Jaz and the islands all to ourselves* went unsaid. "I think Jaz is too."

"Jaz isn't going. She's taking a hospital project in San Diego. She wants to work solo," Hep said, as Kyle disappeared.

The words "Jaz isn't going" rang in his ears as Kyle strode down the hall and into her office.

"Jaz, we have to talk." He barged in on her team meeting and leaned directly over her, as everyone looked up surprised at the usually super-cool Kyle.

"I'm in the middle of a meeting," Jaz said.

"You'll excuse us won't you, gentlemen." Kyle's knuckles never left the mahogany of her desk as he turned his steely cold ebony eyes upon each of them. "Close the door behind you Marc, thanks," he directed, and they filed out without comment. As soon as the door closed, Kyle whirled back to Jaz, who sprang into action.

"I don't appreciate your coming in here, disrupting my meeting and dismissing my team–"

"Best defense is an offense," Kyle said. "I don't appreciate the runaround and cold shoulder you've given me since we got back from New Orleans." He continued in that killer low voice, she had to strain to hear. "I don't appreciate spending my days and nights alone when I'm used to having you with me. I don't appreciate an empty bed." Jaz jumped up from her desk, and turned toward her view of the city, folding her arms across her chest. "Jaz," he said, softly, moving his body between her and the view. "I know we had something special all those months in New Orleans. We come back here and I'm cut off at the knees. I miss the 'you' I knew there. I want to know why it went away, and I want it back."

Jaz couldn't trust herself to speak, so she just shook her head, only fueling Kyle's press.

"I know for some insane reason you think this is for the best, but it isn't. Only the lucky ones find what we have ... again. We can't throw it away because we came back to a place and people who knew you as a married woman. They'll get used to the idea ... you did."

"No!" Her feelings found voice. "I thought about it and I decided–"

" 'I?' Excuse me but I think there are two of us in this relationship, which means some discussion–"

"No. It's over. It was great while it lasted–"

"Hold up. You've been looking at too many old movies. This was not something to occupy my time while I was in New Orleans. I could've had that with Marisa, Courtney or any number of women." He held her by the shoulders to get her to listen. "This was something deeper, stronger and far more lasting then just a roll in the hay."

"I'm sorry." She broke away. "But that's all it was for me,OK?"

"You're a liar."

"You men. Just can't believe a girl can have a purely physical relationship with a guy–"

"Oh I can believe it ... but not of you–causal sex? Naw. No way." He stalked her move for move. "I know you're anxious, scared of commitment–"

"Ah! Doctor Jagger!" Jaz threw up her hands, "I've heard the 'you're scared routine' before."

"You're scared that I'm gonna do the same thing Qwayz did." Her head jerked at another man daring to speak his name. "You're afraid that you'll love me, and I'll abandon you like he did."

"Now wait just a damned minute!"

"You're afraid that somewhere down the line I'll leave you for some noble cause–"

"You are *way* out of line!" Jaz shrieked against his calm, slamming things in a her attache´ case. "You have no right to discuss him and me."

"I have every right. I'm here and I'm staying. I'm in love with you and I want to marry you, and I'm tired of seeing your life wasted on a ghost."

"Damn you to hell! Let go of me."

"He's dead Jaz, he's not coming back. Let go of him. Let go." He spoke in soothing mantra-like tones. "Let go. He wouldn't want–"

"Don't even pretend to know him or what he would want." She grew as eerily calm as he. "You shouldn't be allowed to speak his name."

"I promise I won't leave you, Jaz."

"Yeah, well, so did he." Jaz ran tearfully down the hall, pressing the elevator button a zillion times before Zeke opened the door. "Close it!" She ordered, just as Kyle reached the shaft. "Down!" Jaz spat, when she realized that Zeke had closed the doors, but hadn't put the elevator into motion.

"Is that a commentary on the relationship?"

"Mind your own damned business!" She collapsed onto the bench, fishing for her sunglasses, car keys and a tissue.

"Yes, Miss Jaz."

"Don't call me Miss Jaz."

"I don't think you should drive Mis–" Zeke caught himself, but not her before she was through the garage doors and in her Jag heading out of the lot.

Jaz yanked a tissue from its box, the tears flying as fast as the car was going, her hair trailing in the wind. Inside her regal feline, she wailed aloud like a wounded animal, talking to herself, wavering between trying to calm herself down and inciting herself up. For the first time she admitted that she was mad at Qwayz for leaving her, and, then, for not coming back, despite his promise.

"Damned you Qwayz for leaving me!" She screamed within the confines of the car. She was mad at a dead man and scared to try again–to open herself up for hurt, again. To be loved copiously and be left, again.

Then she was mad at the man who brought it to the forefront, who had the guts and caring enough to risk it all to heal her. To force her to come to grips with the total reality of the situation.

"Kyle." She banged out his name on the steering wheel. "Arrogant SOB. 'Let go, Let go.' I let you go. Sh–." She turned up the volume of the radio and laughed at the irony of vintage Jackie Ross taunting her with "Selfish One."

"Qwayz, Qwayz," she said dreamily. "If only you had come back to me, or hadn't gone at all, I wouldn't be in this fix now." She almost missed the turn to Ruidoso, she slammed on the breaks turned the wheel and the car skidded out, clinging to the side of the cliff before cutting itself off. Jaz banged her head on the padded steering wheel.

"Aw shit!" Jaz looked at the blood trickling from her forehead then sighed. "C'mon, do what you always do." She instructed herself, after eliciting only a mocking whine from her car. "Call on your ancestors from the past who say you can handle this and anything else life has to dish out." She rested her head and became mesmerized by the ocean. The image of calm and infinity.

She fell asleep, until a Ruidoso Canyon cop found her and escorted her to Paradise Rock, where she made Formosa oolong tea, lit a roaring fire and went to bed.

After a restless night, the only real brightness was the rising sun and the flickering red light of her answering service. Ignoring Kyle's messages she called her parents to assure them that she was fine, that she didn't want company, and she'd return to work in a couple of days. Her father didn't mention Kyle, which meant he hadn't said anything to her father.

Jaz sorted out her emotions. That Qwayz was as irrevocably in love and flawed as she, and his decision forever affected her. During the course of the next few days Jaz forgave him for going and not coming back, and herself for harboring such feelings for so long. She reconciled herself with Qwayz in his absence, and finally, Jaz accepted his death on all levels.

She didn't return any of Kyle's phone calls before he left for Hawaii. Walking the beach of Paradise Rock, she admitted to herself, if to no one else, that she did love Kyle Jagger. By the time she returned to work, Kyle had stopped calling her. When he called Hep, he did not inquire about her.

Jaz treated AJ and Avia to lunch at Gary's in Monterey, telling them about the times she and TC had their May dates there, and how she and Qwayz had frequented the popular bistro. Both AJ and Avia silently marveled at Jaz's being able to speak of Qwayz in the past tense at last. Then she led them from the restaurant down Ruidoso Canyon Road to the house perched upon the rock. Jaz watched the couple make over the house and the view. AJ spotted the familiar tarped-wrapped red Karman Ghia in the carport.

A wide grin washed his face. "I always wondered what happened to the old girl. May I?" AJ whipped off the cover. "The hours I spent in this car. I was small enough to fit back here."

"At one time," Jaz agreed, and Avia let the two venture down memory lane without explaining details to her. "I want you to have it." Jaz dangled keys in front of him. "If you promise to take care of her."

"Most definitely, just like I did Akira. Thanks." He hugged his Aunt Jaz. "I'll take her home and polish her." He began removing the car keys from the chain.

"Keep all the keys. This car comes with the carport and the house."

"What house? This? We can't afford this." He gathered Avia in his arms. "Not for awhile yet. Maybe never."

"It's a gift. From Qwayz and me to you. I bought it as a welcome home gift for him." They fell into silence. "This house was built and designed for lovers, and that's what you two are, even if you are married."

"Ah man, can you believe this!" AJ swung Avia around. "Jaz, are you sure?"

"I am. Qwayz would want you to have her, and this house. We called it Paradise Rock, but I'd appreciate it if you'd call it something else."

"Home," Avia said simply.

"I like that." Jaz smiled at the handsome young couple.

Over the next couple of months, Jaz quietly made the transition from Qwayz's widow to single woman, doing so without outside pressure. Completing her hospital project in San Diego, she survived without Kyle's attention. She missed him, hoping that in the interim he was not engaged in another out of state project or another relationship. If he were, then perhaps they were not meant to be, but that little reserved piece of her heart had reintegrated with the rest, making him the center of its attraction. When he got back Jaz decided she would initiate the long awaited discussion of feelings and future. Jaz had grown up, and caught up with the tail end of the Seventies, and her perspective was clear.

Kyle was in town, but didn't join the Culhanes for the Fourth of July celebration on Hep's boat in the bay. Jaz's disappointment continued when Kyle didn't come in to work for several more days during normal working hours. Jaz thought of going to his house but decided she wasn't ready for the possible rejection on his doorstep. At least at work she could slither down the hallway, close her door and busy herself.

"OK that looks good," Jaz complimented Dory on his work. "The Chancellors are gonna love it. I hear we're talking award time for the Botanical Gardens of Hawaii."

"That was a good project. You know Kyle ... perfection personified." Jaz didn't bite. The couple had been the talk of her team since Kyle put them out of her office months ago. "He worked us with a vengeance, but it's a fantastic piece of real estate now."

"That's good. Where's he off to next?" Jaz tried sounding casual.

"Not sure. Why not ask him?" Dory smiled. "He's in his office."

"He is?" Panic hit her face as she bit her bottom lip.

"Go on. It's worth a try–all he can do is tell you to get lost."

Jaz straightened her hair, smoothed her hands over her suit skirt and tugged on her jacket, as she walked down the corridor musing how she was always painting herself into corners.

"Hello Kyle." Jaz knocked and opened the door with the same motion.

"Jaz." He acknowledged without getting up, not trusting himself to look at her.

"How was the project?" Ah yeah! Jaz knew she was stone in love with this brother. You can play games with your mind when miles separate you, but up close and personal–seeing him–she was in love with this man.

"Almost complete."

"That was fast."

"I had alot of time on my hands."

"AJ and Avia are expecting."

"That's nice. Listen, I got alot to catch up on, so if you'll excuse me." He rifled papers, returning to them in a blink.

He didn't want to be cruel, but he wanted it known that his time chasing her was up. His father and grandfather had taught all six of them, if you want something go after it with all your might, give it your best shot, and when the deed is done, rest easy. Know the difference between what can be got, and what can't. Know when it's time to give up the reigns and try another filly. It'd be awhile before he could, but Jaz had let him know the filly wasn't gonna be her.

"Fish or cut bait," Jaz whispered one of Papa Colt's sayings to herself. "Kyle Rawlings Jagger, I got some talk for you."

"Listen Jaz, if this is the speech about how we should try to be friends for the sake of our professional careers–no. I don't want to do lunch or an occasional dinner meeting. I don't want to work on any joint projects–"

"What do you want?"

"I'm not up for playing games." He looked at her for the first time.

"Neither am I." Their eyes locked. "What do you want? An open public relationship with a future?" Kyle reared back in his seat but didn't utter a word. His eyes never left hers as he held an inner conversation with his wants, needs and the reality. He wasn't going to be jerked around, especially by someone he loved.

"With whom?"

"With me!"

"Let me get this straight." He got up and rounded his desk towards her. "You are offering me a 'normal' exclusive relationship?"

"Yeah."

"Why?" A smile began to play at the corners of his lips, and Jaz was immediately relieved.

"Because ..."

"Because what Jaz?" He moved within inches of her, looking playfully down at her, egging her on with his eyes.

"Because ..." She wanted him to touch her, to hold her, to stroke her, to smell his natural scent. "Because ... I love you."

"Was that so hard?" He took her in his arms.

"That was physical blackmail."

"I didn't touch you." He kissed her cheek. "I missed you Topi. Being in a romantic place like that without you." He kissed her again. "Set a date."

"It just so happens I'm free this evening. We could eat out at The Cliffs, get baked goods from Grimaldi's."

"Cute. I'm talking wedding date."

"What?" Jaz reared back.

"You said a relationship, and I quote, 'with a future.'"

"I didn't mean now ... this year."

"Hey, time is of the essence when you fall in love with an old broad like you. Tick, tick."

"That's coldblooded."

"Why wait? We know we're compatible, we have no money problems and now we're both in love. There is one thing we have to get straight up front." He walked her to the couch and they sat over the lion skin. "If we are to have an honest, trusting relationship I have to say something about Qwayz."

"I can't let go of him completely."

"No one's asking you to. He was a very important part of your life, and the love you shared will always be. You can't trade one love for another. Every one has a special place which no one else can occupy. It was because of your relationship with Qwayz that you can have one again ... with me. It was never my intention to replace his memory with ours, it cannot be done. To pretend Qwayz never existed is to court misery." He lifted her chin in his hands so their eyes met.

"I have a big heart, Jaz. Big enough for you, me and Qwayz's memory. As long as we can talk about him, he'll never come between us. I choose to make a place for him, because I'd be no place without you." He wiped a solitary tear from her cheek. "I could never love and respect a woman who didn't do the same for her first husband. I love you because you had the capacity to love him so deeply." He hugged her. "There's something else, Jaz." Kyle stopped and, looking down, played with her fingers. "Just recently, I realized that I met Qwayz once."

"When?"

"Remember the hyped Tulane/Stanford game of '66 between Magic and Midas?" Jaz nodded. How could she forget. "I was Midas. After the game I nodded at Qwayz in the lobby, and saw this beautiful girl beside him–it was you. I guess in a way I've been looking for you all my life."

"Oh Kyle."

"Now, I have no more secrets, now you know that Qwayz and I have the same taste in women." He brushed his lips against hers and they kissed.

"You are some piece of work Jagger. And I do love you."

"So what do you say, do we pick a date?" He pulled her to her feet.

"Isn't the fact that I love you enough?"

"No. I didn't get where I am today by half-steppin'." His deep dimpled smile claimed his face.

"What do you mean 'We' white man? I thought you said I could pick a date?"

"Nag, nag, nag already. You want to pick the date? Pick it." He encircled and hugged her in a slow dance.

"I know you'll be there."

"With bells on." As he bent to kiss her, neither heard Hep walk in, excuse himself and walk back out.

Hep pondered how unusual it was for Kyle to breech his office etiquette. "Jaz is a lucky lady." He stopped abruptly in his tracks. "Jaz?!" He catapulted back. "What's going on?!"

"You're going to be invited to a wedding as soon as my fiancee´ picks a date," Kyle beamed.

"Who? Jaz?"

"Yes Daddy, although I haven't been asked properly yet." Kyle sat her down, and sank to one knee.

"Jasmine Bianca Culhane Chandler would you do me the honor of becoming my wife, to love, honor and–"

"Uh-uh," Jaz nixed the obey.

"Love and honor ... until death us do part?"

"I do."

"I'll be damned." Hep remained flabbergasted. "When did all this happen? How did it? If I'd known, I would have promoted it." The realization began to hit him and he slapped Kyle's back heartily. "Congratulations! I never thought of you two together. I thought of you as a son; well, this is down right incestuous! I couldn't be happier. Lemme go call Lorette. Son of a gun."

"I'm not sure I like this." Jaz returned to the bed from the bathroom where Kyle awaited with cardamon-laced coffee. "Just how many other women have preceded me in this bed of hedonism?" She challenged from a kneeling position.

"Doesn't matter who was here before you. It's who's here now, to stay forever and ever." He gathered her to him, unfurling the sheets they'd knotted during their lovemaking. "If you'd prefer, we could trade this bed for that gorgeous brass bed of yours."

"Never mind." Jaz vetoed her bed, which was slated to join the rest of her life with Qwayz in her parents' attic. "I'll wipe out every memory you ever made here with any other heffer."

"You already have. Before I even knew your name, all I had to do was look at that Topaz on my mantel there, and it was you I was with." He kissed her again.

"Negro, puleeze." She resettled on his chest. "I may have been out of circulation for awhile, but I'm not fresh from the farm."

"Why is it that when a guy finally finds someone he's committed to for the rest of his natural born days, and finally speaks from the heart–his woman never believes him?"

"Oh I believe you, but I don't believe this is your first time loving–"

"You are the first woman I have loved enough to propose to. I love you, Jaz."

"You can never hear it enough, Jagger, don't forget that. I don't wanna spend my days remindin' you either."

"You won't have too, I guarantee it." Jaz intertwined her bronze legs with his brown ones.

"Pretty combination, isn't it?"

"The best. You set a date yet?"

"No. I will. What is the rush?" She sat straight up, her brown nipples as piercing as her eyes. "You in love and trouble?" She giggled and he joined her.

"I'll be in love and trouble if you don't marry me–soon."

"There's so much to clear up. Where to live?"

"Between here and The Cliffs, until we decide where along the coast we want to live. Then we'll buy the land and build."

"Suppose we find one already built that we can renovate to our liking."

"Just so it has a fireplace in the bedroom and in the bathroom."

"The bathroom?"

"Right next to the sunken tub with an ocean view. I want my kids to have close to what I had growing up. Not too big, I remember. First things first, when will you make me an honest man? When will you walk down the aisle with me and tell thousands of folks you love me and want me forever?" He turned her over devouring her with kisses which tickled her. "You could have this every morning, noon and night?"

"I do have it every morning, noon and night."

"Aww, I make it too easy for you." He lamented playfully.

"I'd marry you in a second if we eloped," Jaz said after a gulp of spicy java. "It's so romantic, just the two of us, all alone, private, intimate, maybe a very few close friends."

"Sounds like you've had experience."

"I have, and it's highly recommended."

"Then definitely not. Not for us. I waited too long for this day. It's gonna be my first and last marriage." Jaz looked at him quizzically. "There were two things I envisioned growing up. One was becoming an architect and the other my wedding day."

"Oh Jagger, you would never had made it in Watts."

"Naw, now, you're jumping to conclusions. All men have an idea of how they want their lives to pan out. Mine included my wife and children. And I've been looking for you since my senior year in college. I decided that when I found you I wanted a big wedding with all the trimmings–"

"Kyle, I don't want a circus, those marriages are over before the warranties on the gifts run out. And I hate that wedding march. I'm not dressing up in all that fussy frilly stuff and I won't–"

"Jaz, Jaz," he soothed holding her close. "How about a nice garden wedding in your folks side yard around the fountain? You can wear whatever kind or color dress you want. All I want is to marry you."

"No press or media."

"Not a one."

"They're already having a field day since you gave me the ring. 'Money Begets Money,' 'The Merger of A Lifetime–Jagger and Culhane,' 'The Black Dynasty,' 'Heirs Extraordinaire–Publishing and Building.' It's offensive!"

"No press. Two hundred white lawn chairs arranged in rows with flowers everywhere. A harpist."

"Harpist? I want my aunt and sister to sing."

"Great." It was the first progress he'd made with her.

"One hundred ultra-close family and friends each."

"Deal. One hundred–that'll be just my family." He chuckled and she hit him with the pillow. Then he began to sing "When We Get Married" ala The Intruders, and Jaz chimed in. Kyle got out of bed and took Jaz's hand as they sang and D.C. bopped in the nude.

"I don't need a dress," Jaz could barely speak through convulsive laughter. "I'll wear my birthday suit."

"We'll be the talk of the wedding circuit–an original gown!" They laughed at themselves.

"Honeymoon."

"Kyle."

"We're on a roll. Definitely Kenya, the rest of Africa and Europe."

"You've been to Europe a thousand times."

"True. But never with you. I want you to show me your Italy. So what do you say?"

"I say." Jaz looked at him intently. "That I'm pretty damned lucky."

"I'm the man with the plan." He moved close to her, matching his body parts with hers.

"I'd say you're a man with much more than a plan." Jaz felt his rise, and their lovemaking began once again.

With only six weeks until their wedding day, both Jaz and Kyle tried to clear their desk and calendars to accommodate the one month Kenyan-Italian honeymoon. Jaz made a call to Glaviano, a designer from her Tawny days, who agreed to make the wedding dress she'd designed–a tea length peach chiffon with a bugle-beaded drop waist and sheer bodice with fitted sleeves complete with Juliet points. Jaz also commissioned the exquisite matching peach-beaded cap, which would fit snugly on her head with only an opening for her chignon in the back.

When Jaz ended her phone call to Glaviano, she grabbed the

structure analysis and estimates from her desk and rode down to finance. When Tre' wasn't around Jaz left a note. She then pressed the executive elevator button, deciding to wait for Zeke.

"Miss Jaz?" Zeke opened the elevator door.

"Not for long." Jaz stepped into the tiny hot chamber.

"Marryin' a good man. Couldn't do no better."

"I kinda like him too. If I died tomorrow I must say I've loved and been loved by two of the most exceptional black men ever to grace this earth."

"You said a mouthful Miss Jaz." He opened the door for her.

"What will you call me after I get married?" Jaz paused over the threshold as Zeke thought.

"Mrs. Jaz," he said, finally, and they enjoyed a laugh.

"You're wanted in the conference room," Lita said in passing. Jaz checked her watch and opened the door.

"Surprise!" yelled Tre', Marc, Derek, Dory and the rest of the crew.

"Guys." Jaz closed the door behind her accepting kisses, presents and a cake that said, 'Another One Bites The Dust'. "So romantic."

Everyone lapped up expensive champagne and eats. While Jaz opened her gifts of lingerie, they made wisecracks about her getting pregnant on the honeymoon and never coming back to work. Her guys' surprise shower had been the first of three; the other two hosted by Denny and Tracy in L.A., and Lorette in Frisco. The former ambassador's wife was in her world planning an "impossibly small" but elegant wedding. The first she'd planned for any of her children.

As Lorette's mind was still conjuring up fantastic images of ideas she could set to money and music, Jaz addressed more realistic concerns–cleaning out her closet at the apartment. Pulling out Qwayz's Air Force trunk, Jaz opened it and the smell of Southeast Asia stung her nostrils. She paused a moment to look at the contents, which he had packed himself before taking that fateful flight–the last things he touched. Over the years she hadn't disturbed the trunk except to move it from one house to another. She eyed the things she'd placed in there. Bypassing their love tapes and her letters, neatly secured with a red ribbon, she went straight to the Rolex box. She held the watch he never received. "Till the end of time,'" engraved on the back, shiny and brand new.

She patted her heart as if to quiet it, returned the watch to its box, and reached for the deed to Paradise Rock. She thought how he loved that place and how surprised he would have been when she led him to it. The documents shared an envelope with the tickets to Myrtle Beach, yellowed and unused. "Qwayz, Qwayz, Qwayz," she lamented.

There were pictures of them peeking out from under his clothes. Of her leaning against his red car when she couldn't have been more than fifteen; of both of them dressed to kill–him in jeans and Chuck Taylors, her in a mini. Then with Akira, her in stirrup stretch pants, and he in bell bottoms, and of course his everlasting leather bomber jacket.

Jaz wiped away her tears, accepting them as fact, and went to the halltree. She stared at his red baseball cap and jacket for a long time before she slipped them from their brass hooks. Hugging, then folding them, she returned to the trunk. She closed her eyes tightly as she unhooked the gold star her husband had placed around her neck when she was sixteen years old. She held the necklace, the bracelet of interlocking hearts and her wedding rings in the palm of her hand, looking at them for the last time, and when the sight became too painful, she balled up her fist and tears fell upon her closed fingers. She slipped them into the pocket of the leather bomber, and placed the jacket and red baseball cap in the trunk as if it were a grave accepting a long awaited body.

"Goodbye Qwayz." She closed the lid, locked the lock and kissed the brass edges. "I will always love you."

She pushed the trunk as close as she could to the covered wedding portrait and the other things relegated to the Culhane attic. Then she walked to the fireplace, picked up Amber and strummed it the way he'd taught her too. There was only one place for Amber to go.

"Jasmine!" The surprise lady backed away from the door to let her in.

"Hello, Ma Vy." She kissed her on the cheek.

"I wasn't expecting to see you for another eight days."

"Then you're coming?"

"I wouldn't miss it for the world. Hanie is flying in from London. I've been waiting for this day for a long time."

"Well good. I brought something for you." Jaz unstrapped the guitar which hung over her back, so Ma Vy hadn't seen it until this instant. "There was no place else for it to be, but here with you."

"Oh my." She began crying. "Those men of mine sure loved this guitar."

"Yeah, they did."

"Got just the place for it." Ma Vy propped it against the fireplace near the picture of Qwayz and his Dad.

"Perfect. I don't know why I didn't think of giving it to you before."

"It was where it needed to be. Now you don't need it anymore."

"I dunno 'bout that Ma Vy."

"Just butterflies."

"I didn't have them with Qwayz."

"You had pimples with Qwayz," she chuckled. "You're braver when you're younger. You don't know no better." She patted Jaz's hand. "That Kyle, he's a good man, Jaz. I like him. It's clear to see he's crazy about you. All we ever want is for our children to be happy. I think he can make you so."

"He brought music, humor and happiness back into my life, Ma Vy ... I gotta go." Jaz could barely speak as she turned and walked towards the door. "Next time I see you Ma Vy, I'll be marrying somebody else."

"Well, at least I get to go to this one," she said. "I envy you Jasmine. To start over again. It takes courage and the love of a good man. I think you got both." She patted her cheek. "See you in eight days."

Chapter Thirteen

Jaz sat at the vanity staring at–but not seeing–her image in the mirror. Her wedding day had come, her makeup as perfect as her manicure and pedicure, her twisted chignon coiled at the base of her neck, not a wild, loose tendril in sight.

"I wish we had eloped," she said to her reflection as she sprang from the vanity stool in the room she used at her parents house. "You're a wreck."

She paced, trying to calm herself.

Why are you so apprehensive? Kyle is a great man from a terrific family. You liked his parents and his brother and his wife, the sisters and their spouses. What is the problem?

She peered out the window at the crowd below. On the front row a space for her parents, then Mel and Lee Harker sat with Hud and Star, who was climbing from one to the other. AJ, Avia, Ma Vy, Melie, Hanie and Aubrey Sr. comprised the second row, then the guys from work, Gladys Ann, Sloane and their husbands.

"Jaz! You're not dressed yet?" Denny was a whirlwind of activity.

"All I need to do is put on my dress, cap and step into my shoes–"

"Well do it! Do it!" She held the dress over the bride's head. "It's gorgeous." Denny smoothed it down. "You know the trades have guestimated the price of this Glaviano original at twenty thousand."

"I wish."

"Where's your cap? Oh Lordy!" Denny ran from the room, returning in seconds with it. "Don't move–you'll get all sweaty!" Then disappeared again.

Jaz looked beyond the eight foot wall which surrounded the grounds, to the arriving limos. There was a crowd of folks in the street out front, a mixture of press, and the fans of Selena and Zack in from Paris, and Mel–the Broadway and television star had recently given up her hit variety show to stay at home and raise her family. Hired security kept the onlookers at bay, but it was as festive outside the walls as it was elegant inside.

Jaz saw Lloyd, Denny's husband, lead Little Lloyd to an aisle seat, as Denny rushed in, this time with Tracy.

"You all look really nice." Jaz eyed the pale green attendant dresses.

"Thank you," Tracy beamed.

"Will you go and get her shoes ... please?" Denny snapped.

"OK," Tracy sauntered off.

"Denny, calm down. I'm the one getting married." With those words out of her mouth, panic set in on the bride. "Oh Denny ... I'm getting married?"

"Shush, shush," Denny soothed, placing the jeweled cap upon her head like a queenly crown. "Oh Jaz, you are simply ... gorgeous!" A tear fell from her eye.

"Don't start Denny, or I'll be forced to join you."

"We can't have that." She blotted her eye carefully. "I'm so happy for you. How do you feel?"

"I'm happy for me too."

Tracy poured into the room with Amber, a junior bridesmaid in a muted peach and green floral dress. Kyle's niece and nephew were the flower girl and ring bearer. Mrs. Pemberton, the wedding coordinator Lorette had hired, fluttered in announcing "picture time," and the photographer orchestrated various poses.

"It's time! It's time!" The rotund woman sang as she escorted them to the bottom of the back stairs off the kitchen, setting the pace.

"You OK?" Denny asked before descending the steps.

"I'll be glad when it's over. Where's my father?"

"Here I am, Punkin'." Hep wrapped her hand over his arm. "You OK?"

"Yes, cheeze. I really hate all this!"

"Uh-oh, that's classic Jaz pissed off." He identified and they chuckled. "Punkin' I think you got a good deal. I think you both did."

"Well, I'll give it the old Culhane shot."

"Your grandparents would be proud."

Kyle was in such a hurry he and Cass entered the bridal trellis well before time. Father McCaffery, who had baptized the groom, laughed at his eagerness. They watched as the procession began.

"Finally," Kyle said.

"I've never seen a man so anxious to end life as we know it," Cass teased.

"You don't have a woman like Jaz."

"You got me there brother." They watched as one of the ushers escorted Addie, her husband and Zeke to seats in the back.

"Oh God Daddy." Jaz shook, as father and daughter stood on the back stoop waiting for their musical cue.

"It's alright Punkin' I'm here," he said, and stroked her hand. The harpist began her solo.

Jaz stepped onto the ivory carpet that led to the trellis and saw Kyle. Her eyes fastened to her future husband and her lips smiled when she recognized the stringed rendition of "When We Get Married," recalling how they had danced nude to it and decided to use it instead of that godawful wedding march.

"I dunno man," Cass said. "Mixed marriage may not work."

"Wha?" Kyle asked without removing his gaze from the vision of his bride.

"You're jazz and she's strictly rock and roll."

"If that's all we have to deal with, we'll be just fine." Kyle could see that beneath her veil, Jaz was wearing the diamond earrings he'd given her. A compromise they arrived at when she balked at the nine carat diamond engagement ring, calling it gaudy and pretentious. So they'd decided on a five carat, rare pink Australian diamond ring, if she'd let him put five on her ears, "two and a half on each precious lobe."

Jaz joined Kyle beneath the trellis, the magical trickling from the Italian fountain was interrupted by the light laughter of the guests when Jaz anxiously took his hand before directed to do so. He squeezed and held it firmly, and they barely took their eyes from one another during the ceremony. They were wrapped in the hush of the moment, only their love screamed loudly at one another.

Forced to look at the priest when vows were exchanged, Jaz caught a glimpse of another wedding party behind the clergyman and the trellis, beside the ivory baby grand where Selena sat, and beyond the imported fountain. Wavery, filmy images of her ancestors, on whose shoulders she stood. She couldn't make out the ones in the back, but was sure the dark, purple-blue-black woman was Great Grandma Saida, who stood next to her son, Papa Colt, with Canary. There were her grandparents Javier, with a tribe of folks of many hues behind them, and TC. It was as if all her friends and relatives from the world beyond ventured back to bear witness and approval of this happy union.

"TC," Jaz whispered.

"Jaz?" Kyle said gently. She looked at him not realizing it was time to repeat her vows. She did, and returned her gaze for ancestral approval, but there was only sunlight where they'd been, and a milky, ghostly outline of Qwayz.

"I now pronounce you man and wife. What God has joined together, let no man put asunder. You may kiss the bride."

Kyle slowly lifted the gossamer tulle from Jaz's face, allowing it to fall over her chignon in the back. Taking her chin in his hand, he raised her lips toward him and kissed her. The guests shrieked.

"I give you Mr. and Mrs. Kyle Rawlings Jagger," the priest introduced, as doves fluttered and helium-filled balloons exploded to the heavens.

"This is where our happy ending begins Jaz," Kyle vowed as if they were the only two people in the universe.

The next few hours were a melee of best wishes, congrats, picture posing, hugs and kisses, champagne toasts and dancing, provided by Aunt Selena's jazz combo. Jaz was gracious yet ravenous, sneaking sushi or a lobster salad boat from any traveling waiter.

Finally the cake was cut, the bouquet was thrown and both had transformed wedding attire into traveling suits, as the pair ran full gallop down the circular staircase across the harlequin tile to the waiting ivory antique car. The license read: Topi.

"Your first gift from me as Mrs. Kyle Jagger." Kyle kissed Jaz as he opened the door to her Excalibur amid the rice throwing.

"I decorated the car, Aunt Jaz." Hud, Jr. ran up to kiss her goodbye.

"You did a wonderful job, Sweetie. Thank you."

"Be happy, Jasmine!" Ma Vy elbowed her way to Jaz for a final kiss.

"Thank you, Ma Vy." The newlyweds pulled away from the waving family.

"Oh Kyle–it's over." She nestled right up under him.

"Happy?" His dimpled smile was never wider.

"Indescribably. And famished beyond words."

"First stop, a full meal."

"Bless you." She kissed him. "Oh, I have to stop by the office."

"What?"

"C'mon. I have to get something. It's my first marital request."

On the thirty-fifth floor, Jaz ran around to her office and grabbed the music box and the rock, juggling with them a bit before realizing she hadn't brought her purse, so she left the music box and palmed the rock.

"I'll get you later. Goodbye office–for awhile at least!"

"Sure was some wedding," Zeke said closing the elevator.

"It was rather nice." Jaz didn't remember his being there. "Why did you leave so early?"

"Ah, I'm not much for crowds–alot of those children didn't

know me."

"Well, I'm glad you came." It was suffocating in the tiny little elevator, made worse by her lack of eating, the wine bubbling in her head, and the excitement.

"What's that you got in your hand?"

"This – it's a lucky rock from Hawaii. Good luck charm ... part of my dowry," she chuckled.

"You know Mrs. Jaz, you and Kyle are special people. He's a good man, didn't just tolerate me, but actually cared about me. One of the few genuine men I've had a pleasure to meet in my long life. You–well you take some getting used to," he chuckled and coughed. "I think you two deserve a shot. Got a real good chance of making it."

"Why thank you, Zeke."

"So is that rock a wedding gift to your husband?"

"No, but I carry it with me all the time."

"Didn't you tell me it was from your first husband?" He slowed up the elevator a bit.

"Yep, last thing he *gave* to me on a runway in Hawaii. Cheeze, it's hot in here."

"Why take it on your honeymoon?"

"Why not?"

"Because you're starting out a new life and there should be nothing between you and Mr. Kyle." He slowed the elevator down even more so it drifted from floor to floor. "If you're not going to tell him about the rock, you shouldn't take it. You startin' off on the wrong foot, with a rock between you that can grow into a mountain."

"Zeke–" Jaz began, weariness, nerves and a lack of sleep had caught up with the bride, and she felt a weird weightlessness. Her head began spinning in the heat of the dark chamber and the smell of liniment only added to her dizziness.

"You can have no hope for the future, if your past keeps crossing it. One foot in yesterday and one in tomorrow is only a half-assed commitment." Jaz had never heard the old man cuss before and she looked at him as he went on. "You love that man downstairs waitin' on you don't you? And it's easy to see how he feels about you.

You're starting a new life. Don't carry any old baggage."

"I don't need a sermon–" She felt faint.

"Listen to me girl." The old man had turned toward her, grabbing her about the shoulders. "You're gonna have to let Qwayz go. All of him. He's not coming back and you can't hold on to him any longer." Jaz stared at Zeke's one good eye which changed from black, to brown to hazel and back to black again.

"He's dead. Bury him and the love you had for him ... now. Jaz, let go. Let him go. Let me go, please. You gave me paradise here on earth but you're making my life in heaven ... hell. Jaz and Qwayz? It's over."

Jaz eyed the old man upon whose melted face a superimposed milky, ghostly vision of Qwayz appeared.

"Qwayz?" Jaz rocked and swayed, she thought she heard the lilt of his voice, or was it a carry over of Ma Vy, Melie and Hanie's she'd heard only moments before.

"Qwayz is gone forever, Jas-of-mine. Let me go Jaz, so you can live again, and my tired soul can rest, and my heart can rejoice in your happiness. I loved you more than life itself but we are not together and won't be for all eternity. Go, be happy so I can rest in peace. You have my blessing."

Jaz stared at the image on the contorted face, realizing Qwayz had used Zeke for his blessing and the sign she sought all along. As the elevator reached the ground floor, his vision disappeared.

"Goodbye, Qwayz."

As Zeke opened the elevator door, a shaft of sunlight lit the eerie chamber, and Jaz eyed the grotesque man, not sure of what, if anything, had just occurred.

"Zeke, would you take care of this for me?" She handed him the rock.

"Sure, Mrs. Jaz." He tipped his hat and smiled on the side of his face that could.

"Jaz?" Kyle met her halfway in the open foyer, and they walked off together into the ray of light. Zeke watched them pull away in the new automobile.

"Did you get what you wanted?" Kyle asked negotiating traffic.

"I decided I didn't need it. I've got everything I'll ever need right here." And she lifted her lips to his as Jeffrey Osborne from the radio, told them they were going all the way.

MYRTLE BEACH, SOUTH CAROLINA
1985

Far from the beaten path in a small cottage on its own private inlet, the flickering of a projector shot light into the darkness of the house and its surroundings. From the back pier through the kitchen, voices from long ago cut through the heat and the smell of medicines and human decay. In a corner of the overheated house, an artificial leg was propped against an antique halltree with brass hooks. There was a wheelchair by the table that held an imported music box, which played Nat King Cole's "Too Young;" and next to it was a rock from a Hawaiian runway, and dozens of photographs of the young lovers littered about the room. Old European magazines with Tawny gracing their covers and some more recent ones with articles on CE, rare pictures of Kyle and Jaz, and never of their children. Jackie Wilson, Johnny Mathis and Nat King Cole albums scattered about the floor. Words from "Everlastin' Love," pumped life, hope and romance into the otherwise dreary dankness.

The film showed Qwayz and Jaz, singing one of his songs, then leaving the control booth into the congratulatory arms of Selena, Zack, Hep, TC, and Gladys Ann. As the old man rewound that segment, he started the VHS tape which showed Jaz and AJ frolicking on the beach that Malibu summer. From there the old man rewound and replayed the young lovers.

Zeke sat alone watching the images of two very young, very in love people singing to each other as if there was no one else in the world. It was the usual way he spent his time, fishing, or watching every inch of film he could get on these young lovers. When the film ran out, he had a series of photos made into slides and for hours he'd press that single button that would project their larger than life images up on the giant screen.

"It's four in the morning." His gnarled hand reached over to cut off the projector, plummeting the room into a pitch except for a lone bulb in the kitchen.

This was the dog's cue that his day was beginning. The old man seldom slept. These days the old man couldn't lie flat, and had to sit in his overstuffed Murphy chair with its hassock, surrounded by bottles of pills and liquid medicines he could barely take without choking.

"Time for some fresh air." He maneuvered his stiff leg onto the floor and shifted his weight to scoot to the front of the seat. He sighed heavily and the dog relaxed, knowing it would be some time before the man would mobilize himself.

"Better take these pills before that bitch nurse badgers me to death today." He struggled to pour some lukewarm water from a carafe into a glass. "Is Hep suppose to come today or is it my IV day?" He asked his canine companion. "He'll bitch at me too." He screwed the pills into the side of his mouth and choked on the first swig of water, coughing convulsively, causing him to collapse back into the chair.

"Whew!" He sighed rewinding the VHS, as the dog resumed a sleeping position. "Hep thinks this is 'unhealthy.' What else I got to do?" He asked the dog and began coughing again. "Won't be the first time we disagreed, won't be the last." His breathing was difficult and labored. "Not the first time we haven't seen eye to eye. Get it? Eye," he pointed to his one good one, gone bad, "To eye."

Hep had nixed his request of a picture of Jaz pregnant or with one of her babies or with her "sharp new" haircut. The old man hadn't confessed that he'd called her a couple of times. He got her number from the address book Hep left during one of his monthly visits. Every time he called, the maid answered. What did Hep think he was going to do to her anyway? He would never hurt Jaz or destroy what she had.

He couldn't complain about Hepburn Culhane. Over the years he'd been mighty generous: the job, setting him up in this house with everything he could possibly ask for and some things he didn't. He thought of the seven phones in this tiny little place so when Hep called daily to check up on him, the old man wouldn't be taxed. And the nurses who came daily from ten to ten. Hep had provided him with several live-ins over the years, but he'd chase them off until they had finally compromised on a twelve-hour-shift about six years ago. Neither he nor Hep thought he'd live this long.

After all these years, hard as he tried, he still couldn't remember the actual explosion. Whether they had drawn enemy fire or if it was engine malfunction. He just remembered waking up in a pool of his own blood in the midst of the most excruciating pain his taunt athletic body had ever experienced. Surrounded by an eerie quiet only a jungle forest can produce–one in which, despite the pretense of calm and being alone, a thousand pairs of eyes watched your every move. It was still and dim; the sun was blotted out by the dense foliage. He called out, but only a monkey's high cackle answered. He didn't know how many hours he'd been there before the pain awoke him. A merciful pain which caused him to shut down and blackout. Sometimes when he woke it was pitch black, as if his eyes were still closed. The acrid smell of burned flesh was undeniable.

He finally decided to move at least out from his own liquid, and in determining his direction, he noticed he could only see through one eye. Struggling to move, he noticed his blood soaked clothing had become encrusted with tiny, minuscule bugs feeding on the plasma. One arm was burned beyond repair, and a contorted leg held on by a thread of flesh. It was himself he smelled. The sight and realization of his condition, coupled with the pain, caused him to black out once again.

The next few hours and days were a blur–a series of him hurling his charred shattered body down the hillside. He crawled through thick vegetation through buffalo dung, over rocks and ridges. In and out of various stages of consciousness, of sleeping and waking and talking to himself.

He prayed that Jaz wouldn't mind his missing a limb or eye. That their love was strong enough to endure the physical. He also prayed that he was rolling toward a road and not a river. He didn't have the strength or limbs to negotiate the water.

The dusty hot roadway accepted the lump of humanity, baking him unmercifully in its heat. Qwayz could roll no further on the flat surface, so he lie there sizzling in the heat, until he could feel the vibrations of an approaching platoon.

"Make 'em mine, Lord, not VC. If they're mine I go home to Jaz. If they're Charlie ... I'm gonna die. It's your call, Lord."

The scuff of marching feet shuffled around the pile of rags in the roadway. Qwayz hadn't strength to raise his arm or the voice to cry out as his own men passed him by.

"Hendrick!" A commanding officer barked after identifying the uniform as theirs. "Get this carcass in a body bag!" He marched on.

"Whew!" Hendrick fanned off the stink. "Wonder how long this has been layin' here."

"Why bother?" The other soldier bent beside him, arranging a body bag.

"I guess the folks back home will be glad to get anything," Hendrick said looking for dogs tags but found none.

"Could be a gook for all we know." The other soldier surmised. "Got no face, just a little beady eye."

"Looks like he was cooked pretty bad," Hendrick said, as they placed the torso with a dangling leg into the plastic.

"Hendrick . . look ... is that eye moving?"

"Can't be." Hendrick began zipping up the heavy black plastic.

"It blinked!"

"Impossible, lemme see." Hendrick spit out his toothpick and straddled the body, blocking out the sun, so he could see the eye himself.

Qwayz tried with every fiber of his mangled body to blink the eye over which he no longer had control. He knew that if they zipped him up in that plastic bag, he'd suffocate to death. He moved his fingers but they weren't looking. And suddenly his hand grabbed the ankle of the soldier.

"Shit!" The soldier jumped scared.

"I'll be damned!" Hendrick bent to one knee and listened for a heart beat. Feeling for the familiar pounding, he saw the mush of lips moving. He held his nose, and inclined his ear to the lips of the man.

"What's he saying–kill me? It's the humane thing to do, man. Shit."

"Naw ... he said jazz." Hendrick stood. "I guess he wants us to know he's a brother. No sweat, Blood, me and Anderson will take real good care of you, Soul Brother," Hendrick pledged as Qwayz passed out.

Qwayz was told he went from a MASH unit to a sea hospital onto Japan where he awakened from a coma six months later. He'd undergone several extensive operations, was bandaged from head to toe and on life sustaining equipment when he came out of his deep sleep. He'd become the challenge and pet project of Doctor Maeda Yamamoto who was hoping the GI would remember who he was since there was no ID and his fingerprints had been burned off. Dr. Yamamoto was touched by this soldier who, from all practical indications, should have been dead, but had an insatiable will to live against all odds. The least the doctor could do was to help him, and his dedication astounded the medical community as much as Qwayz's awakening.

Between the trauma of all the operations and the painkillers, Qwayz suffered from amnesia. It was another six months before he finally realized who he was ... and he cried. Not tears of joy but tears of despair.

He had been a robust, talented basketball player, a musician, had a future as a brilliant lawyer, and a loving family, and the most beautiful loving wife in the world. Now he was a grotesque piece of flesh, with one eye, one arm, one leg and paralyzed on one side. He'd been burned over most of his body, and what was left had been scarred from grafting. His handsome face was now a melted contortion of pinkish flesh, a Cyclops eye, collapsed nose, sealed lips and no hair. He was hooked on morphine and wanted to die. He tried suicide several times. Dr. Yamamoto believed Qwayz knew who he was, but when asked, he'd simply answer, "Frankenstein."

In February of Seventy-two, Qwayz began the long road to rehabilitation. His muscles had severely atrophied so he began with bed exercises before learning to walk with an artificial leg. He learned to maneuver his arm, care for himself hygienically, and to feed himself. It was quite a task for the superb athlete who broke records, packed sports arenas, and graced the covers of all notable sports magazines. The only way he could reconcile himself was to believe that Qwayz had died in Vietnam. This was the Qwayz of today. This was who he had to deal with, live with and be. His only beacon was Jaz and his family. He didn't want to contact anyone until he was ready. He hoped Jaz wouldn't remarry, but then he thought, she just couldn't take another man so soon, not if what they had was real, and he knew it was.

It was still months later that he finally contacted Ambassador Culhane in Italy. It took several attempts.

"Yes? Ambassador Culhane here." Hep had taken the phone from his secretary. He listened in horror as a cracked old voice claimed to be his son-in-law. "This is some kind of sick demented joke. Do not call here again!" he boomed, and hung up. But the calls kept coming on his private line, which only his family had privy too. For that reason he couldn't tell Antonella not to put the man through.

"I'm afraid you leave me no choice but to contact Jaz directly," Qwayz threatened not really knowing where Jaz was, knowing Hep's number only because of their scheduled trip to Italy in Sixty-five.

"That would not be advisable!" Hep thundered, closing the door to the sight of his precious daughter and Antonella conversing. "Just so happens that I will be in Tokyo next week," he lied. "Perhaps, I'll stop by then."

Qwayz's memorial had been over long ago, the calls had begun two months ago, and with their persistence, Hep hadn't slept much in the last few weeks. Perhaps the art of denial was an inherited trait–Jaz denying Qwayz's death, and he denying his existence. Hep thought of calling an investigator in, but he didn't want anyone else to know about it. He hadn't confided in anyone, not even his wife, which worried him as much as the use of his private line. If those calls were really nothing as he pretended, he would have told Lorette.

The voice was not one of a man in his early twenties. It was old, weary, but there was familiar cadence and rhythm to his speech, a familiar unusual choice of words. If it were Qwayz, in what kind of shape would he be? But of course it couldn't be him. What could this man want from him–money? On what basis could he make such a claim? Blackmail? Was Qwayz living in Vietnam with another family? No way! Was he a prisoner of war, and this guy the link to getting him out? There were no dog tags as with TC. No body, not even part of one, just the Air Force's word that Quinton Regis Chandler IV had been killed in action.

Hep walked the long antiseptic hallway of the hospital with its medicinal smell and an occasional unbearable vision of the remains of a man. It was all too painful.

"Here we are sir," the nurse said. "Sorry to stare but Jazzman hasn't had any visitors."

"Jazzman?"

"Used to call himself Frankenstein but now he's the Jazzman. We're fellow music lovers." She didn't go into the private room. "I'll get his doctor."

Hep didn't want to be alone, but the nurse disappeared. He approached the back of the shrunken man, immediately relieved that it couldn't be Qwayz. He was about to leave, to get out before the doctor came, but the shriveled hand of the old man fanned Hep closer.

"I am Ambassador Culhanc," Hep boomed with his usual intimidating ploy, but the old man didn't respond with the characteristic jerk.

"Don't be so relieved, Mr. C." The man turned slowly facing him, his voice coming from a hole in his neck. "It's me and you're still doing that thing with your voice, huh?"

Hep almost collapsed at the sheer sight of this monstrous mush of a face. Ribbons of pink scar tissue about his face and neck covered one eye completely and left only a pinhole of a pupil in the other. Hep fought the fact that this was his son-in-law, but in some twist of fate, he knew. For the first time he was glad that TC had died and not come back ... not like this.

Hep fired questions about Ma Vy, Denny and Hanie, about Qwayz's sports records, his singing and affiliation with Champion Studios and Raw Cilk. Qwayz answered them all without hesitation.

"For all I know you could have been in a prison camp with Qwayz. That would certainly give you time enough to study up on him."

"I know you wish, Mr. C. You have no idea how many times I've tried to kill myself, but I'm still here." He lay back on the waiting wealth of pillows. "You've asked about everyone who's dear to me but the two I loved best, TC and Jaz." Hep began to pace nervously. There was no denying that this man was his Qwayz, the pride of Watts. The prize sought by nine colleges, and six ivy league universities. The most superb athlete of the sixties. 'Magic' Chandler of Stanford. Scholarship to law school. The love of his daughter's life.

"Lemme check the medical records." Hep read that this man's only word on the dusty road of Vietnam had been his daughter's name. To review what this young man had endured over the past few years, the operations, addiction, rehabilitation, only proved that one man could survive this tremendous agony for the love of one woman.

Hep returned to the room and wept for Qwayz, for TC and for Jaz.

"I'll make arrangements to take you home," Hep said quietly after several hours of telling Qwayz everything he knew about Jaz.

"I figured a little house in Myrtle Beach would be nice."

"Jaz is in Italy right now."

"I'm not going to see Jaz. She was my reason for getting better, but I'd be a burden pure and simple."

"You can't be serious. That girl has never given up hope on you. Even when everyone else considered you dead, she never let anyone say different."

"She was wrong, Mr. C. The Qwayz she knew is dead–scattered in Laos. I ruined her life once by leaving. I won't do it again by returning."

"You can't be serious–"

"But I am. I've had plenty of time to figure out all the angles. I couldn't live with her pity, her sense of duty and obligation. It would be no life for her. You remember once I told you I loved Jaz more than life itself ... my own life and I'd do anything to prove it. You told me you hoped it'd never come to that. Well, it has. The ultimate price of my love is to live out my last few remaining days without her–and to let her get on with her life. I could be selfish and let her be my nursemaid, but I'm not that kinda guy. I guess this proves that my love for her was everlasting after all."

"But she knows you're alive."

"So what do we do after she gets an A on the big test, and a F in the course?"

"Boy we went around and around with that one didn't we?" The old man's voice pierced the silence and the dog looked up. "Then Jaz came back home and went to work at CE, and I just had to see her, be around her as often as my health allowed. It was hard to ride in that Jaguar she wanted all her life, to go to Addie's wedding with her, sit beside her and hear vows of love until death do us part. I almost lost it when we went to Paradise Rock." He looked about the dismal surroundings and grunted.

"Amber really hurt when she called me a monster on the elevator–the little girl I named. I expected as much from Scoey, but it still hurt. Then there was AJ," his voice choked. "All grown up, handsome–in med school, and I wanted to say 'I am your Uncle Qwayz.' I wanted to stand in the middle of Jaz's thirtieth birthday party and say 'Hey! Denny, Zack, Selena–I am here!' That would have been something, huh. Then what ... everyone would cower and cry–well." His voice broke and he thought of Jaz's wedding when he saw his sisters and mother, all who avoided him like the plague.

"Love supreme, Akira II." The dog rose at the sound of its name. "The supreme sacrifice ... so that all the folks I care about can remember me as I was. It was too painful seeing Jaz happy, even though that's what I wanted I still couldn't take it. Ready for some fishing girl?" He maneuvered his stiff leg ignoring the wheelchair, and grabbed the cane Kyle brought him from Africa. "He's a good man, a lucky man." He shuffle-scraped towards the kitchen door, quietly remembering that Hep said Jaz asked about Zeke's absence when they returned from their two-month honeymoon. He glanced at their oil wedding portrait which hung over the splendid brass bed as he steadied himself.

"Ah." He made it to the doorjamb. As the screen scraped open, the dog accompanied her master for the two minute walk down the pier, which took him fifteen. He thought of Jaz, and how if he hadn't picked, pried and prodded Hep for information, he wouldn't know anything of her life now. Hep was stingy and made Zeke work for every morsel. But he persisted, otherwise he wouldn't have known that Jaz only took three projects a year to keep professionally fit so that when her youngest daughter, Savannah, began school Jaz could resume her career. He wouldn't have known that Kyle came home from work nightly in time for dinner and prayers with his wife and three children. That they took three vacations a year; one to their Kenyan retreat, another to their villa in St. John and the third, a trip dictated by Gabrielle or their son, Cully's, school studies. Hep was most guarded in describing the Jagger home, but over the years Zeke had gleaned that it was an Italianate style villa, constructed of limestone and split-rock built in the 1930's, remodeled by the Jaggers, and situated on ten prime acres of Santa Barbara coastline.

Zeke sighed as he sat on the custom bench Hep had had built for him by the water. It housed duplicates of his oxygen tank, medicine, spring water, cups, dog food and his fishing gear. "Well ..." He looked to the mouth of his inlet where the ocean and wider horizon met. "Looks like it's gonna be a good day. Huh, girlie?" He patted his dog clumsily. "Ah, death is a slow process." He kissed the Irish setter. "Jaz wouldn't like that. Does she have a dog? Oh yeah, two Airedales named Osiris and Isis after those black Egyptian gods–that's Kyle's doing I bet. Those kids know their roots. Our kids would have known theirs too." He patted the dog once more, before dropping his line in the water.

"Yep, yep, yep another beautiful Myrtle Beach morning will be breaking soon." He situated himself on the custom bench and began coughing convulsively, hacking and sucking up the thin oxygen. "Whew!" He wiped his brow wanting a sip of water, but dared not drink. The man and his dog sat in silence for awhile and he finally murmured. "The stars are in their heavens and all's right with the world." Tired and spent, he closed his eyes and his rod fell into the water.

INDIGO SERIES

Sensuous Love Stories For Today's Black Woman

NOW AVAILABLE . . .

BREEZE

Her father, whose life was his music, adored but abandoned her. Her mother, disillusioned with musicians, and a bitter life, discouraged and deceived her. Her first love, lost through treachery, returns to teach her the rapture and dangers of unbridled passion. She is successful. She is a superstar.

Her name is Breeze.

EVERLASTIN' LOVE

In 1967, Jaz believed she had everything, a marriage to her high school sweetheart and a secure future. But the Vietnam War caused her fairytale to end. Jaz was left devastated and alone.

As Jaz struggles to pull her life together, recollections of the past overshadow all attempts at relationships. That is until Kyle Jagger, a co-worker, dares her to love again. His patience and unselfish love breaks through the ghosts of her past, and together they find everlasting love.

ENTWINED DESTINIES

Exquisite, prosperous and stunning, Kathy Goodwin had a bright future. Her professional accomplishments as a writer for an international magazine have given her admittance into the most prominent and wealthiest of circles. Kathy Goodwin should have had a clear passage to happiness. But, after suffering the tragic death of her parents and the breakup with her fiance, she was withdrawn. Then into Kathy's life comes an extraordinary man, Lloyd Craig, an independent, and notable oil company executive. His warm gaze makes her flesh kindle with desire. But Lloyd is tormented by his own demons. Now, they both have to discover the ties that entwine their destinies.

RECKLESS SURRENDER

At 29, Rina Matthews aspirations are coming true . . . A safe relationship with her business partner . . . A secure career as an accountant . . . And, physically, she's more stunning than ever.

Into Rina's life comes the most self-centered but sensuous man she has ever met. Cleveland Whitney is, unfortunately, the son of her most influential client.

While she tries her best to elude him, she's forced to encounter him again and again, during a three month assignment in Savannah, GA. The handsome lawyer seemed to be deliberately avoiding her . . . until now. While Cleveland's gaze warms her body, his kisses tantalize, Rina recklessly surrenders to the power of love.

COMING IN SPRING 1996

SHADES OF DESIRE

Forbidden . . . Untouchable . . . Taboo . . . Clear descriptions of the relationship between Jeremy and Jasmine. Jeremy, tall, handsome and successful . . . and white. Jasmine, willowy, ravishing and lonely. The attraction is unquestionable, but impossible. Or is it?

DARK STORM RISING

Every time Star Lassiter encounters the wealthy and mysterious African Daran Ajero, things start to sizzle. Its more than coincidence that he keeps "bumping" into her.

Soon, his charm combined with his hot pursuit of her begins to cause major problems in her life, especially after she meets his sexy live in maid.

Star tries to say "no" in every language she knows, but Daran arrogantly refuses to accept her refusals. Sparks continue to fly until they end up stranded at his Delaware beach house . . . where their passions reach their peak . . . as the dark storm rises.

Dark Storm Rises . . . SIZZLES

LOVE UNVEILED

Julia Hart, art director for a thriving magazine, is thrilled to learn that her younger sister, world renowned fashion model Sammi, had fallen in love with Brad Coleman, an affluent entrepreneur. When Sammi brings Brad home to meet the family, Julia senses a forbidden fascination and desire for her sister's fiance.

Brad, instantly captivated with Julia, finds himself trapped between a link to his painful past and his obsession for the entrancing Julia. Engulfed in flames of desire, Julia and Brad succumb to a love that unveils.

WHISPERS IN THE SAND

Lorraine Barbette, a beautiful American filmmaker, on business in Senegal falls in love with a Senegalese Diplomat. Torn between making a new beginning in Africa with the man she loves, or going home to America to continue the career to which she has devoted so much of her life, Lorraine is confronted with making the ultimate decision.

Set in exotic Senegal . . . the worlds of film and politics . . . the powers of love and desire and one woman's final moment of truth.

CARELESS WHISPERS

Whispers abound at Westgate Publishing where Dyana Randolph is the star reporter . . . murmurs about Dyana's relationship with the retiring editor-in-chief Michael . . . rumors that the magazine is about to go under . . . gossip that the new talented and handsome editor-in-chief Nicholas, is a tyrant determined to put the magazine back on top. Predictions are that Dyana and Nicholas won't see eye to eye about how to run the magazine.

Locked in a contest of wills and bound by blazing passion, Dyana and Nicholas discover that thc truth of the whispers about them, is undiscovered emotions and burgeoning love.

Now Available From Noble Press

UNCIVIL WAR: The struggle between Black Men and Women

by Elsie B. Washington

Elsie B. Washington, a former senior editor at Essence Magazine, spent over two years researching the answer to the often asked question: "Why are healthy romantic relations between Black men and women so difficult to come by and so hard to maintain?"

Uncivil War examines the many factors that make maintaining a healthy relationship so difficult: economics, discrimination, Eurocentric values and declining spirituality and increasing emotional dysfunction. It also provides valuable insights from Black family therapists, sociologists, and Black couples who have found the keys to making their relationships last.

Uncivil War is a enlightening and practical guide for Black men and women seeking enriching and loving partnerships.

$24.95 Hardcover

ISBN 1-879360-25-X

SPIRIT SPEAKS TO SISTERS
An Empowering Testimony of Love for Women of African Ascent

by Reverent June Juliet Gatlin

"June Gatlin's insight has brought light to my life and the lives of c ountless others."

–Susan L. Taylor, Editor-in-Chief, ***ESSENCE*** Magazine

Spirit Speaks to Sisters lovingly instructs Black women on how to have a more intimate relationship with the Spirit of God. And as a result, achieve greater fulfillment, power, and love in their lives.

Spirit Speaks to Sisters offers chapters on how to achieve spiritual fitness, loving and spiritually enhanced relationships, a more positive point of view, and a new partnership with the Spirit.

Spirit Speaks to Sisters will serve as the standard bearer for books of inspiration and spiritual guidance for decades to come.

$20.95 Hardcover

ISBN 1-878360-39-X

Available at Fine Bookstores Everywhere